THE AVION MY UNCLE FLEW

"Full of vitality and suspense . . . The most ingenious feature of the book is the fascinating way in which Johnny learned to speak French. This is a wholly new idea in a story, worthy of special notice."   —*The Horn Book*

"It is one of the few instances when the most transitory form of fiction—the mystery-adventure-spy story—makes a permanent contribution not only to boys' books but to understanding how a boy's mind works and how, on occasion, he can change it."   —*New York Herald Tribune*

Mon oncle threw le maire out of the door

[page 134]

The Avion My Uncle Flew

by Cyrus Fisher

Pictures by Richard Floethe

PUFFIN BOOKS

PUFFIN BOOKS
Published by the Penguin Group
Penguin Books USA Inc., 375 Hudson Street, New York, New York 10014, U.S.A.
Penguin Books Ltd, 27 Wrights Lane, London W8 5TZ, England
Penguin Books Australia Ltd, Ringwood, Victoria, Australia
Penguin Books Canada Ltd, 10 Alcorn Avenue, Toronto, Ontario, Canada M4V 3B2
Penguin Books (N.Z.) Ltd, 182–190 Wairau Road, Auckland 10, New Zealand

Penguin Books Ltd, Registered Offices: Harmondsworth, Middlesex, England

First published in the United States of America by Appleton-Century-Crofts,
an affiliate of Meredith Press, 1946
Published in Puffin Books, 1993

1 3 5 7 9 10 8 6 4 2

Copyright Darwin L. Teilhet, 1946
Copyright renewed Hildegarde T. Teilhet, 1974
All rights reserved

CIP data available from the Library of Congress
ISBN 0-14-036487-0
Printed in the United States of America

Except in the United States of America, this book is sold subject
to the condition that it shall not, by way of trade or otherwise,
be lent, re-sold, hired out, or otherwise circulated without the
publisher's prior consent in any form of binding or cover other than
that in which it is published and without a similar condition including
this condition being imposed on the subsequent purchaser.

ODDLY ENOUGH, this book about the unusual adventures of young Mr. Littlehorn last summer in France is dedicated with much affection to three young ladies whose great-grandfather came from that very same part of France:

MARTA JEHANNE
SARAL DIETER
and JEHANNE HILDEGARDE LEORA

FOREWORD

I don't expect you to believe every word that is laid down in the following pages, because now and then, perhaps, the truth has been stretched a little, here and there; and, between Johnny Littlehorn and me, we might have kicked up a trifle more dust in spots than may have actually existed. I wouldn't want to have to swear that everything contained is the pure gospel. However, you might like to know about that airplane or glider —or "avion" as the people in that part of France claimed it was supposed to be called. I'll leave it up to you to decide if Johnny Littlehorn did do what he allowed he did with it. That's for between you and him. But one thing I do know and can swear to—I saw a glider something like Johnny's take off from that very same mountain, and about the same sort of thing happened that Johnny claimed happened to his glider. I can testify to that; I can testify, because I was there. I was in that glider. It happened to me. If it happened to me it ought to be able to happen to Johnny. In addition to this testifying, I think Johnny Littlehorn would like to have me thank Miss Edna Wilbur, of Mountain View High School, Mountain View, California. Miss Wilbur spent time going over this book and where Johnny or I (I'm not going to try to explain here how I got mixed up in it) made mistakes in some of the words she was good enough and kind enough to give us a lift, and set us dead to rights.

Cyrus Fisher

CONTENTS

ILLUSTRATIONS

xi

1

MY FATHER RETURNS

My father says I should write down all about what happened to me last summer when I got planted in that little French mountain town which was probably one of the awfulest sells in the world because nobody there ever had learned a proper language to speak—I mean, a language like the kind of language you and I and sensible folks speak. These Frenchmen in this little French town didn't know any better than to speak something they called French.

It all started early last summer just after the war in Europe ended. My father had been away for three years. My mother tried to manage the ranch while my father was away fighting. It wasn't very easy for my mother to do that. You see, my mother is French; she was born in France. She came over here to school where my father met her. She never had much experience with ranches or cattle or horses until my father took her out here to Wyoming.

All the same, while my father was away in Europe my mother did what she could to keep the ranch going. We had old Jake Tolliver to help. He is our foreman. He'd been on the ranch when my grandfather was alive. Without Jake, I suspect, we'd never been able to keep the ranch. A year and a half ago I was twelve. That winter we had a lot of snow. Except for Jake and a couple of the older men there was hardly anyone left on the ranch. I knew my mother was worried. So one Saturday, right after the big snow, I figured I was old enough to start earning my keep, especially while my father was away. I saddled up my pony. I went out after the men to help them bring in the cattle from the east range, where the drifts were high.

I don't know exactly what happened. Maybe it was colder than I thought. Later, old Jake told me they'd had men out looking for me before my pony came in. Luckily, it had stopped snowing. They traced back on the pony's tracks and got me into the house before midnight. By and by when I woke up I found I wasn't frozen to death after all but something was wrong with my left leg. I must have fallen off the pony when I got cold and sleepy and didn't know what I was doing; and I evidently hit a fence post or something sticking up through the snow.

Well, they had the doctor drive out from Piedmont. He set my leg. A month later he came back. He had to set my leg again, because something still was wrong. My mother kept me home from school.

Then, in the spring, my mother took me down to Salt Lake City where they have important doctors. Here, they made more X-rays of my leg. I was worried because I didn't know then whether I'd ever be able to run or play football or ride a bicycle like the one my friend Bob Collins had bought. Bob'd bought a wonderful second-hand bicycle and painted it red. Probably it was about the fastest thing in the whole country. Ponies are common as dirt in the part of Wyoming where I live, but you don't come often across red bicycles with a high gear and a low gear like the one Bob Collins owned. It had seemed to me it was the most gaudy bicycle in the world and I pestered my mother to get me one like it.

She explained that right now things were hard on the ranch. That was why, to be honest, I'd wanted to help, thinking maybe if they had another man working on the

I went out after the men to help them bring in the cattle

ranch, such as me, why, things would get enough better for me to have a bicycle like the one Bob Collins owned, with a high gear and a low gear. The low gear was for climbing montagnes—as the French call mountains—and the high gear was for racing.

On the way back home from Salt Lake City I asked my mother how soon I could begin to walk around like anyone else did without having all the hurt and pains in my hip and if she thought maybe by this summer I could ride a bicycle.

I said, "How much longer have I got to use crutches? I can't do anything with crutches. I don't like crutches."

Mother said, "I don't know if you can ride a bike this summer. Dr. Watkins gave me the name of a man in Chicago and another man in New York. Both of them are supposed to be very wonderful. You don't exactly have to have an operation. They have to twist the bone just right and I'm afraid it will be rather painful and after that you have to be very brave and make yourself walk without crutches, even if it does hurt—" And then she sort of stopped and looked quick out of the window and I heard her say, as if mostly she was talking to herself, "Oh, Johnny, if your father were only here."

Old Jake Tolliver, the foreman, met us at the train with the ranch truck. He carried me down, crutches and all, like I was a baby. He must have noticed something in my mother's face because he didn't ask her any questions at all on the way home.

For the next couple of weeks it was pretty bad. Most of the time I stayed in my room, going over my coin collection or reading—or not doing anything at all. I told my mother I wasn't going to see any bone-twisting doctors. I'm afraid I didn't give her much peace. The fact is, if you want to know, I was plain scared. My mother was gentle, and no one could have been any kinder than she was. Because my father was in the service, mother learned she had the right to take me to an army hospital. Mr. Collins— who was Bob's father, and an old friend of my father, and sort of looked out for us while my father was away—

well, he said that it would save expense if we could find
someone just as good as the men the Salt Lake City doctor
had recommended. Mr. Collins got busy. He wrote letters. He sent telegrams. He found the Chicago man was
almost the best bone specialist in the country. But the man
wasn't in Chicago any more; he was a major, and in the
medical corps; he was located at the Letterman Hospital
in San Francisco. The very best bone specialist in the
country was off somewhere else, over in Europe with the
army, so even if we'd have wanted to go to him in New
York we couldn't.

It was all fixed, then, for my mother to take me to San
Francisco. Meanwhile, they'd been cabling to my father
in France. They'd cabled him about me, so he wouldn't
be concerned when he learned we'd left the ranch—and
they cabled him about an idea Mr. Collins had which was
to combine the ranches and form a business, with a place
for my father as one of the heads of the outfit just as soon
as he was released from the army.

But we didn't get any news back from my father. . . .

Mother cabled again. So did Mr. Collins. They waited
a week—and no reply came. They couldn't understand
that. Mother delayed our trip. They got worried. They
knew the war in Europe was ended but they had read in
the newspapers how the Germans were still causing
trouble with what is called gorilla fighting. Mother, I suspect, was afraid something might have happened to father.

Time stretched out three days—four days—a week. Mr.
Collins again drove over. He said maybe he ought to take
it up with the War Department; he couldn't understand it.
While he was talking, with mother just sitting there, her
face awful pale, we heard thunder from up in the sky.

I can tell you, we don't have much thunder in Wyoming. When we do have it, we don't have it usually in late spring. That thunder rose up big and huge—and then we knew it wasn't thunder. It was a low flying airplane. Mr. Collins said maybe one of the big transports had lost its way and he ran out of the house and mother went to the window and I grabbed on to my crutches and limped for the door.

With a kind of whish and roar to it the thunder went right over our house. Next minute somebody was shooting off revolvers outside. My mother rushed out of the house. Old Jake was yelling. I got as far as the door and accidentally slipped on the rug, the crutches plopping out from under me on each side. I crawled over to get one of the crutches. Then I was crawling over to the other side of the room to get the other crutch. There I was on my hands and knees, like I was still a year old and didn't know how to walk, when the door opened.

My father walked in. My mother was holding his arm. Her eyes were glistening. He'd flown straight from Washington in an army plane going on to Salt Lake City. The pilot who was flying the plane was a friend of my father and had circled our ranch and come down behind the barn where the meadow is straight and even clear to the crick; and afterwards he took off again for Salt Lake City.

"Hi, Johnny," said my father, looking down at me. He seemed bigger than I remembered him to be, lots thinner. His hair was gray around the sides. There was a big ugly red scar he never used to have down from his cheek to his chin, nearly. But his eyes were just as laughing as ever. His voice had that same funny deep sound in it I used to remember it had when he'd come up and hint around that we might take a Saturday off to go fishing or for a tramp up into the montagnes.

I was so excited seeing him that I clean forgot about my leg.

I got about halfway to him and my mother, too, when it was like having someone open a trapdoor underneath me. Probably I'd have gone on down clear to China if my father hadn't given a jump. He grabbed me. He picked me up and carried me to the sofa and laid me down there.

I guess I have to stop now. Tomorrow night I'll write some more. I'll tell you why my father hadn't answered our cables and why he'd come back for only a short time; and what he decided to do, after listening to my mother, and hearing what Mr. Collins proposed to do with the ranches. And, oh, yes, I'll explain what Dr. Medley said about my leg.

2

THE MAN WITH THE CROOKED BEARD

On Saturday I heard the news.

We were going to France! All of us. My mother and my father—and me. It was like falling off a horse again to hear such a thing as that. Falling off a horse? A house. A whole skyscraper.

You see it happened this way: Almost a year ago, my father had been pretty badly hurt when a German shell exploded near him. He'd written us he'd been in the hospital but we never realized it had been anything very serious. He'd almost lost an eye and he would carry that scar on his face the rest of his life.

After he recovered, he wasn't strong enough to go back to his outfit—and I guess, not being able to rejoin his men nearly killed him. But anyway, after he was released from the hospital he was transferred from his outfit to Paris. He had to work on what he called "liaison"—which is a French word, I think—helping our army staff in Paris tie in their plans and actions with the British and French. My mother's family name was Langres. Her mother and father had died when she was a little older than I am now. She'd come over here to live with an uncle in New York, who was an importer, and go to school; but her brother had been too young for any traveling, only a baby then, so he'd stayed in France to be brought up by friends of the Langres.

I'd never seen my oncle—as the French call it—Paul;

but by now he was about twenty. This may seem like a roundabout way of explaining something but it isn't. Even though my oncle Paul was only fifteen or sixteen when the Germans took over France, he had managed to escape from the pre-engineering school he was attending in Paris and run away to the montagnes and join other Frenchmen who kept on fighting. Toward the end of the war, my father told me, my oncle Paul had done some flying, even.

Well, when my father went to Paris, he ran into Paul who had been hurt and had been in a French hospital and now was out, acting as a French liaison officer between the French command and the Americans.

Although my oncle Paul was the only man remaining of the Langres family, he had important friends in the French army, who had been friends with my mother's father—that is, my French grandfather who'd been a colonel, too, only in the last war. In addition my oncle Paul knew how to speak the English language that people like me and my father and my mother and everyone else I knew spoke before I was taken over to France. He introduced my father to his friends.

As a result, I gather my father found he had a whole barrel of new friends in Paris. Some of them were pretty high up. Consequently, when the American army heard about that, they said that was helpful. They kept him on his new job. They never did let him go into Germany with his outfit. After the Germans quit they asked him to keep on, and help clean up all the details that follow any war. They gave him a furlough of one month to return home; and the reason he hadn't ever replied to our cables was, first, he planned to surprise us; and second, when mother's and Mr. Collins' last cables were sent, he was on the way to us.

He told my mother he was expected to stay in France for at least another year. You can guess that news made my mother pretty sad. But he told her he had more news for her: With the war ended now for nearly a half year, ships and airplanes were beginning to take regular passengers back and forth, between our country and Europe. He said he'd talked with Washington, D.C. There wasn't any objection if mother and I bought tickets and went over to Europe and took a house in Paris and lived there to be with him.

Another thing, he said, when he'd learned about my leg, he'd discussed it with the army doctors over there. There was a colonel named Colonel Melvon, in the medical corps, in Paris. Father knew him. And, father said, this Colonel Melvon was supposed to be the greatest expert on bone surgery and bone troubles we had. At that, my mother started smiling. This was the same doctor that the doctor in Salt Lake City had said I should see in New York. So before coming back, my father had talked with Colonel Melvon and arranged for him to look at my leg and see what was wrong providing my mother and I came to France.

And that was the news. . . .

You never saw such a stirring in all your life. Of course, my mother had known we were going for nearly a week. My father had arranged with Mr. Collins about the ranch. Everything was attended to. On Sunday we even had a big dinner with half the county there, I guess. But all that time I'd been doing a power of thinking.

One thing, until my father returned and I knew we

were going on the trip, I hadn't ever thought of my mother as being French.

Sometimes when I'd see her out of my window, watching her swinging along toward the barn or toward the corral, holding my father's hand, it was almost like seeing two other people down there and not my own father and mother. I can't exactly explain. They'd be laughing and talking away, sometimes in this new funny language they had together; and, it was as if somehow they were a couple of kids not so much older than I was, and they were all interested and wrapped up in themselves and their own plans, and they forgot they had me, too, that I belonged with them. I'm not explaining very well, I know. The fact is, of course, with my father gone away for three years I'd gotten too used to hanging on my mother's apron string. After having that accident with my leg, I was cottoned to and sort of babied. Although I don't like admitting it in writing, I'd not only been spoiled but lost a lot of my gumption.

Anyway, I had the sense of this strangeness. It was coming to me, along with the idea of being uprooted and taken over to France where some fellow over there was going to twist my leg around.

Finally, I told my father I didn't reckon I wanted to go. I told him that the day before we were going to take the train. He didn't say much. He just looked down at me, with that scar red and jagged on the side of his face. He looked down and studied me for a long time, maybe three or four minutes. It sort of scared me. His eyes weren't even laughing. Presently he said something so queer I didn't understand it then—and it was a long time before I did.

He said, "Johnny, did you ever realize a war can cause casualties away from the front line as well as on the front line? That is one of the things so terrible about a war. It can reach out and hit behind the lines where soldiers are fighting. Sometimes it can reach clear back and hit a man's home and hurt the people in his home he loves best. In a way, Johnny, you're a casualty of war, too."

I said, "Me?" and tried to laugh because I thought he was joking but he wasn't joking. He was quiet and serious. I said, "Thunder. I just fell off my pony. That isn't like being shot at."

He said, "It's more than just falling off a pony. In the hospital in France I saw men a lot sicker than I hope you'll ever be and they hadn't even been touched by bullets. They'd been wounded but you couldn't see any wounds on them, Johnny. They'd been hurt inside of them, by the war. In a way, something like that has happened to you. We've got to get your leg fixed but that isn't the important thing." He started smiling. "We've got to get you to want to run on your leg, even if it hurts you to run for a time. We've got to get you to want to see new people and have new experiences instead of depending on your mother and me, and staying shut up in a house and—" He halted a minute. Then he said, "We've got to work out some way for you to go on your own again and not be afraid, just like when you weren't much higher than my knee and you set across the room on your first steps with neither your mother or me holding you, although both of us were scared you'd fall and hurt yourself."

I said, "I bet if I had a bicycle I could pedal around and—"

He laughed, "Maybe we'll fix it for you to have a bicycle, Johnny, someday, but not right now."

We took the train Monday with everyone at Piedmont to see us off. I can't tell you how I felt as I saw the montagnes slip away behind us, and all the land and the meadows and the town go off toward the horizon.

We got to New York and stayed at a big hotel. I never saw anything of New York except through the windows of our taxi and through the windows of my room. My father had some army doctors come and look at me. They handled my leg. I don't like to tell how I acted. It's all right to say I was nervous and excited, I suppose, as an excuse—but it was more than that. What I wanted was to be back in my own room on the ranch with my mother bringing up my food and reading to me and feeling sorry for me and making everything easy, or with Bob coming over, and being sympathetic, and letting me have my own way because his father'd told him I was sick.

I upset my mother, too. For about the first time I can remember, my mother and father nearly quarreled. My mother said, "But, Richard—" which is my father's name. "But, Richard, those Army doctors were very rough with him. After all, Johnny's only a little boy."

"A little boy?" said my father, his voice going kind of queer. "He's almost thirteen, and in another three or four years, the way he's starting to shoot up, he'll be bigger than I am. Those doctors weren't rough on him. They were busy. They came up here to look at him as a favor to me, my dear."

"Perhaps," my mother said, "we shouldn't plan to go to France with you, Richard. Perhaps we've made a mistake to do this with Johnny."

My father got a gray sort of sadness in his face. "I've been gone a long time, haven't I?" he said; and that was all he said.

He walked out of my room. My mother looked at me and went out. After a little while she came back and she looked at me again. Her voice wasn't quite as soft and sweet as it generally was when she said, "Johnny, these last three years while your father has been away, I have tried to do the best I can for you. But if *ever* I hear you shout and scream again, just because a doctor is trying to examine your leg, and say it was all your father's fault because he came back and made you leave Wyoming—if *ever*," she said, "you do such a thing again, I won't speak to you. I'll *never* speak to you. We're going to France. I *want* to go to France. Even if you don't seem to, *I* want to be with your father!"

After that, somehow, something changed between my mother and me. She remained just as sweet and pleasant as ever, but it was as if a thin curtain or shade had been pulled down between us. The worst part of it was, I blamed my father for it. I know it was wicked of me to think that—but I couldn't help it. I lay in that bed in New York, most of the time alone while my mother and father were running around in New York, having a gay time for all I knew. I thought how much better it had been back in Wyoming before my father returned, when the whole house and ranch more or less circled around me.

Well, we stayed about four days in New York. Afterwards, my father went to Washington. From there he flew to France. My mother and I had two more days of it, and it was pretty dismal. I wanted to go back home. I said if she'd agree to go back home I'd even let her take me to San Francisco where the doctors there could tinker with my leg.

On that subject she spoke a lot more sharply than she ever did before my father came home. She said it was silly for me to talk that way. I was big enough to understand there wasn't anything so dreadfully wrong about my leg that couldn't be fixed. It could go on this way for six months or a year, possibly, maybe two years. There was a chance I'd grow out of the trouble. She and my father had talked about it together, before he departed. The thing was, it wasn't good for me to stick to bed all the time and wait to see whether I'd grow out of the trouble. The operation wouldn't take very long; in the hands of a top-notch specialist, the job was simple and—she said—it hadn't ought to hurt too much. It wouldn't hurt—she said —nearly as much as my father had been hurt. By having it done in France, we could all be together instead of having the family split up once more. She thought I should be glad to go to France. She didn't understand why I acted this way.

I turned my face away from her when I said, "Nobody likes me any more."

Well, you'd have thought that might have brought some sort of response because I felt as low as dust. Do you know what happened? She laughed. Yes sir, my own mother. She laughed. I never heard such a heartless thing.

It was because my father had come back and filled her head with ideas about France and the two had made plans of their own, leaving me out. There I was sick, practically alone in New York, in bed, my leg hurting, wanting sympathy and kindness and maybe a big dish of chocolate ice cream or a promise from my mother I'd get a bicycle—and all that happened was my own mother laughed at me.

Perhaps if I died, they'd think back and feel sorry and wish they hadn't acted as mean as they had. After I died, I'd probably haunt them. It would serve them right.

I nearly did die, too, on that boat, although nobody but I realized it. I never have been so almighty sick in my life as I was on that boat going to France. Sick? Now I'm writing it down, even at the thought of how sick I was, I turn green around the gills and wish I hadn't eaten so much tonight for supper. . . .

The ship's doctor said I had to expect a touch of seasickness. He said he guessed almost everyone had it now and then. That man was the most casual person about sickness I ever did see. He seemed to think being seasick was something ordinary and cool like having a case of measles or scarlet fever or something on an even lower level.

At least my mother worried. She changed around when she saw I was likely to die and stayed up with me all the second night. I think maybe she had melted enough to promise a bicycle if I hadn't gotten hungry and told her, the third day, what I wanted was a couple of pieces of that mince pie and some ice cream they were serving for dinner. You'd think a proper mother would realize, wouldn't you, that a fellow can still be sick enough to die, maybe, and yet be starving to death, particularly for hot tantalizing mince pie?

Anyway. It was a mistake asking for the mince pie. I can see that now. Mother's eyes flashed sparks. She said she understood better than ever what Richard—that is, my father—my mother wasn't like some mothers who go around saying "your father" in the same tone of voice they'd say "your bicycle" or "your trousers need scrubbing," or "your teacher is coming to dinner," but she called my father Richard when she was speaking about him to me as if he was somebody important and real and human and—come to think of it—he was all of that. Where was I?

Oh yes. She said she understood better than ever what Richard meant about me needing to get well all the way through.

She said she hated wars. She said she hated wars for many reasons. One of them, not the least, was that wars split up families and did things to families but the Littlehorn family—which was our name—was one family that wasn't going to be licked by a war. When she said that she put down her foot hard. She said, "Do you understand, Johnny Littlehorn? Your father wasn't licked. I'm not going to be licked. And you're not going to be licked."

I didn't get any mince pie that night. I didn't get mince pie or a promise to be given a bicycle. When I was sick again that night and yelled for her, where she was sleeping in the next stateroom, do you know what she did? She closed the door. That's what she did. She closed the door. Although I yelled some more she kept the door closed, and I got so mad I guess I forgot I was seasick. The rest of the night I just thought about how my mother and my father were changing on me, and felt sad and sorry for myself, and homesick, with the ship we were on going up and down, creaking to itself, sloshing through the almighty blackness toward a place hundreds and hundreds of miles away.

My father met us at a town called Cherbourg. I won't try to tell you what a French town looks like yet, because I was too scared and worried about what was to happen to me to care anything for French towns or the special smells that French towns seem to have. They lugged me on a train which was less than half the size of our trains, with a little engine up front; and we got to this city that was Paris. They carted me out to a hospital and I was there for nearly two weeks.

Father and mother had taken rooms in a big hotel. After two weeks I was moved to one of these rooms in the hotel. The doctor who had worked on me, a little short white-headed man, Colonel Melvon—he came to the hotel a day or so later.

This time, though, he was in uniform. He didn't have his white clothes on. And somehow the hands didn't look as terrifying as I'd remembered them from those days in the hospital. They were still big, but they looked worn and thin, with brown spots on the skin. They were old hands. The yell slid back down into my throat and vanished. I found he was kind of smiling at me, and he said, "Johnny, I've come to tell you good-by. I'm on my way home. Are you feeling any better?"

He was smiling still more. Something in his eyes seemed to reach out to me. It was as if there was a special secret between him and me. He knew I was lying to him. He knew I didn't feel any better and never expected to feel better and the pain and hurt would always be in my leg, forever and ever.

He bent over and said, "I want to tell you something. That's why I came. Johnny, your leg is as good as an old man can ever make it. I can't do any more. From now on it depends on you whether you'll be able to run as well as you used to run. I can't help you. Your father, he can't help you. Your mother can't help you. If anything," he said, and he said it thoughtful and slow, "if anything, they'll hinder your getting well, Johnny. That's a funny thing for me to say, isn't it?"

I didn't answer.

He wasn't talking so much to me now, I could see, as to my mother and father who were in the room listening.

He said, "If they try to help you too much, they're liable to prevent you from recovering completely. They can't baby you, Johnny. If they do that, you're done for. You've got to want to get up. You've got to want to walk and run, no matter if it hurts like blazes. You've got to want to run and jump and make that leg of yours adjust itself to acting like a normal leg again and make that brain of yours realize the same thing. Good-by, Johnny. Good luck."

I blamed Colonel Melvon for the decision my father and my mother reached. My father was to go to England for a couple of months—not right away, but in a few weeks. He and my mother talked over what Colonel Melvon had said. They concluded England wasn't the place for me. I should be in the country, with sunshine and trees and grass. My father would have to stay in London.

They proposed sending me down to St. Chamant, in the middle of France. The first I heard of it was a few days later. My mother opened up the subject to me. She said she'd received a letter from her brother, Paul Langres. He was finishing his military work. He was in a city called Rouen, somewhere north of Paris, and planned to come to Paris in a week or so to see us, just as quickly as the military people would allow him to go. He was eager to see all of us. He'd written, after visiting us, he planned to return to St. Chamant, where he and my mother had been born. He hadn't been back to St. Chamant since the war had started. He wanted to stay there during the summer and part of the fall to rest and work on one of his projects and he suggested perhaps we'd like to go with him.

Well, that had given my mother an idea. She'd written to ask him if I could go with him and stay with him in St. Chamant. Of course, I protested. I wanted to be with my parents. My protests didn't do much good. My father thought it would help me. A day or so later, mon oncle wrote back and said he'd be delighted to take me.

I complained I wouldn't be able to walk or move—and I'd be a bother to him. By now, you see, I'd become accustomed not to move. As long as I remained in bed or stuck to a chair, it was all right. And all I wanted was to go home. I didn't even receive any enjoyment when my father brought home a collection of German coins for me. You can see how low I was.

The only friend I had was the hotel porter, Albert. My father had hired him to wheel me around Paris, hoping I'd pick up and find more interest in life once I got out of the hotel room. I told Albert how I might have to leave my parents and go down to a little no 'count French village. Albert spoke English, although he didn't speak it very well. He was fat with tiny eyes and puffed like a leaky kettle as he pushed my wheel chair.

"I'd rather die than be shoved off to St. Chamant," I said.

"St. Chamant?" he said, stopping.

"That's the name of the place," I said.

"St. Chamant?" he said once more, his voice having a squeaky sound to it. "You say it iss St. Chamant, Master Littlehorn?"

I said, "Sure. My mother was born there. She was a Langres."

"A *Langres?*" he said, the same way he'd said the name of the town, as if he was echoing me.

I twisted around at him. His mouth was open. I said, "My uncle's Paul Langres. He ought to be here in a couple of days. You don't know him, do you?"

"Know him? Ah, no," said Albert, giving my chair a jerk as he started pushing it. "For why should I know him?"

"You haven't ever been to St. Chamant?" I asked, hoping he had.

He shook his head. He said he'd never heard of it before. A little later he explained he'd been surprised to hear I was going because he enjoyed wheeling me in the chair and that seemed a reasonable explanation too. I said I wasn't sure I was going. I was going to get out of going if I could and he supported me in that. He said he didn't believe a lame boy such as me would enjoy being away from his parents. Well, that didn't hit me exactly right. I allowed I could exist without my mother and my father for a couple of months. But he went on and sympathized and pitied me and I began to feel sorry for myself. That night I argued louder than ever against going.

The following day Albert wheeled me into a little parc. He asked to be excused a few minutes. He said he wanted to buy some tobacco across the street. A tall man happened to walk by me and went on and returned and sat on one of those iron benches the French have in parcs. He was one of the tallest men I've ever seen, all bones, with a white face and a beard that was lopsided. I mean, it grew thicker on one side than the other. He had green-

From the start something about him wasn't very pleasant

ish eyes. He watched me with those greenish eyes. They made me uncomfortable. I wished Albert would hurry back.

He noticed my legs and my crutches. Pretty soon his eyes became soft and round. He hunched over toward me, the dark cloth of his suit wrinkling on him. I wanted to draw back. From the start something about him wasn't very pleasant although he did his best at first to be easy and friendly. "Bon jour," he said, in a voice soft as mucilage.

I said, "I don't speak French."

At that, his eyes opened wider. "Don't you now?" he said, in English just as good as mine. "I'm surprised at that, my young friend. If I had a son as intelligent as you appear to be, I'd quickly teach him French and take him with me and show him a good time instead of foisting him off with a stupid hotel porter."

It never occurred to me to ask him how he knew I was with a hotel porter.

My first feeling against him changed as he continued talking. He said he had a son who was lame, too. His son was in Marseilles. Telling me about his son more or less broke the ice between us. He said he was here in Paris on business and felt lonesome. He didn't like the people in Paris. I replied I didn't either. He smiled, all the sharp yellow teeth showing. Just for a second again I had that odd feeling toward him—but right away it passed. I forgot it as he told me how easy it was to learn French. "Now, take what I said. I said 'bon jour' to you. That means 'good day.' 'Bon' is 'good' and 'jour' is 'day.' You observe how easy it is? Bon jour. You say it."

So I said "good day" in French. I said, "Bon jour."

"There," he said, very cheerful. "It is easy?"

Albert seemed to be taking his time getting tobacco. We must have talked about fifteen minutes. The tall man said his name was Mr. Fishface—that's right. I didn't think I'd understood, either. He repeated it, calm and placid. He didn't appear to realize it was a funny name. He spelled it for me: "Fischfasse," which was French. I don't think he knew it was an almighty funny sort of name in our country. I managed not to laugh, though.

He said his son was coming to Paris in a few weeks. He hoped we could meet. His son was fifteen years old and knew English. Of course, that pleased me. Then—I remembered. I said I didn't think I'd be here. He lifted his eyebrows.

"My parents want to shove me off to St. Chamant with my uncle," I told him.

"Oh," said this Mr. Fischfasse. "St. Chamant? You and your uncle will live there?"

"I expect so. I don't want to go, though."

"Ah," said he, "no wonder. A dull little place."

"You've been there?" I asked.

"No," said he, "no, I have not been there. But I have friends who have passed through it. I am surprised any parents would send their boy there."

"My mother was born there," I explained. "Her family had a castle there or something. I expect my uncle and I will live in the castle."

I don't know why I stuck that part in about the castle. I shouldn't have. It was stretching the truth considerably; and later I paid for it. But he had kind of sneered when mentioning the town my mother came from. I didn't like that. I wanted him to realize my mother's people and where she lived were important, even if the town wasn't.

"You're going to *live*—" He broke off. He got up, joint by joint. "I must go now. Perhaps if you are here tomorrow we shall see each other again, Mr. Littlehorn. I will teach you a few more French words and you'll surprise that good father of yours." Then, he said, "Bon jour," and off he went.

I replied, "Bon jour," and waited for Albert to arrive and take me back to the hotel.

That evening, I started to tell my mother and my father I'd run into a Mr. Fischfasse, but they never let me finish. My mother said, "Why, Johnny. You mustn't call people names like that."

I said, "I can't help it. That's his name. He looks like a fish, too."

My father laughed. "Johnny, don't let that imagination of yours run away with you."

I said, "But I *did*—"

My father laughed again. "You've been cooped up in bedrooms for so long you'll be seeing giants and monsters, too, if you don't be careful."

And my father and mother got to talking, again, about shunting me away from them. I didn't care to hear any more about it. I dragged off to my bedroom. Here, I tried playing with my coins. When my mother came in to put out the lights, I asked, "Did you live in a castle in St. Chamant?"

She halfway smiled. "It wasn't a castle, Johnny. But it was a very wonderful house. I haven't seen it for years. Paul hasn't either since the Germans attacked France. I hope they haven't hurt our house too much. I shall want you to see it. Good night."

I tried my French on her. "Bon jour," I said.

This time she smiled all the way around. "Why, Johnny. Bon jour. But when it's night, you don't say 'bon jour.' You say 'good night' or 'bonne nuit.' "

I tried that on my father a little later. He understood it and grinned and replied, "Bonne nuit, Jean."

I asked, "What's that last word?"

He said, "Jean?"

I said, "Yes sir. That one."

He answered, "That's you. 'Jean' is your name in French. 'Jean' is 'John.' "

Well, that did it.

I didn't mind trying a couple of words in the lingo but when I heard the French had gone and changed my own name to Jean it was too much. I was through talking French. I was finished. I said, "Father, can't we go home now?" I said, "Please."

He stopped smiling. His face got the same tired gray look it had before we started saying "Bonne nuit" to each other. He shook his head. "I'm sorry," he said. "The government has made me an officer in the army and I have a duty and I can't run from that duty, can I? If I'm ordered to report to London on the Allied Aviation Committee it's my duty to go and not complain. I'm sorry." He shook his head and said, "I'm very sorry, Johnny." He turned off the light and shut the door. He'd sounded sorry, too. I won't ever forget how sorry he'd sounded. It was as though I'd done something to make him sorry.

I couldn't go right to sleep. I thought about the French changing my name into "Jean" and how queer names were and about Mr. Fischfasse and all at once I remembered he'd known my name. He'd called me "Mr. Littlehorn." I couldn't understand that. He hadn't ever seen me before. I hadn't told him my name, either. I couldn't get over it. I was bothered. I went to sleep and had dreams about him, only he was like something made out of dry wood in my dreams, about a mile high, his white face stuck on top of the sticks, like a dead fish.

3

THE BARGAIN

When it was time, the next day, for Albert to
wheel me outside I told him I didn't want to go back to the
parc. I didn't explain the true reason; I merely said to Albert to push me through some other part of Paris because
I was tired of seeing the same old streets. He nodded and
replied, "Yess," and shoved along, humming to himself.

The fact was, I had a notion Mr. Fischfasse might be
waiting in the parc and I didn't want to see him again. I
can't explain exactly why. Maybe it was because of the
dreams I'd had last night, seeing that fishlike white head
of his miles up in the air on sticks, grinning down at me,
as if it held a secret against me and was waiting for me to
get in trouble.

Despite being bundled in the blanket, I shivered a little.
Albert wheeled me around the big opera house. He trun-
dled me along through another street. I got to thinking I'd
imagined everything, and was wondering why I'd been
scared—feeling secure, of course, not expecting to run
into Mr. Fischfasse again.

Well, Albert either didn't understand my directions or
was just dumb. He ran smack into that parc again, this
time from another direction. I didn't want to kick up a row
about it. It wasn't important enough. Albert let go of the
handle to the chair. He said if I didn't mind, he'd leave me
here a minute and buy himself more tobacco.

I did mind. I was telling him I was tired and he could

buy himself tobacco in the hotel but he merely smiled, pleased and cheerful, as if he hadn't heard me, and thought I'd given him permission to go.

I called, "Albert—"

But he nodded. "I be back in vun minute," and away he trotted, his fat legs moving faster than I realized they could go. I sunk down into the chair, wanting him to get back. When I looked up, Mr. Fischfasse was sauntering toward me through the trees.

I tried not to notice him, hoping he'd go on.

He didn't. He halted. "Ah, bon jour, Jean," he said to me.

"Bon jour, Mr. Fischfasse," I said, knowing how to answer that. Next I asked, "How'd you know my name?"

He looked perplexed. "But you told it to me yesterday."

I probably blinked at that. I never remembered telling him, but I must have done it after all. It explained everything.

His greenish eyes lit up again. He smiled. He sat down on the bench, taking his time about doing it, as if he might break some of those sticks inside his dark suit.

I don't mean he really had sticks inside his clothes. However, he was so tall and skinny and stiff, it was as though his arms and legs were made of sticks nailed together.

I thought maybe he'd been sick or perhaps during the war he hadn't had much to eat. But right away, I learned I was wrong on that guess. Confiding and friendly, he told me how he and his family had been forced to run away when the Germans came and he had gone to Spain to live. He and his family had returned to France only a few months ago. He said Spain was better than France. People ate better in Spain. I'd read newspapers. In the newspapers the facts were different. People were starving in Spain. I wondered what he meant. He didn't explain.

He leaned over. In his soft way he said, "You mustn't call me 'Mister Fischfasse.' You must say 'Monsieur Fisch-fasse.' Monsieur is French for mister."

So I repeated, "Bon jour, Monsieur Fischfasse," wanting Albert to come quick.

He said that was fine. Then he said, "Le jour est beau?"

I didn't get any of that at all. At least, at first I didn't think I did. I must have looked puzzled because he started laughing. He had a queer laugh. It was soft and short and the only way to describe it is to say it was like the way some of the coyotes laugh, even though some people might tell you coyotes don't know how to laugh. I've heard coyotes laugh; and when they laugh it's because they've worked out some plan to fool people and are tickled by it. If you hear that laugh you'll find you've got shivers running down your spine. Well, hearing Mr. Fischfasse's soft short laugh somehow put shivers down my spine.

I forgot right away his laugh had bothered me because he reached across and laid those long dry fingers of his on my arm and said gently, "Le jour est beau, non?" repeating his question.

Well, I got a couple of words out of it. I got "jour" and I got the "non." "Jour" was "day"—and I guessed the "non" was our English "no." I told him that was all I understood.

He explained he'd been asking me a question in French. Nobody had to tell me it was in French. I knew that much! He said "*le* jour" meant "*the* day" and probably I ought to have known that. And "est" was "is;" and "beau" was the word the French had for "beautiful." So he was asking:

"The day is beautiful, no?" Simple. In other words: "Isn't the day beautiful?"

I asked, "What do I say?"

He said, "You can reply 'oui.' That means 'yes.' "

The fact is, le jour was beau. It was a beautiful day, all right, but I wished Albert didn't have to take so long to get tobacco. I didn't enjoy being with Monsieur Fischfasse, even though he was laying himself out to be agreeable.

He didn't try any more French on me. He asked if I'd heard any more about being sent to St. Chamant, explaining he'd received a letter from his son this morning and wanted to write him telling about me. I replied it looked as if I was stuck unless I could persuade my mother and my father to take me with them to London.

He said, "You must try to persuade them, Jean. Yes, indeed." His face twisted suddenly and looked mean. "I do not think you would like St. Chamant. I do not think so, at all."

I asked, "What's wrong with St. Chamant?" looking around, hoping to see Albert.

"The people are most disagreeable there."

That didn't make sense to me. He couldn't know whether or not the people were disagreeable, having never been there himself. Inasmuch as my mother had come from St. Chamant I didn't appreciate the fact he was so much against it and I said, "I might like it. My mother was from there, you know. Her family has a big house there, like a castle. If I went there my uncle and I would stay in it."

"But the house no longer is there. The Germans have burned it."

"How do you know?" I asked, puzzled.

"You are a very stupid boy," he said in a sudden rage.

He jumped off the seat and came toward me—and stopped.

He whirled around and walked away before Albert arrived. It happened all at once. I was tremendously glad to see Albert. I told him I didn't want to come to this parc again. "Yess," he said, amiable as ever, puffing on his pipe. I tried to drive that fact into his head. I'd been pretty much scared for about a second. He said, "Yess," again, smiling, puffing on the pipe, not paying much attention.

He didn't take me back to the hotel as soon as I expected, either.

He wheeled me around the streets for nearly an hour more, although I asked him to get on back to the hotel. I was dead tired. After that experience with Monsieur Fischfasse, I wanted—I might as well admit it—I wanted to be with my father and my mother. I didn't feel secure anymore when I was away from them. I kept seeing that white face looming at me.

Along about two or three in the afternoon we reached the hotel. Albert wheeled me into the elevator and up to my room. He pushed the chair into my room and bowed, as he always did. I shut the door after thanking him, although today I didn't feel very thankful.

After laying myself down to rest, I heard voices coming from the next room. I was surprised to hear my father's. Usually he worked all day. I heard another voice, too, muffled through the wall. I thought it was mon oncle who had come to Paris. I got out of bed, using my crutches.

I managed to lump it into the sitting room. I suppose I should have knocked first, but I was too eager to see mon oncle. Anyway, I just pushed the door—went on through.

When I looked up, the first thing I saw was the man whom I'd met in the parc. He and my father and mother were sitting in the parlor, talking. I exclaimed, "Monsieur Fisch-fasse—" saying it the way he pronounced it, "Fish-face!"

I wish you could have seen my father and mother then.

My mother said, "Why, John!" and jumped up.

The tall man smiled weakly. He gave me a look as if he hadn't ever seen me and was embarrassed at having a boy jump out at him and call him "Fish-face." My father asked, "John, what's gotten into you? Apologize at once to Monsieur Simonis."

I stared at the man. "But he *is* Monsieur—"

"That will do!" said my father in a big hard voice. "John, do you hear me?"

The man said, "It is nothing, monsieur," to my father, with a weak-as-milk smile on his face. "This is your son?" he went on.

He knew I was the son. He knew who I was. I never heard of a man acting the way he did. My father said, yes, I was his son, and repeated he didn't know what was the matter with me, and was embarrassed. My mother rushed to me and whispered, "Johnny Littlehorn, you apologize instantly to Monsieur Simonis."

I said, "But I know he's Monsieur Fish-face—"

My mother bundled me out of the room, with my father standing, his face red, embarrassed clear through.

For the first time in years my mother locked the door on me. I stayed there nearly half an hour, until my father entered and sat down. He said, "John, I simply can't understand how you would do such a thing."

I tried to tell him I had met the man before.

My father shook his head. "No, that won't do, John. It

won't do at all. It's bad enough to have you jump in on us and call a guest 'Fish-face' before our very eyes, but to have you try to wriggle out of it later and lie—"

When my mother came in she listened to my explanation. She said perhaps I'd seen a man in the parc by that name. That was possible. But she said I couldn't have seen Monsieur Simonis before. He was a dealer in wines who lived in Tulle before the war, escaping into Spain when the Germans came. Excitedly, I said Monsieur Fish-face had done that, too. He'd lived in Spain.

My father said, "Be reasonable, Johnny. Suppose Monsieur Simonis had met you in the park. Why should he tell you his name was something else?"

That stumped me. I couldn't answer that one. It was an absolute, livid mystery to me and I didn't get the answer to it for months afterwards. All it did now was to confuse me. More than ever it convinced my parents I'd been imagining something or out of sheer contrariness had tried to show off in front of their visitor by calling him "Fish-face."

My father saw I was too stumped to reply. He said, "There you are, Johnny. Monsieur Simonis never saw any of us before. He arrived in Paris today. He is buying vineyards around St. Chamant. He heard from friends of your mother in St. Chamant that we were here. He came here to ask your mother if she and her brother wanted to sell their property. He offered a very low price for it, too, telling her the Germans burnt down the Langres house two years ago."

I tried once more. "He told me that too. The house is burnt down."

My father sighed and shook his head.

My mother said, "Johnny, it isn't good for you to imagine things."

It wasn't any use to attempt to make them believe me, even when I said that they could ask Albert tomorrow when he came for me if he hadn't seen the man.

My mother must have talked with my father about what I'd said at dinner, that night. I didn't feel like eating—I was too much disturbed. They brought in food for me to eat later on, and stayed there, to make sure I'd at least try to stuff it down. I could see they were worried about me, too.

It was such a mess, I didn't half believe what had happened myself any more. I repeated I was sorry if I'd made a mistake. My mother said she was sure it wouldn't happen again. I asked, "Are you going to sell your home?" hoping she would. That would mean I could stay with my parents and not go to St. Chamant.

My mother shook her head. "Half an hour ago, I talked to Paul long-distance. He doesn't want to sell. If he doesn't, I don't either. He hopes to rebuild the Langres house. *I* want him to, too," she said, lifting her head, proud and trusting. "You and Paul can live in the little hotel in St. Chamant. It will be quite comfortable."

My father said, "Johnny, your uncle Paul is coming here tomorrow or the next day. I think you'll like him. He plans to try to build an avion he's invented." My father stopped, as if he was doing his best to interest me and cheer me up. "Do you know what an 'avion' is, Johnny?"

I didn't care what an avion was.

He said, " 'Avion' is French for 'airplane.' "

Well, when somebody starts talking about avions—airplanes—it's almighty hard not to be interested even if you have an idea the whole world is coming apart. I said, "My oncle's inventing an *airplane?*"

"That's right. As I've told you I've written him a couple of times about you. Today when we talked to him on the long-distance telephone, he said he'd be here tomorrow, or the next day, maybe, so your mother and I can leave for England."

I said if I went to England with them I could learn to walk there just as well as being shunted off to a little French town where I didn't know anyone.

My father replied that was the difficulty: In England, my mother and he would live in London. He was going over there as a member of the Allied Aviation Commission. Because of a shortage of trustworthy translators, he had arranged for my mother to be put on as a temporary government employee, to help translate documents. Both of them would be very busy, and have no time for me. It couldn't be helped. This was government work, for our country. They hoped I would understand and realize how important it was.

I couldn't argue against them.

I was stuck. After eating, they left me alone for a time. I kept thinking about the white-faced man in the parc. They came in to tell me "Bonne nuit" and afterwards, in the dark, I still thought of that man. I wondered if I'd see him again if Albert took me to the parc. If I saw him, I'd know for sure whether he was someone else or the same man who'd tried to buy my mother's property in St. Chamant.

All that night, I didn't get much sleep.

A couple of times I thought I heard noises at my door. Perhaps no one ever actually came down the hotel corridor. I don't know. Anyway, both times I thought I heard the noises I lifted straight up in bed. Probably it doesn't make sense, but immediately I imagined Monsieur Simonis or Fischfasse, whatever his name was, was attempting to get in at me. I don't know why. I can't explain that. I simply had the fear. The first time I got to the door and listened and got back to bed, too, despite my leg. I walked. I was so scared and concerned I didn't have time to worry about my leg or how my leg hurt when I used it for walking.

It's a funny thing what you can do when you have to do it. Once I was in bed I lay there and sweated and felt the pain and wondered how I'd ever done it—but the second time that noise came, I didn't stop to wonder. I just did it again.

Halfway back to the bed the second time, I realized what I was doing. I sort of halted. I grit my teeth and deliberately put all the weight of my body on my bum leg. And that leg didn't flop out of joint like it used to at all. No sir, it hurt—but it stuck smack in place and stayed there.

I expected to fall, too. It made me kind of mad, thinking of all the days I'd wasted in bed or had been wheeled around like an invalid. When I did get into bed, I didn't care so much that my leg was hurting. I realized if I hadn't been such a baby and had tried my leg more frequently, my mother wouldn't have asked that hotel porter, Albert, to wheel me around—and I wouldn't have run into Monsieur Fischfasse.

Next morning, my father didn't go to work as early as usual. He stopped in to see me. First, he said, "Bon jour, Jean."

So I said, "Bon jour, father."

He said, "You should say, 'bon jour, mon père.' That means 'good morning, my father.' 'Mon père' is French for 'my father.' "

So I said, "Bon jour, mon père."

He laughed. He was pleased. He sat down. He said, "C'est un beau jour?" and he was still laughing, because of how I must have looked at him. I don't think he expected me to figure out what he'd said this time. But I fooled him, in a way.

I remembered from yesterday when that white-faced man had said, "Le jour est beau, non?" My father had said practically the same words except for that "c'est" thing. I knew already that "est" was our "is." Somehow, after walking last night, I must have felt better. Anyway, I made a guess. I decided "c'est" might be something like "it is"—and I replied, "Oui, mon père. Le jour est beau," and waited to see if I'd answered as I should have. It was like a game.

He said, "Johnny, you *are* picking up a little French, aren't you? That's fine, Johnny." He was as pleased as could be. I asked about that "c'est." I'd been nearly right. It meant "it is"—actually, it meant "it's," so I had guessed almost on the dot when my father had told me, "It's a beautiful day."

He became more serious. "Johnny, I don't want you to think we're running out on you. You know we're not, don't you? All last night I worried. I'm sorry about yesterday when I lost my temper because I thought you were insulting Monsieur Simonis. I'm willing to accept your word you did think he was someone else."

It made me feel weak and funny inside to hear my father

talk that way, as if he'd done something wrong. Yesterday, I'd thought my father and my mother were shunting me off from them. Now when I looked up at him and saw how thin and tired his face was, with the scar red and ugly, all at once I knew I didn't ever have to worry that they were trying to get rid of me. All along they'd known I was *able* to walk—if only I put my mind to it. I'd had to be scared nearly to death before finding that out. I guess I felt a lump in my throat. I'd planned to blame them and tell them I knew they didn't like me anymore and kick up a row for being left behind. . . .

You see, I'm aiming to put everything down here, just as it happened, even if it makes me appear a pretty low sort of person, as I guess I must have been.

But I didn't do what I planned. I looked up and told my father, "If oncle Paul'll let me help build his avion, maybe I'll have lots more fun than going to England."

Well, his face cleared. He smiled. He said, "Johnny, you watch me fix that for you."

I said, "Would you like to watch me do something?"

He said, "You bet, Johnny."

I threw off my covers and I walked clear to the door and almost got all the way back. I wasn't scared like I'd been last night so I could feel the pain more this morning. When the pain came I wasn't used to having so much of it. I had to stop. My father grabbed me. Even if I was going on thirteen, too big to be hugged by my father—he *did* hug me. I'm not ashamed to write it down here. He carried me back to my bed and called my mother. To hear him, you'd have thought I'd done the most wonderful thing in the world.

"Johnny," he said, all of a sudden, "here I've been worrying all night because I was afraid you'd be angry at your mother and me. You've surprised me. You have, and I'm proud of you, too. I'll make a bargain with you. What do you want most to have?"

I didn't have to do any thinking to answer that. I said, "A bicycle with a high gear and a low gear like the one Bob Collins has."

"I'll tell you what I'll do," said my father. "You go down to St. Chamant with your uncle Paul, without complaining. If in the three months you're there you can learn to use your leg again and walk—you don't have to run— just walk, Johnny, I'll *buy* you a bicycle. I'll get one from England. With gears on it."

Mother was smiling. She said, "Bob's bicycle hasn't any lights, has it? I'll tell you what *I'll* do, Johnny. If you can learn to walk again in three months you ought to be able to learn enough French to write me a letter. Remember, I was born in France. I love France. Nothing would please me more, next to having you walk again, than having you stop being so stubborn about the French. If you can learn enough French in three months to write me a letter, not very long, I'll promise to buy you one of those electric lights—" She hesitated. She appealed to father. "Oh, Richard, *you* know the lights I mean. Not the ones with a flashlight battery, but real lights, just like the automobiles have."

"A dynamo," said my father, grinning. "They have bicycles in England and France with electric dynamos to run the lights. That's what you mean."

"Yes," said my mother, smiling again. "That is exactly what I mean. What do you say, Johnny?"

What could anybody say, being offered the chance to

get a bicycle with a high gear and a low gear and electric lights from a real electric dynamo? Nobody back in Wyoming had ever seen such a scrumptious thing. I could just shut my eyes and imagine myself wheeling out such a bicycle on a dark night and simply flicking the switch and putting it in gear and riding over to Bob Collins' or into town, having everyone gaping at me, wondering what in nation I was on.

Why, I tell you: For a bicycle like that, I guess I would have promised to sprout wings and a halo, to go to church every day in the week, to keep my nails clean, to wash behind my ears, and to do my school lessons without ever being told. Instead, all I had to do was go to a French town with mon oncle, build an avion there, probably fly around in the avion and have a noble time doing it—and walk and learn French. Anybody could do that—was what I then believed, at least.

So I said it.

"It's a bargain," I said.

"We'll make it you have to be able to walk two miles," said my father.

I said, "I'll walk twenty miles for—"

"Two miles will be enough, Johnny."

"And write at least two pages in French," added my mother.

"It will be easy," I said.

I was so pleased and excited, all my worries about that white-faced man passed away, as though it had all been a bad dream.

A little later I got to thinking more about the promise I had made to learn French. I put down all the French words

I knew so far. When I was finished, I was surprised I knew so many. Here they are:

1. Montagne	7. C'est	13. Parc
2. Oncle	8. Nuit	14. Oui
3. Bon	9. Jean	15. Non
4. Jour	10. Monsieur	16. Le (jour)
5. Est	11. Mon	17. Bonne (nuit)
6. Beau	12. Père	18. Avion

Knowing how to say "it's" was helpful. With that "c'est" I could make sentences. I could say, "C'est mon père;" "C'est mon oncle;" or, I could say, "Le jour est beau;" and, "Le parc est beau;" or I could ask myself silly questions like, "Est mon oncle le parc?" And answer myself, "Non, le parc est le parc." Maybe it seems foolish, but I found it was fun. It was a start toward getting that dynamo, I figured. I looked at all the words and said them over and I had them down cold and I hadn't even tried to learn them.

4

ONCLE PAUL

I was in bed next morning when that Monsieur Simonis telephoned to ask if my mother had decided to sell the property. By the time I was up, I heard my father and mother talking about it.

Monsieur Simonis had been cross, learning he was refused. My father said he was glad my mother and Paul were keeping the property. It had been owned for generations by members of the Langres family. If Paul succeeded in inventing a successful new avion, perhaps he would receive enough money from it to rebuild the house and settle once more in St. Chamant.

"I hope he does," said my mother. "I do hope so, very much."

My father looked at his watch again. He waited until about eleven, but mon oncle Paul didn't arrive. He said probably Paul would catch tomorrow morning's train. He kissed my mother and gave me a pat and went off to work, late.

At one-thirty, Albert appeared on the dot to take me for my ride in the wheel chair. My mother thanked him for attending to me during the past week and said today would be the last time he'd have to give me an outing in Paris. I was leaving tomorrow for the country.

"Oh, by the way," she said. "Johnny mentioned he encountered a French gentleman in the park. He became

43

rather confused over the name. You don't happen to remember, do you, Albert?"

"I am most sorry, madame." He smiled sheepishly at me.
"I get tobacco. I leave Master Jean, and for one or two
minutes I go get tobacco. Iss wrong to do that?"

"Of course not," said my mother. "Johnny's quite safe
at his age in Paris for a minute or so, certainly. You didn't
see anyone, then?"

"No, madame," said Albert, pulling at his cap. "I am
most sorry."

"Never mind. It isn't important." My mother bundled
me up and watched Albert wheel me to the elevator.

Outside, on the sidewalk, Albert asked, "You see somebody in the parc, yess?"

"Yes," I said, thinking Albert was so dumb it wasn't any
good to try to explain to him.

Albert didn't ask any more questions. He pushed me
around the opera house, waiting on the corner while all
the bicycles and the horses went by. Gasoline was still
scarce; there weren't many automobiles around. The
streets were lined with shade trees, the leaves out and
green and pretty. It was a beautiful jour, the sun shining.

He pushed me up more streets, humming that silly tune
to himself. By and by he stopped humming and filled his
pipe. I was beginning to enjoy myself, thinking that I'd
made a big mistake ever to believe that someone visiting
my father could have been the same man whom I'd met in
the parc. I started thinking about mon oncle, wondering
why he was so set on building an avion and if I'd like him
and whether he was big or little, all the questions you ask
yourself about somebody you expect to meet.

I didn't notice until too late that Albert had headed the

wheel chair down toward that same blessed little parc. I
said, "Wait a minute, Albert—" but it was like trying to
tell a mule where to go. Albert sucked loudly on his empty
pipe. He smiled at me.

He said, "I get a little tobacco, pliss."

"Look here," I said, "I don't want to stop here in this
parc. I don't care for this parc at all."

"Yess," said Albert, still smiling.

But he shoved me into the parc. There under the green
trees, was the man whom I'd met—and he was the same
man I'd seen with my father and my mother. I couldn't
mistake him. Coldness slid all down through my spine. I
gave a jerk—and tried to lunge out of the chair. Albert
stuck his big hand on my shoulder and held me down,
pinned where I was.

Monsieur Simonis—to call him by the name he'd given
himself in front of my father—stood up from the bench,
long and thin, his green eyes cruel. "Bon jour, Jean," he
said, making his face smile!

We were alone, Albert and him and me, surrounded by
the trees, with a little stone fountain over to one side
splashing water into the sunshine.

"Well?" he said, coming to me, his teeth showing in his
white face.

I didn't reply—I couldn't.

"Well?" he asked again, laying his long stiff fingers on
my shoulder. "Perhaps you can help me persuade that foolish mother of yours she should sell her land in St. Chamant." He reached down with his long fingers and dug his
nails into my leg, twisting it.

It happened so suddenly, so unexpectedly, I wasn't prepared at all. I opened my mouth to yell. The next instant,

he clapped his other hand over my mouth. "This will teach you," he whispered, "to pay attention to what I am saying. I want no noise out of you, foolish boy."

I wriggled, expecting Albert to lay in on him and help me—to shout—to do something. But I caught a glimpse of

I didn't reply—I couldn't

Albert, grinning away, puffing at that empty pipe of his, seeming to enjoy what was happening.

Monsieur Simonis removed his hand. I slumped back, catching my breath.

Monsieur Simonis ordered harshly, "Listen carefully, silly boy. I have informed myself all about you. You are an only child and your parents are in the habit of spoiling you. Is that not true?"

Even if it was true, it wasn't pleasant hearing him say that. And in addition to what he said, he had a manner, an attitude, that went way and beyond his words toward filling me with absolute horror of him. I don't think I can ever explain. I can see now, too, how clever he was. He never said anything which could be reported against him. If I told anyone it sounded merely as if he'd stopped me and out of the kindness of his heart had said St. Chamant wasn't a very good place to go to and my parents should know that fact. You see, it wasn't so much *what* he said, but the *way* he said it which conveyed an altogether different meaning to me and let me know he was determined I wasn't to live in St. Chamant. He was sinister and cruel and he allowed me to see he was. He went on, his eyes as green as a cat's. He said, "I suggest—do you understand? I *suggest* that St. Chamant would be a very inhospitable place for a boy of your age. Your parents are making a very great mistake to—" He didn't finish. Albert whistled a warning. Just like a big skinny cat, too, Monsieur Simonis whirled about and sprang through the trees, vanishing.

A big fat Frenchman and a little yellow-haired girl, about five, walked by. The little girl saw me. She ran over to me and said, "Bon jour."

Even though I recognized by now that Albert was in cahoots with Monsieur Simonis, I cried, "Help, help!" to the big Frenchman, my voice probably weak and frightened. The little girl's father asked Albert, "Qu'est-ce que c'est que ça?" and if it annoys you to see that string of French words put together which you can't understand, how do you think I felt when he said all of that?

I knew I was lost. It was the first time in my life I'd needed a Frenchman to understand what I was telling him

—and here he was, big enough to help me, and he wasn't
any more use to me than if he was deaf!

Albert chuckled. He replied. I don't know what he said,
but whatever it was, it was a lie because the big fat Frenchman laughed. He tipped his hat and said, "Bon jour, mon
garçon." The little girl laughed; and *she* said, "Bon jour,"
too. Away they both went.

I heard Albert make a gritty sound in his mouth, as if
he were shoving his teeth together. He said, "For that, I
vill twist your leg hard—" and he came at me. I grabbed at
my crutches and jumped. I landed on the gravel path. I
scurried up, trying to run with the crutches. I didn't succeed very well. I was panting and half crying, thinking he
was right behind me when I ran into somebody.

I fell down. I was picked up, put on my feet. "Ah, now.
What is this?" said a lively voice. I looked up. The man
who had taken hold of me was gazing at me, cheerful and
gay. He was about twenty or twenty-one, I imagine,
dressed in baggy old French clothes. He had black curly
hair and black eyes and a nose sticking so far out of his
face you could hang your hat on it. He wasn't much bigger
than I was, either, although he gazed at me, his head flung
back, as if he considered he was at least six feet tall.

I'd seen photographs of him—and, once you'd seen a
photograph of him from one side, showing the length of
that nose, you'd never forget him. I exclaimed, "Oncle
Paul!"

"Voici!" said he, his eyes sparkling. "Jean!"

Next thing, he kissed me on one side of the cheek and on
the other. Afterwards I learned that was a method all
French had when they greeted friends or relatives of theirs,
men or women, it didn't make any difference. I wriggled

away, remembering about Albert and Monsieur Simonis. All my fear came back. I can see now how I must have confused mon oncle Paul, shouting the men were after me.

When I got quieted down, I saw nobody was in the parc except oncle Paul and me. That Albert had decamped, too. He must have seen mon oncle pick me up and run to keep another and safer appointment. Mon oncle wheeled me to the hotel, explaining his train had been late. He'd arrived just a few minutes ago at the hotel. My mother had told him I'd probably be in the parc and he had gone to surprise me and fetch me back to the hotel.

Back in the hotel I repeated everything that had taken place while my mother and my father and mon oncle Paul listened. Just as I've explained to you, Monsieur Simonis was too clever for me. It was exactly as if he expected me to report on him and had figured out a method to beat me, no matter.

My mother and my father were simply confused. I think they considered I still was set against going to St. Chamant and had worked up a big tale about a mysterious man to persuade them not to send me. It didn't help when I urged them to telephone down to the hotel manager and ask him to send Albert up to them, so they might question Albert. My father did telephone down.

The hotel manager was sorry. Albert had left a note explaining his sudden departure. Albert's sister in Rheims, a city north of Paris, had telegraphed Albert's mother was sick. So Albert had departed. My father hung up and shook his head and said, "This beats me. Johnny, are you *certain* you saw that fellow Simonis?" He asked my mother, "Should I send for a doctor?"

I didn't want a doctor.

From the other side of the room, mon oncle winked at me, as if he understood how dense grown-ups could be. He folded his brown hands around his knees. He said, "Voilà, perhaps I can explain this mystery."

"I certainly wish you could, Paul," said my mother.

According to mon oncle Paul the mayor of St. Chamant was a man named Monsieur Capedulocque. While most of the men, older boys too, of the village had gone away during the war and hidden in the montagnes when the Germans came, this mayor had remained. Mon oncle Paul said no one had ever proved Monsieur Capedulocque had actually worked with the Germans. No. The mayor had kept free from that suspicion. But he had taken over the vineyards and sold pigs and goats and made a lot of money. Now he was the wealthiest man in St. Chamant, with almost everyone else owing him money.

Before the war, none of the Capedulocques had been very important. They were jealous of the Langres family, and the Meilhac family, and a few other important families living near the town. These families had been pretty much ruined by the war. Now the mayor was buying up their vineyards and land and forests. He had attempted to buy the Langres property cheaply. Mon oncle Paul had written him several times, refusing.

Now mon oncle Paul finished, "I zink this—" He never could pronounce "think" as it should be pronounced. "I zink this mayor has arranged for an agent of his to come to Paris, my dear sister, and see you to persuade you to sell our land."

"That makes sense," said my father, thoughtfully. "Then, you believe Monsieur Simonis was trying to purchase the land for that rascally mayor?"

"Oui," said mon oncle Paul, nodding his head, smiling at me. "It is simple. And Monsieur Simonis gives, maybe, a little money to this Albert to find out about you before approaching you. When we refuse to sell the land, Monsieur Simonis goes to Jean here—" He indicated me. "He wishes Jean to help him persuade you to sell by refusing to leave for St. Chamant. Is it not that, perhaps? Monsieur Simonis is most stupid, I zink. He zink if Jean and I do not go to St. Chamant and see how beautiful is our land, very soon my sister and I—we change our minds. We say, 'Oui, we will sell.' Voici!"

My father glanced at me. He began grinning. "Johnny, I guess I made a mistake. I'm sorry for not believing you. Poor old Simonis was merely a French business man trying to make a sale and hoping you could help him. If you hadn't let that wild young imagination of yours—"

"But it wasn't my imagination!" I cried. "He *did* threaten me."

There it was, again. Even if they had worked out a solution which satisfied them, they couldn't realize there was something more to it than merely wanting to buy land owned by my mother and mon oncle. They persisted in believing I'd become excited because I had been sick and miserable and cooped up. My father laughed and picked me up in his arms, big as I was, and carried me into my bedroom and said I wasn't to worry. A couple of months or so in the country, and I'd be well and strong and forget to be afraid of any stranger I happened to encounter.

"Bosh," said my father, and told me to rest now, to take a nap. He was going out to buy tickets. He wanted to give my mother and mon oncle a chance to see each other alone. I wasn't to disturb them.

Mon oncle Paul couldn't remain for dinner. After talking with my mother, he left to arrange for supplies to be sent on down to him in St. Chamant for that avion he was determined to build. At dinnertime, my mother and my father were busy with their own plans of what they would do in England.

That night I slept fairly well. I didn't have dreams about Monsieur Simonis but I did awake early in the morning. I thought about him and about Albert and tried to puzzle out what they actually wanted. It seemed to me this morning, more sure than ever before, that my parents and mon oncle Paul failed to understand there was more to the mystery than someone merely wanting to buy a parcel of land. But if I talked about it any more, they'd consider I was merely attempting to wriggle out of my bargain to get the bicycle with the high gear and the low gear and the electric lighting dynamo. In the excitement of preparing to depart, I pushed away all thoughts about Monsieur Simonis and the mystery. . . .

After breakfast, my mother let me help her pack my duds. I was to leave that afternoon. Ordinarily, I suppose I wouldn't have wanted to go, considering what had happened. But I did want to get that bicycle. I was tired of never walking. It's true, my mother showed she was a little nervous too. She said I was to write regularly from St. Chamant and if the mayor caused me any difficulty—or if, for that matter, anyone caused Paul and me difficulty she wanted to know in a hurry.

While we were packing, my mother also told me a little more about her brother. She said first he'd been in the army and then he'd been with the French underground and had fought against the Germans all during the war. She explained he was dreadfully poor now, because all the money her father had left him had been stolen by the Germans. He had learned how to fly. While he'd been in the hospital he had thought of a new kind of avion. She wasn't very clear in her own mind what kind of avion it was— you know how women are, that way. But I could see she was concerned over her brother. He had a little money the French government had given him while he was a lieutenant, saved out of his pay. With that he planned to live in this little town of St. Chamant during the rest of the summer and fall and hoped to build his avion himself before he ran out of money.

My mother said he wouldn't take anything from my father. So, she said, my father planned to give me quite a lot of money for a boy of my age, almost three hundred dollars, changed into French money. She asked me to look out for mon oncle Paul without hurting his pride and to make sure he didn't spend all his money on his avion and that he ate enough food and took proper care of himself. The result was, I had a responsibility, too.

My father and mother were leaving late that night for London. We had lunch together, all four of us. Mon oncle Paul was still in his old worn clothes, but to look at him you'd never realize he might be aware of how shabby he looked. His clothes were clean. He kept them neatly pressed. His curly black hair was brushed. He was gay as ever, telling my parents they were to have a good time in England and not to be concerned about me.

When he talked fast he made me want to laugh because sometimes he wouldn't say our words exactly right—he'd say "ziss" for "this" and "I zink" for "I think"—but for all his easy, light-hearted manner he was a proud, touchy little fellow, and I didn't care to laugh for fear of wounding his feelings. My mother had told him about the bargain I'd made to earn that bicycle with the high gear and the low gear and the real electric lighting dynamo.

Now he said, "That bicycle, Jean—" He never did call me "John." "Ah, we shall get it for you, I zink for a certainty. I, personally, will teach you the great French language. You will see. I promise. For the honor of the family, zat I promise!"

You know, I thought he was half joking, just making conversation. I never realized he was in dead earnest and privately considered it was his obligation to help me win that bicycle and electric lighting outfit. I could have saved myself an almighty lot of trouble later if I had known mon oncle Paul Langres never trifled when he took on a job, whether it was fighting the Germans, inventing an avion, or taking charge of an American nephew.

When it was four o'clock in the afternoon and time for mon oncle and me to get to our train, all of us, I guess, became a little solemn. My father rolled out the wheel chair. Mon oncle Paul shot a glance at me. I took a long breath. I tucked my crutches under my arms. I remarked I could go to the station without that chair.

"In two months," mon oncle told my father, "Jean will run. Jean va courir, you watch!"

"What does that mean?" I inquired.

"What is what?" asked mon oncle. "Jean va courir?"

"Oui," said I. "What does 'Jean va courir' mean, please?"

Mon oncle said, " 'Va' in French can be both 'goes' or 'is going.' And 'courir' is 'to run.' Now you tell me what 'Jean va courir' is, my friend."

I thought. "Jean va" according to him could be either

"John goes" or "John is going." The first one didn't make sense with "courir"—to run. So I said it meant I was going to run. I hoped he was right. I hoped in two months I was going to run.

"Exactly," said mon oncle. "It is easy."

It was time to shove. I didn't need anyone to carry me. The porters came up for our baggage. My mother and father went into the corridor. I came after them, trying not to let them notice how the pain jogged me every time I used my left leg. Mon oncle waited behind me. So they wouldn't see my face, I looked back at him. Then to say something, I asked, "Mon oncle Paul va?"

I must have said, "My uncle goes?" well enough in French because he grinned and said, "Bien!" giving his fingers a snap. "Très bien! Oui, ton oncle Paul va aussi, Jean."

I didn't know what that "aussi" at the end of the sentence meant but it sounded like "also." Later, I learned it *was* "also." Sometimes you can pick up words in sentences without having anyone tell you what they are. And that "ton oncle," of course, was simple: "Your uncle." I could guess that much.

When we reached the station we had about ten minutes to wait. In France there are three classes on trains, not like ours. There is a magnificent and expensive first-class where nobody rides but swells and lords and dukes, I guess; and a second-class, about like ours; and a third-class where, as nearly as I could find out later, everyone in France actually rode because it was so cheap. Mon oncle Paul said we should have gone third-class and he expected to pay for the tickets. But by now my father knew how to handle him. My father apologized. He said he was sorry he had purchased second-class tickets and he hoped Paul would forgive him for doing it. But he thought I might be more comfortable going second-class this time.

Inside, French trains are cut up into compartments, with the aisle running down one side. The aisle has big greenish colored windows. Mon oncle and I stood in the aisle, watching my father and mother as the train started chuffing out of the station. We waved and they waved and then they were gone. Mon oncle and I took our seats. We were the only people in our compartment.

I felt pretty low, all at once. Oncle Paul opened his old-fashioned black leather valise. He didn't seem to notice how low I felt. He pulled out a long flute and said, "You like music, no?"

I said, "Music?"

He could have asked if I liked the Greek language or moonlight served in toasted sandwiches, fried in butter, for all I cared right then. He gave me a sort of grin, the corners of his mouth going up, his eyes creasing into little slits, the light and sparkle dancing behind the slits. He slid down on the seat and stuck the flute to his mouth and shut his eyes and began playing, softly, gently, hardly so anyone could hear. I never heard music like the music that came out of mon oncle's old flute.

I don't suppose you'd say there was a tune, either. At least, not a tune anybody would recognize. The music seemed to steal out of that flute, only for him and me to hear. It made me forget the sounds of the train. The music stole out of that flute and caressed me and spoke of rivers in Wyoming, although how mon oncle ever knew the way a Wyoming river sounded is beyond me. And it made little laughing noises, like sheep, and the music danced ever

so lightly as if wind was fluttering through our poplar
trees back home and I could almost hear the voices of Bob
Collins and old Jake and then the tune, if you call it a tune,
again changed, and it was like French soldiers marching
down a long avenue, gay and proud and noble, something
thrilling to hear them, with it going deep and quick in your
blood. Oh, I don't know how to tell you. It was a marvel
the way he played on that flute, all so softly. He might
have gone on playing forever, with us rushing off into a
wonderful land that flute was trying to speak to me about,
if I hadn't happened to lift my head.

A man was watching us from the aisle. I caught a
glimpse of that dead white face, and the eyebrows lifted
upwards, sneering and haughty. I shouted, "That's him—"
and tried to get my crutches. I fell smack in between the
seats. Mon oncle opened his eyes. By the time he'd picked
me up and put away his flute, the aisle was empty. I told
mon oncle I'd seen Monsieur Simonis for sure. He was on
this train.

Mon oncle rubbed his nose. Very slowly he asked, "You
are not afraid to stay here a few minutes?"

I was afraid. But after listening to that flute, somehow
I couldn't admit it. I shook my head.

"I'll be back," said mon oncle, lifting up his long nose
and sniffing as if he were trying to sniff out that white-
faced man. Never once did my oncle question the truth
of what I was saying. He believed me. He went out and he
must have searched up and down the train, every car in it.
When he returned, he said, "I am sorry. I do not see anybody like him."

More than ever I was bewildered. Nobody could miss
Monsieur Simonis. He was too tall to be missed. Just de-

I caught a glimpse of that dead white face

scribing him was enough. Mon oncle laid his brown hand gently on my arm. "Have no fear, hein? I zink, back there, when the train slow down a little, he has jumped off. It is a good thing you see him, I zink. Now he will not follow us."

"But why would he want to follow us?"

Mon oncle shrugged. "I do not know, my nephew. I zink the mayor is jealous, perhaps, of the Langres and does not wish a Langres any more to live in St. Chamant. This man wishes to get to St. Chamant as quickly as we do, and inform the mayor he has failed. I have friends in Paris." He laid his finger against his big nose, smiling, encouraging me. "Today I have told these friends about the man and that Albert. My friends, they are with the police. I zink we must not worry your mama and your papa. It is best they do not worry. Your papa has much now to do. My friends in the police will find soon that Albert and write me what is this that has happened. And—pouf!" He snapped his fingers. "We have no troubles."

I hoped he was right.

By and by I asked him if he'd play his flute for me some more, but this time he shook his head. "No, I do not zink you need the flute now," he said. "Only when it is needed very much do I play the flute."

That seemed a queer thing for him to say.

I was going to ask him what he meant by it, but he leaned back against the cushions, closing his eyes, smiling to himself the oddest and most contented and encouraging smile you ever did see. With his eyes still shut, he murmured, "You will walk, my nephew. You will walk and speak the French language and win the bicycle. You will see. I promise."

Outside the windows was darkness, except when lights flashed by. It began raining, the rain streaking the windows. Sometimes I imagined Monsieur Simonis' white face staring at me through the windows. When I shut my eyes I could hear the pound and thud of train wheels on the rails, making a regular clicking and humming. It sounded like, "Jean va, Jean va . . ." and it was true, all right, that John was going. But as Paris slipped further and further behind us, my mother and father miles and miles further away, I wondered just where after all I was va-ing and the idea of going, all at once, wasn't as rosy as it had been back in the warm hotel room in Paris when I'd made my bargain to get the bicycle.

5

LE VILLAGE DE ST. CHAMANT

The best way for me to tell you where we were heading is for you to open up your right hand and imagine it is a rough outline of the map of France. First, say that Paris is on the second knuckle of your middle finger. That would put Normandy and Brittany and the Atlantic Ocean over on the left side of your palm. Now, trace down to the bottom of your middle finger. You ought to find a faint line going down from there, cutting across some diagonal lines, and practically splitting your palm in half. Imagine that to be the line our train followed into the mountainous south-central part of France.

The first horizontal line on your palm that your faint vertical line crosses will be the river Loire. This river extends from the ocean into the upper center of France, a hundred miles or so below Paris. It follows a big long valley. In this valley are hundreds of castles. I was sorry it was so dark when we passed the river Loire because I didn't get a chance to see any of those castles mon oncle Paul told me about. He said some of them were over a thousand years old.

Instead of spending our money in the dining car, mon oncle opened the window and bought food when we stopped at one of the stations. This wasn't my idea of the way to eat on a train ride but I didn't say anything. I hauled out some of the money my father had given me, to pay for it. But at that, mon oncle lifted up his eyebrows. He said I was his guest. He said he wouldn't hear of me paying. He dug out a few pieces of money from an old leather pocket book. He counted out the money to the woman outside the window. In return he took a hunk of black bread and a sausage and sat down again and seemed to think we were having a feast. The bread was dry. The sausage was mainly cereals, with not much meat in it, and filled with garlic. The first taste nearly lifted the hair off my head. He said, "C'est bon!" and he meant it, too. I didn't agree it was as bon as he appeared to think it was, but I managed to nod. I choked down a little food.

We changed trains at nine o'clock. We took a smaller train—older and smellier, too. We were still chugging south. Now look at your palm, again. Where you see the second horizontal crease or line crossing your palm, is about where the montagnes began. That is a good two hundred miles below Paris. Our train followed down that line from your middle finger, the one I told you about. Most of this time I was trying to sleep—but couldn't. You see, we didn't have any berths at all.

We were supposed to sleep on the seat. If we had had both seats to ourselves, we might have been able to stretch out on them and managed to sleep. But all during the night, the train stopped and started. Sometimes the compartment would be crowded. Other times, we wouldn't have a soul in it but ourselves. Consequently, by the time a body had stretched out on the hard seat and wriggled on it and worn down the hard spots and was ready for sleep —the train would stop; people would enter the compartment. You had to sit up. In my judgment, the French didn't know how to run trains or how to travel in comfort. In fact, as the night—la nuit, as they say, if you want to be fancy about it—as la nuit endured and hung on, the hours going slower and slower, in my judgment French trains weren't worth the powder to blow them off the track. And my opinion of the French idea of being comfortable dropped down lower than gravel.

If you'll trace that vertical line extending down from your middle finger, past the first horizontal crease in your palm, past the second, you'll find it touches or comes close to a third line.

This third line starts at the left bottom side of your palm. It slants upward toward your thumb and first finger. Although it's stretching our map a little, pretend this lower diagonal line represents the river Dordogne which goes from the city of Bordeaux by the ocean up through the montagnes. About where the vertical line which we've pretended is the railroad track joins in with this bottom diagonal crease is where we were going—St. Chamant.

The big important cities of France are off on one side or the other side of your hand, never down along the center where the montagnes are. That's why the big important trains travel along the sides, too; and why our train was unimportant and slow and poky. It took all nuit and part of the next jour to go no further than the distance between, say, New York and Washington, D.C., or San Francisco and Los Angeles.

As I've explained, I'd tried to go to sleep and couldn't. For a time, probably, I didn't feel very sleepy, anyway. Too much had been happening. Oncle Paul, too, helped me from being too lonesome during the beginning of our trip. That is, at least he tried. He explained about the avion he was planning to build.

It was to be an avion, he said, without any tail at all.

Eventually, it would be equipped with a rocket motor. Well, that sounded tremendously interesting. He would remove the tail and sweep the wings back so his avion would look something like a big V on its side. He expected his avion to be perfectly stable. That was the advantage of no tail and a shape like a V.

"Anyone," said he, "can fly my airplane when I have finished. Ah yes, assuredly. The difficulty with the airplane today is that a man of experience is required to fly one. My airplane will require no experience. It will fly itself. You will see. When I have finished, *anyone* can fly it safely. A boy can fly it."

"Like me?" I said.

"Assuredly," he said, not thinking about me in particular. "Anyone, my nephew. Anyone at all." He smiled and finished with his bread and sausage and folded up what was left in a big red handkerchief and declared this would be our breakfast. That wasn't *my* conception of a breakfast. But I saw this wasn't the place to explain to mon oncle that breakfast included bacon and chocolate and hot rolls and pancakes with syrup like old Jake used to make on the ranch and toast and lots of strawberry jam. I saw I was going to have to educate mon oncle on breakfasts, later.

I said, "I'm going to fly, too, won't I?"

He swiveled his nose at me. "Assuredly," he said. "My nephew is going to fly. Mon neveu va voler."

"What's 'voler'?" I asked. "Fly?" I knew "mon neveu" meant "my nephew."

He nodded.

"Jean va voler," I said, pleased with the sound. "John is going to fly." I shut my eyes, imagining myself voler-ing around in the sky in mon oncle's avion. "Voler" was easy to remember, too. I remembered old Mr. Collins who'd flown in the last war used to explain about volplaning to the ground which was an old-fashioned way of saying gliding down to the ground.

"One moment," said mon oncle suddenly, as if he hadn't quite understood. "Assuredly, Jean va voler. But not at present. Not in St. Chamant."

"Not in St. Chamant?" I said.

He hedged. "I was speaking—how do you say it? I was speaking figuratively, mon neveu. It is safe for a boy to fly—voler—yes. But—" He lifted up his shoulders and grimaced. "I zink at first we have to find if I build my airplane right, no? I zink it is best I make it and fly it and I zink—" He was speaking excitedly now. "I zink you must wait three or four years to fly it. It is better." Then, right away, without giving me a chance to argue with him, he went on to explain that this avion he planned to build wouldn't have a motor. Not at first, anyway.

It didn't require a motor. He would glide it to demonstrate its stability. When he had proved his design he hoped a big French airplane company would take it over and manufacture it and give him a job. He had it all worked out in his head. He must have dreamed and thought about it for a long time. When I realized all he was planning to build in St. Chamant was an ordinary glider, I was so cast down and disappointed I didn't have anything to say. It would have been fun to have piloted a real airplane. I could have written back home to Bob Collins about doing that. But a glider was something on a lower endeavor entirely. Somehow I'd expected a lot more than that. I'd expected an avion with a real motor, big and powerful, capable of swooping all over the country and

I had imagined me in it and having a noble time of it. Well, I saw the whole thing was a fraud. Of course, I didn't blame my mother for not knowing any better than to call a glider an avion—maybe in French a glider and an airplane were the same thing. But not in my language.

I humped down in my seat. Once more I tried to get some sleep. By and by the train stopped again, with a jerk. It woke me up. Nobody entered our compartment. There were bluish dim lights overhead in our compartment. I noticed mon oncle was drawing designs of avions under these lights. He hadn't even tried to go to sleep. I realized that avion of his was tremendously important to him. Now, as I write and look back, I can see that he was counting on it to get him a job and make him famous. Except for his family—which, oddly enough, was only my mother and my father and me—that avion of his meant more to him than anything else in the world. But I didn't know that then, on the train. He raised his head; he smiled in his engaging way; then he asked, "You do not sleep, mon neveu?"

Crossly I said, "How can anybody expect to sleep on French trains?" and once more our train started off.

Instead of becoming ruffled because I'd answered that way, he smiled placidly and said, "Ah, if you cannot sleep, mon neveu, then shall we speak French together?"

You'd think an oncle might have more sense than to try to drill a body on tedious French during a jolting train ride when all a body wanted was to get to sleep or to go home, wouldn't you? I thought so, too.

I just looked at him. He said, "You do not forget the magnificent bicycle, Jean? With the high gear and low gear and the electric lighting dynamo?"

That stirred me. For a minute, maybe, I *had* forgotten my bargain.

He smiled. "Now," said he, "we will start our leçon in French. I will say certain words in French and you will tell me if you know them." He asked, "Le train? Qu'est-ce que c'est que le train?"

I asked, "What is that 'qu'est-ce que c'est que' thing you're saying? I don't know that."

" 'Qu'est-ce que c'est que—' is how in France we ask 'what is,' Jean."

I said, " 'Qu'est-ce que c'est que—' is an awful long way of saying 'what is,' isn't it?"

He laughed. "Ah, it is very long, I zink. But what can I do? I can make avions but I do not make the language. Now—qu'est-ce que c'est que le train?"

I already knew "le" was the word for our "the" but I didn't see why he had to add a practically English word like "train" after it. That appeared to me an uncommon method of teaching French. Anyway, I replied, " 'Le train' is the train," and felt foolish doing it.

"Bien!" said he. "Qu'est-ce que c'est que l'automobile?"

"The automobile."

"Bien! Qu'est-ce que c'est que le chauffeur?"

"The chauffeur," said I, thinking this was a waste of time.

"Ah, très, très bien!" said he. "Le vinaigre?"

He didn't pronounce it as we'd say it, but he never did pronounce his words as people did back home, anyway. I said, "The vinegar."

"Bien!" said he. "Et qu'est-ce que c'est que le village?"

"C'est the village," said I, adding that "it's" in French because I was getting bored.

"Très, très bien," said he. "Qu'est-ce que c'est que le village *de* St. Chamant?"

For me, the only new thing in that one was the little "de" and that was easy, too. It could mean only one possible thing as used with the other words. So I told him, "The village *of* St. Chamant." And I yawned. It was the dullest business in the world. It seemed to me if he was determined to teach me French he should start by giving me some French words.

He sat back. He was grinning. He said, "Voilà! You have now learned seven French words."

Polite as could be, I said the only words he'd given me had been "le" and "de"—"the" and "of." All the rest were in English.

At that, he laughed. "Ah, non. But they are French words. Train and automobile and chauffeur and vinaigre and village—all," said he, "French too."

I blinked.

"A long time ago," he continued, pleased as pie with himself, "a thousand years ago, I zink, some French knights and soldiers go to England. They fight with the English. They win. They rule England. For many years afterwards, everyone speaks French in England. Ah, you remember?"

And I did remember, as he mentioned it. I'd read about it in school, where William the Conqueror went over and made himself king of England, but reading about all that old history in school hadn't much stirred me.

Now mon oncle explained how the English and French sort of mixed up after centuries. By and by, they became one people. Instead of part of them speaking in French and part of them speaking in this older English language, the two languages joined together. That was why today about one third of the words we use were French words. I've told you what a proud little fellow mon oncle was; and he took pride in the fact that Americans spoke a lot of French without knowing they were speaking French. Maybe he exaggerated telling me that, I don't know. I don't think he did. My mother says he didn't. But the fact is, he went on, making his speech and talking and pretty soon the jars and jolts of the train sort of faded away. The noise of the wheels going "Jean va, Jean va" died away and didn't bother me. I was cross and tired and lonesome and my leg hurt and I was disappointed about his avion being nothing more than a glider. I didn't mean to go to sleep at all. I didn't think I ever would sleep until I was back with my mother and father. But do you know, I went to sleep.

When I woke up we were plowing through green montagnes. It was jour, instead of nuit. The morning sun was shining. Mon oncle's big shabby coat was covering me and I had my seat all to myself. Opposite me were mon oncle and a red-cheeked old French woman and a tall dignified Frenchman about sixty years old and two younger Frenchmen, each with perfectly enormous black moustaches. There they were, all five of them crowded together on a seat hardly large enough for four; and all five of them were looking at me—and they were smiling. I don't know what mon oncle had said to them. I do know, such kindness from four perfect strangers gave me a queer warm feeling.

The red-cheeked woman said, "Bon jour," and I replied. All the men laughed and I sat up in a hurry. The old man and one of the younger men moved over to my side, taking care not to upset my crutches. Mon oncle brought out what was left of the black bread and the sausage. The red-cheeked woman had a basket and in the basket were a couple of peaches, as well as more bread. She insisted I have a peach. You know, the night before I'd never thought I could eat black bread and sausage.

This morning, I found I was so almighty hungry that the black bread and sausage tasted even better than any breakfast I'd ever had on the ranch. I ate every bit. I ate the peach, too. It was juicy and sweet. The French people talked. Mon oncle talked and now and then they'd say something to me I could understand, like "Le jour est beau?" or "La pêche est bonne, hein?" (By myself I wouldn't have known what "pêche" meant, but the woman pointed to the peach.) Once, when the red-cheeked woman asked, "Tu vas à St. Chamant, le village de St. Chamant?" I worked that one out, getting the "tu vas" to mean "you go" and that "à" as "to;" and I answered, "Oui, Jean va à St. Chamant."

Mon oncle seemed to be pleased that I replied. I could see now that French words that meant the same thing sometimes changed a little just as we say "I go" and "he goes." Both the "go" and the "goes" mean the identical thing; and, I guess the French must have copied from us. Or, perhaps, if what mon oncle said was true, we copied from them. Anyway, "Jean va" was "John goes;" and that "tu vas" was "you go." I remembered how, back in New York, I'd been practically paralyzed at the thought of being in a place where I wouldn't understand a word said. Now I was in that place—and it wasn't nearly as difficult as I imagined. I recognized you can be scared a lot more by something before you come on to it than after it's in front of you.

The red-cheeked woman wrapped the remainder of her bread in a checkered cloth. I got to wondering what the word for bread was in French. I remembered how mon oncle had said "what is" and decided to try it out and see if it worked. I pointed to the bread and asked, "Qu'est-ce que c'est que—?"

"Ah," said the red-cheeked woman right away. "C'est le pain."

"Le pain?" said I, thinking that was a queer thing to call bread.

"Oui," said the woman. "Le pain."

And there it was. I'd learned what le pain was. More than that, I found, with that "qu'est-ce que c'est que—" business, I had a key with which I could fathom out other French words without asking for help from mon oncle. . . .

That morning about nine o'clock we changed a second time at a city called Tulle. We were right in the mountains now. We waited at a long gray stone railroad station for our next train. While we were waiting two French policemen walked by with a short, thick, sullen-looking man between them, unshaven and grimy, with a wild furious glare in his eyes. He was chained to one of the police and the other kept his hand near his revolver. As they walked by, several French women made frightened noises. Men in the crowd started talking and pointing and there were angry shouts. A couple of boys ran after them, carrying stones in their hands. The policemen threatened the boys and the boys waited, while the prisoner was shoved into a big blue car and carried away.

I'd never seen people yell at a prisoner before. It seemed wicked. All my sympathies were for the prisoner. I asked

mon oncle, "What's the matter? What are they yelling at
him for?"

Mon oncle hesitated. "Because he is a German."

"German?" I said. "I thought all the Germans had been
captured."

"Not all," said mon oncle. "When the war ended, a few
ran away and hid in these mountains instead of giving
themselves up. They have caused the country people much
trouble by appearing suddenly at night and stealing
and—" Once again, he hesitated. "And killing some of our
people, too, I am afraid. They are very bad, mon neveu.
Very bad."

I hadn't realized Germans were still around here. I asked
if many remained.

He smiled. "Ah, but Jean, it is nothing. They will not
molest you. Only a few remain and soon they will be
found."

I stuck my crutches under my arms and slowly followed
mon oncle along the station platform. Behind us lifted the
towers and the buildings of the old city of Tulle. It was
located in an oval valley in between the dark montagnes,
and was different from any of the cities we have back
home. The buildings were of stone, mostly, high and narrow, with small windows. The streets were paved with
cobblestones or with big rough bricks. I saw the automobile carrying the German go up a long street.

I was glad they'd caught the German. It wasn't right for
Germans like him to hide out in the montagnes and cause
trouble and become no more than robbers or bandits. Seeing the prisoner reminded me of something. I asked mon
oncle, "Do you think by now they've caught Albert to
question him?"

"I zink so. Oui."

I asked, "I don't suppose you could make sure?"

He nodded. "Oui, if you wish. When we reach St. Chamant I will write to my friends of the police in Paris, but you must not worry. The police will assuredly have caught Albert by now. Pouf!" He snapped his fingers. "They have him fast and in a few days we shall learn the truth."

We didn't have time to see much of Tulle because our train arrived. The engine was about the size of a switch engine back home. It had an enormous funnel and puffed out clouds of black smoke. Mon oncle explained this was a little montagne train. The engine probably was fifty or sixty years old. Behind it were four cars only, all small and old. Mon oncle helped me climb upon the rear car. He followed, carrying our bags. In ten or fifteen minutes the whistle tooted. We started chugging up into the montagnes. These were real montagnes, nothing like those we had come through earlier in the morning.

We wound around curves. We pushed up higher and higher. The sun was warm and bright. The montagnes were covered with oak and chestnut trees and every now and then we'd cross a shaky trestle and see for miles below into valleys, dark green. I had the strange feeling I was being taken years and years back into history, into the time of my grandfather. The people who got on the train wore old-fashioned clothes. Most of them had wooden shoes. They'd go for a few stops and get off again. One girl had a small pig under her arm. In a basket, a woman was carrying a live duck.

The houses we passed weren't like houses I'd ever seen before. They nestled down into the trees, and were of stone and had thatched roofs—roofs of woven straw and hay. Mon oncle became more and more excited. Every few minutes he'd look at his watch. Finally he said, "Voici le village de St. Chamant!" The train halted. Here we were.

I don't know what I was expecting but whatever it was —it wasn't at all like what I found. Le village de St. Chamant was located on the side of a huge montagne and consisted of about twenty or thirty houses on each side of a single road, with the small brick railroad station about one fifth of a mile to the south of this road. Waiting at this little station was a sort of reception committee, composed of three men and one woman.

While the train halted, mon oncle threw out the bags and the men caught the bags. I was awkward with my crutches. Mon oncle never once helped me, either. He got down—and he waited. And so did the men and the woman. They didn't say a word; they were grave and composed, as if it was the most usual thing in the world for them to see a strange boy trying to get off a train with two crutches under his arms.

Right after that, the woman and two of the three men gathered around mon oncle. Instead of shaking his hand they kissed him on the cheek as was the French custom.

The third man hung back, scowling. He approached mon oncle and took him off to one side, talking to him in a loud angry tone. Mon oncle merely shook his head, speaking briefly, cold and polite. After that, the third man lifted his hat about one inch above his pink bald head, disdainfully said, "Bon jour!" and marched off. He wore real leather shoes and a black coat with black braid on it and he had gray gloves on his hands, although the jour was warm.

Mon oncle nudged me. "You see? C'est le maire, Monsieur Capedulocque, whom I told you about. I zink he is angry I have come."

He introduced me to Madame Graffoulier, a tall angular woman with kind eyes, who owned the hotel where we were to stay. After her, I was greeted—French style, always, being kissed on the cheeks—by Monsieur Niort, the blacksmith. He was wide as a barrel and when he laughed it sounded like thunder. The second man was Dr. Guereton, the local physician, gray and small and cheerful.

When he finished greeting me, same as the others, he peered over his spectacles at mon oncle and said, "C'est un bon garçon, ton neveu." It was nice of him to say that, which meant: "It's a good boy, that nephew"—or as we'd say it, "He's a good lad, that nephew of yours."

As I used my crutches, mon oncle Paul assisted me along. We reached the main street—the only street, for that matter. We marched down this street until we came to a crossroad, which came south from the meadows and led around an old stone church and north toward the montagnes. Next to the church was the biggest house in town. It had a fair-sized whitewashed tower in front, and a wall around the whole place. Inside were more whitewashed buildings with a lot of chickens and ducks squawking and goats bleating away. Mon oncle pointed to it; he said it was the house belonging to Monsieur Capedulocque, the mayor whom I'd just met. He explained in France farm people lived differently than he understood we did in America.

He said this village was composed of farmers—that is, people who owned vineyards and little fields in the mountains. While a few people lived on these fields, most of them moved into a village to be close to each other, and kept their animals within the courtyards. Often, the animals would live downstairs in the same house while the people lived upstairs. That was hard to believe. I laughed. I thought mon oncle was joking. But it was an actual fact— because later I saw homes with donkeys and goats on the downstairs floor and the family comfortable as anything, living upstairs. They claimed that was the only civilized way, too. They said if they wanted fresh milk all they had to do was step downstairs and a goat would give them all that was required. It saved time. It was efficient. That may be true, but the French method increases the variety of smells in a house.

We continued down the street. For the most part the houses were of two stories, of stone and plaster, with a crisscross of timbers on the upper floors. Shutters would open. Men or women would stick out their heads and call, "Ah, Paul. Bon jour, Paul!" and he'd call back to them. All of this had a strangeness to me. Perhaps it was because I was almighty tired after using my crutches for such a distance—although, of course, it wasn't really very far. But I wasn't accustomed to going even part of a mile on my own, remember. It was like being in a dream, with the wet mist coming down and separating everything from me.

We came to a building longer than the other buildings, of three stories, all of stone and plaster, with green shutters over the windows. None of the buildings had porches or any decorations as buildings back home had. They came square up against the road, with absolutely plain bare fronts except for the shutters. This big building was like all the others in St. Chamant, plain and bare and simple in front. You'd have taken it for a poor mean miserable stone barn back home. Above the doorway was a sign: "Hôtel du Commerce."

This was the hotel belonging to Madame Graffoulier. She was about fifty, I'd guess; her husband, I later learned, had been killed in the war. Paul had made arrangements for us to stay here. We entered the hotel and it was more like stepping inside a barn than in what I'd call a hotel. The big front room was right off the street, and for a floor— they had *brick*. True, the brick was swept clean and had been waxed. But still—a brick floor! In this room were long wooden tables and chairs and that was about all.

Waiting for us were two kids, a boy about seven and a girl of five or six. Both of them were dressed in the blue smocks all French children seem to wear, boy or girl. Shyly, they came forward. Mon oncle said they were Philippe and Jehanne, the nephew and niece of Madame Graffoulier. I looked around hoping there might be a boy at hand, near my age—but there wasn't.

Madame Graffoulier accompanied me upstairs to my room. Upstairs it was more like a home. Carpets were on the floors. Through the rear windows opening into the upstairs hallway I could sight down upon a courtyard, where flowers and vegetables were growing. Beyond the courtyard wall was the old stone church. It was having everything reversed from what we have at home: we have a front yard, pretty and attractive. In St. Chamant the front of the houses were bleak. Their gardens and trees and flowers were hidden behind, in little courtyards. Madame Graffoulier showed me into a large corner room with a great bed in it and a chest of drawers and round faded blue rugs scattered over an uneven oak floor. She smiled. She pointed to that bed. "Va, au lit, mon garçon."

That bed was about the most wonderful thing I'd seen. I was pretty much done for. Even if I didn't know much

French, I understood what she meant. I va-ed to that lit and I dropped the crutches and climbed into the lit and pulled up the covers and shut my eyes.

Later, mon oncle and Dr. Guereton came in to look at my leg. Dr. Guereton examined it, tapped it, making little chirping noises like a cricket. He finished and evidently was satisfied I hadn't overstrained it. For dinner that night I had a big bowl of hot goat's milk, more black bread, slices of thick yellow country cheese, and fresh figs. I was more hungry than I'd been for a long time and stuffed myself.

With the rest, my leg felt better, too. I came downstairs for a time and met people who'd filed into the hotel to see mon oncle. I went to bed early, about seven-thirty or eight, and was too sleepy to write any letters. I don't know what time it was when I was awakened. The room was black as pitch. I lay there in bed and had the feeling something was wrong, not knowing why I'd started up from a sound sleep, finding myself sitting in bed, grabbing on to the quilts, my heart pounding.

My room was a corner room, the front windows overlooking the little narrow street, the side window above a kind of narrow alley, with a bleak dark stone house half a dozen yards distant, invisible now in the dense darkness.

Mon oncle had taken another room, off in back of the hotel, under the roof. It was a small, cramped room. I was surprised he wanted to sleep there but he explained after his experience in the army, living mostly out of doors, he *liked* being in a room small enough so he could reach out and touch the walls. Later on, I discovered the real reason he'd taken that room was because it was the cheapest.

As I sat there in my room, all at once I heard something again rattle softly against the side window, exactly as if

someone was climbing up the wall to the window. You
know how shadows change things in a room at night. I
managed to turn my head. Over by the window, where the
faint moonlight came through, I saw a white hand reach
upwards and grasp the wooden sill. I let out a yell. I let out
another and leaped out of the bed and fell.

*I heard something again rattle softly against the
side window*

Next thing I knew both Madame Graffoulier and mon
oncle were holding candles over me, and I was in bed. I
tried telling mon oncle somebody had attempted to climb
into my room. He went to the window. He was patient
and kind, explaining I must have been mistaken.

My window was a good fifteen feet above the street. He

leaned out, holding the candle, examining the plaster walls. He said there wasn't a mark or sign of any ladder. Anyone attempting to get into my room would require a ladder. He wriggled the big iron handle on the window. The window opened outwards—French style—like a door, instead of going up and in like our windows. In the moonlight, that handle did resemble a hand. He said that must have been the thing that frightened me—and the wind blowing against the window had rattled it.

Well, I was mortified nearly to death. In French he spoke to Madame Graffoulier. Probably he was telling her I'd been sick, and was still nervous and jumpy. She offered through him to bring me up another bowl of hot goat's milk, to help me go back to sleep. But I said I didn't need it. I was sorry I'd awakened them by shouting. I told mon oncle, "For a second I figured Monsieur Simonis had got to St. Chamant and was coming in after me."

Very gently he assured me, "My dear nephew, you must not let the thought of that Simonis individual any longer disturb you. He has failed in his task, and if my suspicions are true, I zink he will take great care not to be seen by you and me when he reports to the mayor. Perhaps he will not come to St. Chamant, but goes only to Tulle and has the mayor visit him there. Have no fears. If I ever catch him skulking in the village, myself, I will ask him what he wished from you. And in a few days, I zink my friends of the police in Paris will have found Albert and from him learn the truth. You will see. Bonne nuit."

"Bonne nuit," I replied.

His common-sense attitude was calming. I shut my eyes, hearing the wind rattle at the window. Pretty soon I fell asleep, and dreamed of Monsieur Simonis trying to climb through hundreds of purple windows, each time falling back and landing on Wyoming spiked cactus plants. . . .

I spent the next morning in the workshop with mon oncle and Monsieur Niort, le forgeron, where they were beginning to build the avion. St. Chamant was deserted. The men were in the vineyards or fields. I asked mon oncle if there weren't any boys around my age and he asked Monsieur Niort, "Où est Charles Meilhac?"

Le forgeron replied.

Mon oncle asked, "Où est Jules Lemaitre?"

Le forgeron again replied.

With a baffled expression, mon oncle asked, "Où est Pierre Guillaume? Henri Brinz? Guillaume Dufourché? Honoré Yvald?" and le forgeron would shrug and reply in about the same words every time. By now I appreciated mon oncle was naming boys he knew, asking where they were.

Mon oncle told me, "Jean, I do not know what to say. Because so many families of St. Chamant became poor during the war, the blacksmith tells me the five or six boys of your age or older have taken jobs in Tulle and Brive to earn money for the winter. Perhaps later on in the summer they will return."

I tried not to let him see how discouraged I felt, hearing that. In an attempt to cheer me up, he assured me in a day or so he would take us up to the montagne where the Langres family place was and I could see that. I'd find things to do, too, in St. Chamant as soon as I began to walk more and got more strength.

Le forgeron said something.

Mon oncle turned to me again. "The blacksmith tells me he has forgotten. The factory where Charles Meilhac is working may close soon. Then Charles will be here. Ah, you will like him very much, I zink."

"Who's he?"

"You will see, soon. He is a little older than you, maybe. Six months. His father was killed in the war. They are old friends of the Langres, the Meilhacs. There are now only the mother and the sister, the twin of Charles. When Charles comes home I promise to take you to the Meilhacs'. That is better now, non? I zink soon you have a friend—two friends," he added. "Suzanne you will like, aussi."

One thing, also—aussi—I knew I wasn't going to like any girl. And at the moment, I didn't have anything to do. I was tired of watching mon oncle and le forgeron. I lumped back to the door, looked along the deserted street. The montagnes were dark. The sky overhead was all blue and empty. That wind which had rattled my window last night still blew down from the montagnes with a low moaning sound. The pig walked back along the street. It eyed me as if it knew I didn't enjoy being in its village. I called, "Here, pig." It went right on, proud and haughty, not having any truck with me.

6

LA MAISON DE TA MERE

That nuit I wrote my first letters from St. Chamant: one to my mother, one to my father, and a third to
Bob Collins, back in Wyoming. I told my father I'd
walked all the way from the station and everything was
going fine although at present there weren't any boys my
age to play with. I asked him if he'd had time to look at any
English bicycles with high gears and low gears.

In the letter to my mother, I wrote about le train and the
trip down, although I didn't mention seeing Monsieur
Simonis on the train. The fact is, now I was away from
them, I'd had time to think over how I had been acting in
the past. I was ashamed. I wanted them to believe I was
growing up and recovering from being so easily scared
and I was determined to make my letters to them cheerful
if I choked doing it. They had worries of their own. I
hoped mon oncle wouldn't write them, either, and inform
on me, how I'd been frightened by the wind blowing
against a window. I should have asked him not to—and I
decided tomorrow to ask him if it wasn't too late.

I ended my letter to my mother with French words I
knew, such as: "C'est bon here in your village de St. Chamant . . . Mon oncle est giving me leçons in French . . .
Le jour est beau although it rains a lot . . . Où are you
now, in London? . . . Jean va to bed . . ." and things
like that.

To Bob Collins, back home, I wrote a longer letter. I stretched the truth here and there a shade, I'm afraid, because I wanted him to believe I was having a gaudy time of it. I told him probably I'd fly mon oncle's avion. I wouldn't be surprised, from the way I described the avion, too, that he might have obtained an idea a motor was in it.

I went to sleep afterwards, and didn't have any dreams, either. Along about morning, I awoke. The sky was pale and cold. You know how it is when you awaken very early in the morning, and are still half asleep, the bed warm and comfortable. Probably I was almost dreaming. The front windows were open. As I lay there in bed I imagined I heard someone passing by in the street, humming. That was all. I listened; and the tune hummed sounded familiar. I remembered—all at once. It was the same tune Albert used to hum, meaningless and senseless, when he pushed me in my wheel chair.

Once again, the coldness came over me. I forced myself, this time, to go to the window. I looked out into the cold dim light. All I saw were a couple of men of the village going off to the fields, their rakes and hoes over their shoulders. I felt silly. Anyone of them might have hummed that silly old tune. I crept back into bed, wishing I were well, like other boys, not ready to jump out of my skin with fright at nothing.

I had breakfast downstairs in the big front room. Evidently, mon oncle had already eaten and had gone to work on the avion. The two kids ate with me. We had bowls of brownish mush, topped with goat's milk. I wouldn't even have looked at such truck at home. Here, in the montagnes, it must have been the fresh clean air that made a body so hungry. When I was finished, the boy, Philippe, began chattering at me in French. I needed mon oncle to translate, but I couldn't even ask if he'd gone to work on his avion.

Finally, I remembered. I said, "Où est mon oncle?"—that is, "Where is my uncle?"

Madame Graffoulier answered, very slowly, "Ton oncle est avec le forgeron." I knew every word except that "avec" and it slipped in like the last piece of a jigsaw puzzle. The only thing it could mean was "with." My oncle was *with* the blacksmith.

I nodded. I said, "Bien!"

The boy pointed to himself. "Philippe," he said.

I pointed to myself and said, "Jean."

Philippe took my hand. He asked, "Ton oncle va voler?"

I knew that one too. "Your uncle is going to fly?" he'd said. I nodded and replied, "Oui."

Next Philippe asked, "Tu vas voir ton oncle?"

That "vas" was understandable; it was the same as "va" —which was "is going." So "tu vas" was "you are go-ing—" but I was stuck on "voir" until Philippe pretended to look all about the room, saying "voir, voir," at the same time. It came clear. "Voir" was "to see." He'd asked, "You are going to see your uncle?"

"Oui," I said, again.

Philippe asked, "Philippe y va, aussi?"

It wasn't difficult after all. I remembered "aussi" was "also." And I supposed "y" must mean "there." So I said, "Oui, Philippe y va aussi."

Out we went, into the deserted street, Philippe leading me toward the blacksmith shop. As we walked, I pointed down to the street and asked, "Qu'est-ce que c'est que ——?"

"Ça?" said Philippe.

That stumped me for a minute. I knew "ça" wasn't the French for "street" because of the way he put a question after it.

I pointed again at the street.

He understood. "Ah," said Philippe, mighty pleased. "*Ça?* C'est la *rue.*"

"La *rue?*" I asked. *That* was what a street was called in France.

"Oui," said he. "C'est la rue."

We walked along la rue until we reached le forgeron's. There was mon oncle talking to Monsieur Niort. "Bon jour, bon jour!" cried mon oncle. He saw Philippe and clapped him on the shoulders. He said something to him in French. Philippe laughed. He pointed to me and explained. Both mon oncle and le forgeron laughed.

Mon oncle said, "Now Philippe teaches you French, aussi?"

I said he'd told me "la rue" was a street but I didn't understand exactly. Was "street" two words in French, both "la" and "rue"? Well, mon oncle explained that easily. "La" was another word for "the." That puzzled me. I never knew a language to spell "the" two ways. It meant that in French both "le" and "la" were the same thing? He nodded. "Oui, c'est ça."

I asked, "What is 'ça'?"

" 'Ça'?" said mon oncle. " 'Ça' is 'that,' for pointing out something. For example—" He pointed to the street. "Ça est la rue."

I got it. I said, "Oui, ça est la rue."

He pointed to a house across la rue. "Ça est la maison."

I said, "Où est my maison?"

He waggled his long nose. He stepped outside and

pointed up la rue toward our little hotel. "Là—there. *Là est ta* maison. You understand?"

That ended French leçons for this jour. Mon oncle asked how I'd slept last night. I said, "Fine," not wanting to admit I'd been briefly scared early this morning, thinking I'd heard Albert pass below my window, humming. I inquired if he'd received a letter from the Paris police yet and he said it was too soon, but he expected it before the end of this week. Next, I worked around to asking if he'd written my mother how I'd acted the night before. . . .

He laughed. "It was such a little thing, already have I forgotten it. I do not think ta mère—your mother—would be interested. We both forget, n'est-ce pas?"

That cheered me a lot. I knew he was on my side. At the far end of the next building a couple of workmen were laying pieces of wood on a table, joining them. Mon oncle explained this was to be one of the wings. Over to one side he showed me a huge brass pan, big around as a cart wheel, filled with hot water. In here he was steaming other sections of wood in order, tomorrow, to clamp them in forms which bent them into the shape of ribs.

All this time he had been regarding me with a peculiar expression on his face. Suddenly he asked, "Where are your crutches?"

Until that moment, I'd forgotten all about them. I'd walked the twenty or so yards from the hotel to the workshop on my own power, being so interested in learning the French words for street and house. A funny thing happened: the minute mon oncle reminded me of my crutches my leg felt weak, and began hurting. The pain got bigger. Probably I had strained it a little. I was scared.

Mon oncle sent Philippe back for the crutches and the

rest of the jour I stuck to them, as usual. Late that afternoon, Dr. Guereton dropped in and examined my leg
again. He chirped cheerfully and looked over his square
glasses at mon oncle and appeared satisfied nothing had
been damaged.

In the evening, the men returned from the fields. After
dinner, mon oncle had me down with him in the courtyard.
Monsieur Niort played on his accordion. By and by, the
people there persuaded mon oncle to join in with the flute.
All sang French songs and some of the younger women
danced folk dances and it was pretty and cheerful and I
hated being sent up to bed because it was so late.

In my room, instead of going right to sleep I got out my
German coins and wrote Bob another letter, asking him to
find out how much German coins might be worth. I told
him I was living in a place where people had picked up old
Roman coins and I meant to keep my eyes peeled. I'd like
to find a Roman coin, myself. The wind made its sound. As
I wrote, it seemed to me there was another sound outside,
in addition to the wind. I opened the window and looked
out. A long shadow flickered against the opposite wall and
then it vanished; it was gone. It was as though a man had
been standing across from the hotel, looking up at my
lighted window, humming to himself.

I got as far as the door to yell to mon oncle and returned.
I knew I was wrong to imagine things so easily. I mustered
up all my courage. Once again I stared out of the window.
All I saw was a pear tree scraping against the wall over
there. The moonlight made it throw a shadow. I was glad
I hadn't yelled for mon oncle this time. I got undressed
and lay in bed for a time and by and by I got up again and
locked all my windows. After that, I went to sleep.

For the next week or so nothing much happened. Nearly every jour now, mail brought a letter from my mother or father. In her last letter, my mother wrote they were hoping to take a little vacation, themselves. My father's work had progressed more rapidly than he expected. He had asked for a two weeks' leave to allow him and my mother to take a walking trip through Scotland.

My mother said neither of them would go if it worried me in the slightest to know they might be out of touch with me for a little while. She wanted me to write and let them know. I did, too. It seemed to me both of them had earned a vacation. I said of course I'd like to be with them but I couldn't do that much walking yet although I hoped to be able to, sometime. I said everything here was going along wonderfully and mon oncle was about a third of the way finished with his avion. They could take the vacation any time they wished. I mailed that letter the next jour and I was pleased I'd recovered enough not to be scared if they went walking in Scotland where I couldn't telegraph them and receive a reply right away. I hoped they'd go.

Mon oncle and le forgeron were busy with the avion, working like beavers. That boy mon oncle had spoken about—Charles Meilhac—he never did appear. I gave up expecting him. In the daytime the village was deserted. The men were in the fields, the women working in the houses. I did meet more younger kids, but they weren't much fun. Philippe continued to tag after me as if I belonged to him. At the far end of the street I discovered two girls about my age. But they weren't interested in me and I wasn't interested in them. About half the time it rained.

I pestered mon oncle about the letter he was to receive

from Paris. He didn't get it, although time dragged. He wrote a second time, saying perhaps his friend had been away and was too busy to think—"zink," *he* said—of writing about a trivial matter such as questioning a hotel porter.

I practiced walking more. I felt better, too. I ceased dreaming about Monsieur Simonis. Mon oncle had asked the mayor about him. But the mayor flew off into a temper. He claimed he never sent a business agent to Paris to buy property—and, privately, mon oncle told me he didn't believe the mayor. He said the mayor probably had gotten into a rage because he was discovered, and had lied.

From Philippe I learned more French, too, not forgetting the bargain I'd made with my mother—ma mère, I should say. I learned, "Voici Jean!" meant, "Here's John!" More than once Philippe asked me, "Jean va voir la maison sur la montagne?" Finally, I got on to the fact he was asking if I was going to see the house upon the montagne. That "sur" was French for "upon."

I was waiting for mon oncle to take me to the house where my mother was born, but he had to apologize and explain that at present he was in the middle of attaching ribs to the wings of his avion, and couldn't take the time. He promised he'd knock off for an afternoon in just a few jours. He said the waiting wouldn't be wasted because it gave me time to practice walking and put more strength in my leg. He explained the house and land was up on the montagne. It would require a tolerable climb for us.

Along toward the third week, I received a shock. The letter from mon oncle's friend in Paris arrived. It was a long letter. After dinner he went up with me to my room and shut the door and admitted the news wasn't what he expected. The police hadn't been able to locate Albert. He had vanished. Mon oncle stroked his nose and looked at me, pausing. He said that wasn't all there was in the letter. I waited, feeling a funny shiver pass through me.

The man, Monsieur Simonis, wasn't a Frenchman at all, according to the police. According to the description I'd given mon oncle which he had passed on to his friend in the police, Monsieur Simonis was a German agent who'd lived in France and pretended to be a Frenchman. A couple of times they'd almost nabbed him—and each time he had escaped. His real name was Heinrich Simonz.

"Oh," I said, pretty weakly, too.

The police had a theory I'd brought most of the trouble on myself in Paris by chattering away to Albert during those afternoons, telling him my mother was French and had been born in St. Chamant and had a castle there. They figured Albert was in cahoots with Simonis and that Simonis was pretty desperate and needed money. All Europeans, you know, think Americans are rich. Of course that isn't so, but Europeans don't understand. According to the Paris police, Simonis had learned about me from Albert. The two planned to grab me and hold me for money. Simonis had hit upon that excuse to buy my mother's property, as a chance to see my parents and later on would have come back to them, after nailing me, threatening them with what would happen to me if they didn't pay and if they went to the police. That was all there was to the whole business. The police said they were sorry they hadn't learned about it sooner. They didn't think either Albert or Simonis would go very far before being captured. They thought Simonis had been heading south toward the montagnes, to hide in them, and when he saw us on the same train had jumped off, more scared than anything else.

Mon oncle folded the letter. "Voici," he said. "I am better at building avions, I zink, than making guesses on police matters." He smiled. "Ah, and that poor Mayor Capedulocque. I have worried him needlessly. No wonder he was so very angry. I suppose now he zinks somebody else is also attempting to buy our land. He will be very worried. I hope, *very* much." The smile broadened. Mon oncle enjoyed thinking about worrying Mayor Capedulocque, who had been causing trouble the past few days, trying to have mon oncle put out of the workshop. He looked at me. "What do you wish to do, Jean? Shall I write to your father?"

I didn't know what to do. It might spoil their plans for a walking trip if they became concerned about me.

I said, "Maybe you better not write."

He shrugged. He went out and came back with his flute and sat on my bed and played for a time, almost as if playing to himself, soft and low. Pretty soon he raised his head. "It is better here, n'est-ce pas? Even without a boy your age?"

"Better than Paris," I admitted.

"In a day or so, too, I zink you will have a friend. I have heard that Charles Meilhac is expected to return very soon." He wiped off his flute, polishing it. "I will not write. It is not necessary." He stood. "Tomorrow, I tell you what we will do. We will visit la maison de ta mère. You comprehend? The house of your mother. It is a promise."

For all these weeks I'd been looking forward to seeing it. That promise drove any remaining concern I might have had about Monsieur Simonis clear out of my head.

I went to bed early and next morning stuffed myself and for a couple of hours hung around the shop and after an early lunch mon oncle looked at his watch and said it was time.

We were to meet a friend of his, Monsieur Taggart, who was going part way up the montagne in an oxcart. The ride would save our legs. As he spoke, I heard a creaking outside the hotel. A big cart halted, pulled by an ox. A man shouted, "Tu viens, Paul?" Mon oncle lifted me up from the table and carried me to the cart and dumped me into the straw and away we went—at no more than two miles an hour. You can't hurry an ox.

We took the road past the church and Mayor Capedulocque's place, his hens and ducks squawking at us from beyond the wall. We rolled up and up, the big wheels squeaking. White clouds blew across the blue sky. We reached a cross-roads in the montagne where the path branched in two different directions. Here, mon oncle jumped off. He lifted me down. Monsieur Taggart waved his hand and called, "Au revoir," which meant "Good-by," and we answered, thanking him for the ride.

Mon oncle said, "Now, you and I must climb the mountain. In French, you would say, 'John and his uncle Paul mount upon the mountain—Jean et son oncle Paul montent sur la montagne.' "

But I remained right where I was, hanging on to one side of an old stone wall, protesting I couldn't mount sur any montagne without my crutches. "Pouf!" said mon oncle, snapping his fingers. "*I* shall be your crutch, Jean, for a time. You need more confidence, not crutches."

For about half a mile more, mon oncle and I montent sur la montagne, going through a chestnut and oak forest.

At a turn in the little lane, we came around a ridge. Through the trees we had a vista before us, hills and valleys. Five or six miles to the south were tiny houses and steeples of another village, with the silver shine of a river running by the village. Mon oncle stopped. He said that village was Argenta. The river was the river Dordogne.

Two or three thousand years ago, the Romans had made a camp near Argenta, a big camp. They'd stayed there for centuries, lording it over all this part of the country. He took my head and had me sight along his outstretched arm. I saw a kind of round, doughnut-shaped hill which he pointed out, about a mile southwest of le village de St. Chamant. He said that mound of earth was the site of another Roman camp.

That excited me. I said, "Maybe if I do some digging tomorrow, I could find old Roman coins. They're super-valuable. We'd sell 'em and make money."

One thing I liked about mon oncle—he didn't laugh at ideas, even if the ideas were impractical. Perhaps that was because people had laughed at his idea of building an avion. Instead of laughing, he explained Roman coins *had* been dug up from around Argenta and in the river and from that big mound near St. Chamant. He admitted I *might* find a coin—but he said it wasn't likely. Professors from French universities had spent several summers here before the war, with fifty or sixty trained workers, sifting and sorting through everything.

"Come along," he said cheerfully. "Viens, mon neveu. Viens voir la maison de ta mère!" And he gave me a lift with his arm. In another ten minutes we crossed a flank of the montagne and came into a meadow, rich and green. Tall shade trees lifted up toward the blue sky. Birds were singing. Except for the birds, everything was silent. It was almost like walking into a church. I followed mon oncle, using his shoulder as a support. Without saying anything, we walked through the tall grass. We came upon a brick covered lane, with blackberry brambles grown wild on each side.

Ahead were the ruins of an old maison. Two sides of the walls were standing, with enormous empty windows and a great door. Mon oncle halted. "Voilà," he said. "Voilà. C'est la maison de ta mère."

It had belonged to my great-great-great-grandfather. It was hundreds of years old. The Langres family had lived here all that time, generations of them. They had been lawyers and soldiers. Here my mère had been born. Here mon oncle had been born. This great stone house had been what is called a château—that isn't actually a castle, but it was something like a castle. It had overlooked the valley. Many of the people in the village de St. Chamant had worked for my grandfather; and, I assume, from what mon oncle Paul told me, for my grandfather's grandfather, too.

When the Germans came down from Paris they had taken the Langres maison. Before they had departed, they had burnt it. I can't explain how I felt. Mind you, I hadn't seen this maison before. But the minute I saw the ruins, it was as though I'd been here many times and knew about it. I know that sounds funny. For nearly half an hour we walked around the grounds. Mon oncle explained the reason he was working so hard on his avion was he hoped to sell it for much money and he planned to use the money to restore the maison and the grounds. Just as I wanted my bicycle with the high gear and the low

gear and the electric lighting dynamo, so mon oncle also
wanted something—he wanted to rebuild the family home.
I could understand now. I could understand a lot more
things. I wanted him to get his avion completed and sold.
No longer was his avion an ordinary glider, not very
important. I felt the urgency of what he wanted.

By and by he glanced at his watch. "Ah!" he said. "It
is nearly two-thirty. I'm late, Jean. I told Monsieur Niort
I would return to the workshop by two-thirty. Instead
of taking the path we came up on, I zink I shall descend
straight down the mountain. It is quicker."

"But—" I was worried. "I'm not sure I can descend
straight down a mountain without crutches."

He cocked his head at me, something like a quick
lively fox who listens a minute before darting away. He
shrugged. "Then you must descend by the path," said he.
"Descend by the path, mon neveu. You will not become
lost. You do not require crutches. It is confidence you
require. Au revoir!"

"Wait!" I called—but he was gone.

He leaped over the wall and ran toward the trees and
vanished. I hadn't ever expected him to do a thing like
that to me.

For about ten minutes I was so stunned I didn't do a
thing. This was what came of having mon oncle and me
montent sur la montagne. I simply sat where I was. The
breeze was soft and warm. It was the finest jour we'd had
yet. I could sight across the meadow to the edge of trees.
Beyond the trees, the montagne dropped away, sloping
into the valley below. Across to the west was a range of
lower montagnes, purple and green in the distance. Voici
Jean, I thought—stuck. I got madder and madder.

By and by I grabbed hold of the rough bark of a tree and pulled myself up. Butterflies floated above the flowers. I limped to the stone wall surrounding the ruins. Here I sat for a time, almost forgetting my leg as I tried to imagine ma mère as a young girl, playing in the grounds when the grounds were smooth and even and tended to, with the noble old house high and stately on the side of the montagne. No wonder she had always thought of France and loved it. In a way, I was glad she wasn't here to see her family's house—her family's maison, I mean, destroyed by the Germans.

The big front door was still here. It had pillars on each side. It was almost as if ma mère was waiting for me, on the other side of that door. I never saw such a friendly, inviting door. I slid off the stone wall, taking it easy on my leg, gritting my teeth. I got as far as the door and my leg still stayed whole; it hadn't dropped off. It hurt, yes. It hurt off and on but at least it had carried me to the door. I decided I'd stay here and wait. After I didn't show up in le village de St. Chamant, my oncle would begin to worry. I'd teach him a trick, too. He could come for me.

I entered the house, hearing my steps echo. The roof was gone. Part of a big stairway lifted upwards—and ended, abruptly, pointing to the open side. It was sort of fun exploring la maison de ma mère. The wood was blackened from the fire, charred through in places. I followed along the hall, with the sun shining down upon me. I got as far as the stairs and rested and started again around the rear of the stairs. Here, under the stairs was a door. It was on its hinges. The fire hadn't eaten through it at all. I tried the door; it opened, just as if it had been waiting there for me and was inviting me to open it.

When I opened it, something flung around and smacked me in the face. You can imagine how surprised I was. I wasn't scared; at least, I don't think I was. Everything here was so peaceful and friendly, as if I was coming back almost to another home of my own, there wasn't anything frightening at all about the place. I wasn't nervous, or anything like that, either. I was mad—sure; but, now I'd determined to teach mon oncle a leçon, I was recovering from being mad.

So, when that thing flung around and hit my face I stepped back, nearly falling, because I'd stepped back on my punk leg. On the other side of the door leading down into the cellar was swinging a dirty gray knapsack. That was what had hit me, swinging around as I opened the door. I thought perhaps this was a knapsack that might have belonged to mon oncle. I looked more closely at it. Words were printed on it. They were foreign words. And —they weren't French words, either.

One of the words was "Panzergruppe 156." As if from a long ways off I remembered panzer was a German word from reading about the German panzer columns of tanks in our newspaper back home. If the words were German— why, then this was a German army knapsack! It was like having a cold wind blow clean through me. My hands were shaking when I opened the knapsack. Inside was an old tattered dirty paper-covered book titled "Mein Kampf." Underneath the title evidently was the name of the author: "Adolf Hitler." Well, I knew *that* name all right. Last I'd heard of *that* name was quite a few months ago when our papers back home had a couple of lines about him on the inside pages saying he was dead, probably having killed himself.

Something flung around and smacked me in the face

Nothing else was in the knapsack but a whole loaf of French black bread. I touched the loaf of bread, expecting to find it old, solid as a brick. It wasn't old. It was still soft. It couldn't have been more than a jour or so old. That meant the owner of this knapsack hadn't hung it behind the door more than a jour or so ago, perhaps even this morning. Whew! At that thought, I just dropped the knapsack and started to shove out of this place. I didn't want any Nazi holing up in these montagnes to come upon me; I'd had all the experience with them I needed with that Monsieur Simonis to last me the rest of my life.

I was limping away, when I heard a second and softer clunk. I looked back. The knapsack had spilled open after being dropped. The loaf of bread had rolled out—and do you know what? That loaf evidently had been broken in two pieces when fresh and stuck back together again. The second clunk I'd heard was when the long ugly black pistol hidden inside the scooped out portions of the loaf had rolled on to the charred wooden floor.

7

THE PIG OF THE MAYOR

I limped back and gingerly picked up that big German pistol. In Wyoming, old Jake had taught me about guns. This German pistol wasn't much different from an American automatic, except that the muzzle was longer.

The thing was loaded. I saw that.

I skinned through the door, starting across the long bare stretch of meadowland to the stone wall. I had the feeling that German was somewhere in the house, right now, *watching me*. I'd whirl—but, no—I didn't see anyone. The ruins of the place were unchanging, gaunt and huge, not a sign of anybody.

Clouds had swept across part of the sky, hiding the sun. The wind came up, blowing the leaves in the trees beyond, rattling the branches and ruffling the long grass behind me exactly as if a man was crawling along, quiet and careful, not wanting to be seen.

The weeks I'd practiced walking came in helpful now. Probably being scared clear down to the bone helped too, the fear pouring along through the muscles and temporarily making me forget my bum leg.

I flung myself over the stone wall, panting, landing on the bad leg. I felt the jab of pain as I landed. I squatted on the grass, turning my head back and forth, hanging on to that loaded pistol, determined to let blaze with it at the first sign of someone.

Everything came back to me now, about Monsieur Simonis in Paris, meeting him on the train. The police must have been wrong. Monsieur Simonis probably had followed me as far as St. Chamant. Now he was hiding in the ruins of la maison de ma mère and this could be *his* gun.

I don't know how long I crouched against the stone wall. You've seen animals, small ones, when they're scared? Some of them will halt instead of running and try to burrow into the ground. That always had puzzled me, why they did that instead of trying to escape—but now I understood. I had the same impulse. It seemed to me that I *couldn't* move.

I forced myself to crawl away from the wall. I had to get to le village. I found I'd lost my way to the lane down the mountain. Ahead of me was nothing but the dark forest. The moving shadows of clouds passed along the meadow and the ruins. Over toward the east, in the brambles growing to one side of the ruins, it seemed to me as if something had moved—and dropped—and was wriggling toward the wall.

I gave a jump. I snaked through underbrush, crashing away, with the branches reaching for me, trying to grab at me as if they were the long dry fingers of Monsieur Simonis. The land began to slope. The trees became thicker.

I ran into a tree and stopped, winded, my leg hurting more. I laid flat, hanging on to the pistol. The leg was throbbing. It was like having a charley-horse—you know how that is, an awful sort of cramp.

Presently, I heard a rustling from behind me.

The brambles and long green grass were dense, like

moving screens. The rustling came again, louder. I hugged the ground, about paralyzed. For a moment everything was silent, the way a silence comes into a forest. You hear little sounds, the birds, perhaps a chipmunk. In between there isn't anything except perhaps the wind—and all that, somehow, makes a bigger silence than ever, a sort of lonely silence. Next, the rustle was there once more, off through the brambles, exactly as if some tall big thing was crawling forward on hands and knees.

In a minute or so I expected to see Monsieur Simonis' white head thrust itself through the bushes, his teeth grinning at me, with a hand reaching out for me. I hauled up the German pistol. I'd forgotten the cramp in my leg. I dragged to another tree and from there limped to a second tree, zig-zag style. It was as though everything in the forest was watching and holding its breath and looking to see if I was going to be nabbed by the Germans tracking after me.

By now I recognized there wasn't any chance of it being my imagination, either. Every time I halted, straining my ears, by and by, I'd catch a sound of something soft, sliding closer and closer to me through the brush under the trees. The branches overhead were so thick they shut out a lot of light. It was gloomy here, with the ground all slanting, uneven, hidden by brush, the trees high and dark like pillars in some enormous old church.

The next minute I saw a dark thick shape about twenty yards away, above me, on the slope. I shoved my pistol forward—I said, "Don't move another step or I'll shoot!" It had the great enormous head of a man, peering at me. I pulled the trigger.

The pistol didn't go off. I'd forgotten it was an automatic and that you had to jerk the slide back to cock the trigger. I just stood, holding that pistol.

The thing came on through the bushes. When I saw what it was all the tension broke. I was so relieved and weak I laughed in a silly fashion and lowered the pistol and had to lean against a tree to keep from falling.

It was the same French pig I'd seen a few weeks ago in the rue—the one to whom I'd called, the one that hadn't noticed me. It was a well-fed pig standing a little higher than my knees. It had a long bristly snout, and tiny eyes. Looking at it head on, in a way it did resemble a man crawling on his hands and knees. Now the pig gave me a glance. It marched toward me, showing its fangs. I moved backwards—tripped—fell. The pig shoved its snout against the roots of the tree, where I'd been standing, and began to push at the dirt, no longer interested in me.

I got up. I wiped dirt off the pistol, slipping the pistol through my belt and pulling my jacket down. I started moving off when from somewhere behind the trees a man's voice sounded, "Oh, Hippolyte! Où es tu? Où es tu?"

I stopped. That was a French voice. I figured if a Frenchman was up here I'd be safer with company. I started shivering again, waiting for whoever it was to come. In about four minutes Monsieur Capedulocque pushed his way through the bushes, halting when he saw me, scowling. He was wearing a corduroy coat hanging nearly to his knees, with enormous pockets. Today he had wooden shoes stuffed with straw to keep his ankles warm instead of the black leather shoes he usually wore in le village.

Even if it was the mayor of St. Chamant, I can't tell

you how glad I was to see him. I ran to him and gestured
and signed to him, trying to explain a German was hiding
roundabouts and I wanted protection. We had to go to
le village at once. That mayor never did understand me.
I was nearly frantic, too. He considered it was—the *pig*
I was scared of.

That pig of his must have meant a lot to him, because
he took it as an insult that I'd allowed myself to be scared
of his pig. He grabbed on to my arm, scowling all the
time, pointing to the pig, saying, "Hippolyte est un bon
cochon, un *bon* cochon!"

Meanwhile the pig—cochon, in French—had rooted up
something. That cochon wriggled its little twisty tail. It
turned around. Like a trained dog, it trotted over to the
mayor. It had something in his mouth, something round
and dark, about half as big as a baseball.

Still hanging on to my arm, the mayor took the thing
from the cochon's mouth and thrust it at me. "Truffe,"
he said crossly. "Truffe," he said again, very loudly, the
way people do when they think you don't understand
them. Then he let go of my arm and hoisted his sack from
his shoulders and dropped this truffe into the sack and
snapped his fingers at the cochon and again started up the
mountain, as if he didn't care what happened to me.

With sinking heart I watched the mayor vanish, leaving
me alone, lost, not having any idea of how to get down
to le village. Later on I learned about truffes—I discovered
they were a kind of fungus that grew on oak roots only
in this part of the world. They were immensely valuable,
cherished as a delicacy by restaurants and the mayor had
made a sizable fortune before the war with his cochons—
yes, cochons, trained to root up these truffes for him just

the way you might train hunting dogs to track down birds.

But at this time, all this was a mystery to me. It made me more addled than ever. In a few minutes the forest once more was empty. The mayor and that cochon of his had gone—and, it seemed I might have dreamed what had happened. They hadn't been there. Again, I was alone. Somewhere, hiding, watching me, that German was waiting to tackle me.

The fear came, greater than before.

I struck straight through the forest, knowing enough at least to follow the slope of land downwards when I was lost. My leg was causing me more trouble, too. Even with all the time I'd spent strengthening it, my leg wasn't ready for a couple of mountain miles at the speed I was attempting, floundering through brush, panting, sweat in my eyes, the panic surging over me more and more.

It must have been close to three in the afternoon, along toward the time mon oncle would be expecting me to return. I was going more slowly—I couldn't go fast as I wanted on account of the pain shooting through my leg. The forest got gloomier and gloomier. Pretty soon I came upon a little creek, sparkling away, clear as glass.

I fell into the thick grass and drank from the water and rested a minute, feeling dizzy. I was about done for. In a few minutes I found I could open my eyes without having the trees move around in a big dizzy circle. I drank a little more water. I shoved my hands against the moss to push me up. I couldn't wait here. I had to go. I had to reach le village before that German found me.

As I unsteadily heaved myself back on my legs again, I heard yells through the trees. Those yells seemed to nail into me. It was like being frozen suddenly in a cake of ice.

I was caught. I knew I was caught. The yells came more plainly; they sounded like, "Va-hoo! Va-hoo!"

Now I decided I was crazy, out of my mind. I staggered a little forward to reach a tree, hoping to hide behind it. If I'd been home I would have known what those yells were from: They would have been yells from live Indians or from somebody playing at Indians. However, I knew as well as anyone one thing France didn't have was live Indians. No German tracking after me was going to lift up such a commotion by shouting those yells.

I waited, getting my breath, feeling for the pistol in my belt, while those yells continued. Something came crackling and shoving through the bush. A second later and I'm hanged if an arrow didn't wobble out from the bushes and plunk against the tree to fall at my feet!

I say it was an arrow. It was the most unlikely looking arrow I ever did see. It was crooked. It didn't have any proper feathers at the tip. The point was a small lump of wet mud. An arrow like that couldn't shoot dust. I felt sorry for whoever made such an arrow. The surprise almost drove from my head the panic I'd had about being tracked by a German. No German ever manufactured such a mean, unhappy arrow as that. I wasn't so scared that I didn't know that much.

As I was watching, the bushes parted. A boy about my age, stockier and heavier possibly, and not quite as tall, came out into the clearing. He saw me. He gaped at me and stopped dead.

He had red hair. It was violent red hair. It was the reddest hair ever to exist, I think. He had a freckled face and blue eyes and a wide mouth and the rest of him was covered with one of those ratty old sweaters I've seen

Frenchmen wearing, the bottom so long it came almost down to his knees. He had patched baggy trousers and no stockings or socks. In his hand he had what I suppose he thought was a bow. It was no more than a stick with a piece of string tied to the ends. Any boy back home in Wyoming could have constructed in one minute, with his eyes closed, a better bow than that. Any boy at home would rather have been dead than be seen with a bow like that one.

He took a breath. He advanced, pointing to his arrow I was holding. He reeled off a whole flow of words, ending by putting his hand to his mouth and shouting, "Va-hoo, Va-hoo," like as if he actually thought he was an Indian over here in France and probably expected me to fall over on my back in mortal terror.

While he was jumping around in that silly style, the bushes opened again. This time a girl came out. She had red hair, too, but its color wasn't such a violent red as the boy's. Where his was an orange-red, hers was more a brownish-red. It hung down long, old-fashioned style. Some leaves were caught in it, and a piece of bark, too, from where she'd passed under the trees.

When she noticed me, she stopped quick. She gave her head a shake. She snatched away the leaves, trying hastily to smooth her hair the way girls probably do anywhere in the world the instant they think anyone's looking at them.

Her brother stopped dancing. He aimed his arrow at me. He said, "Peau-rouge," a couple of times. That was too deep for me.

The sun was sliding down the sky and the light was dimming. I had the sense once more of something waiting and watching me, and I didn't want to be stuck up here with a French boy and a French girl and get caught by a German. After the first surprise of finding them the astonishment wore off and I became more anxious. I started down the montagne. The boy and girl came along with me. I said, impatiently, "Look, I need help," even though I knew it wouldn't do any good to try to talk to them. I was desperate.

I was afraid I was lost.

"German," I said. "German!" and pointed.

That didn't catch any fish either.

The boy stopped. He scratched his head perplexed while the girl calmly looked on as if she considered all boys were strange articles and she'd been taught to put up with them and not complain.

Finally the boy pointed to himself. "Charles," he said. "Charles Meilhac." He pointed to the girl. "Suzanne Meilhac." He waited.

It was like having a great illumination break through the forest. I should have realized sooner. This was Charles Meilhac! The boy mon oncle had told me about! He could be a friend. He could be somebody who might help after all. I grabbed him in my excitement and he didn't know what to make of it. I shouted a couple of times, "Jean! Jean Littlehorn!" pointing to myself.

Then Suzanne understood. *She* became excited. "Jean Littlehorn!" she exclaimed. "Tu est le neveu de Paul Langres! Ah!" She snatched at her brother's sleeve and jabbered at him. Charles' freckled face seemed to open. His eyes became blue as the sky. He laughed and danced around me and shouted and was pleased and I guessed he'd heard about me from somebody.

Then I worked back to what I was trying to say. I said,

"German—" and realized that didn't make sense to them, so I said, "Nazi!" and that was a word they both understood. "Nazi!" I said again, pointing.

They nodded. Charles solemnly said, "Oui, un Nazi," and looked ferocious and took hold of his bow and arrow and began stealing around the clearing, as if he were an Indian looking for a Nazi.

Well, I could nearly have cried out of vexation. Yes— they *had* understood when I'd said, "Nazi." But they had been playing at Indian and now they figured I was playing along with them, playing we were *all* Indians—peaurouges, in French—and we were hunting Nazis!

The sweat sprung from me. I could imagine us all walking square into that grinning Monsieur Simonis before any of us ever had a chance to get to le village for help. The afternoon was waning. It grew darker. I asked at last, "Où est le village de St. Chamant?"

Probably they thought it was time to quit playing and I wanted to go home.

Charles pointed southwards, through the trees. "Là."

It was wrong of me, I know, but I didn't let on I understood, because I wanted their company all the way to le village. Finally he took my arm and showed all his white teeth in the friendliest smile imaginable, as if he'd forgotten ten minutes ago he was an Indian trying to hunt a play-Nazi. He indicated he'd go along with me to St. Chamant. Nothing could have pleased me more. His sister followed after us. He stopped. He motioned her back and ordered, "Suzanne, reste là!" Well, that order was clear enough to be luminous.

She answered back, "Non, je viens avec Jean et toi." She was saying to Charles, "No, I come with John and you." "Toi" wasn't anything more than "you," and "moi" was me.

"Viens," Charles told me, and marched off.

I did as he told me: I came.

Suzanne repeated, "Je viens avec toi et Jean," and came along, too, just as she said she was going to do. That "viens" was easy as falling off a log, nothing to it—"come"—"I come with you and Jean" was what she'd said.

When we happened to enter another montagne clearing, Charles suddenly halted and pulled me back. I thought it was the German, sure enough. "Sh-h," he whispered. He motioned to Suzanne and said, "Viens," and waited until she'd done as he told her to do, and had to come to us. She sat down quietly between us. "Tu vois?" he asked, meaning, "You see?" and pointed through the bushes in front of us toward the clearing.

On the other side of the clearing was a fat rabbit. It was bigger and rounder than our own rabbits. At the same time it wasn't as big as our jack-rabbits. Charles whispered, "Nazi," to me, smacking his lips as if he was confusing Nazis and Indians and cannibals in his mind. He rubbed his stomach hungrily. He said, "Très bon. Très bon." He crept forward, fixing his arrow. He meant to get that rabbit.

Now, with everything else pressing in my mind I wouldn't have thought another second about that furry rabbit if I hadn't happened to glance at Suzanne. She was regarding that rabbit as intently as if she hadn't eaten for weeks and was seeing a whole Sunday dinner before her.

The hollows under her cheeks showed. She stretched out her skinny arms without realizing what she was doing, wanting to grab that rabbit. I sighted at Charles. He was going forward with the same intentness. It might be, for my benefit, he was pretending he was an Indian shooting —but it was more than that to him. That rabbit meant food.

I'd heard how the French had starved during the war and how poor they were now, with very little food. But this was the first time I actually had it brought up smack to me how important food was to these people. Charles took another step, getting closer, the rabbit staying where it was, wriggling its ears. I found I was becoming just as interested and intent on what Charles was doing as Suzanne was. I *wanted* him to get that rabbit.

Of course, I should have realized he never had a chance —and so should he and Suzanne. He lifted his little bow and shot the arrow. It wobbled across the clearing. Before it was halfway across, the rabbit took notice of it and without any great hurry ducked into the bushes. The arrow hit against a tree, over six feet to the left of where the rabbit had been. The arrow broke. Suzanne made a sad little cry. "Oh, Charles," she said. That was all. She clenched her fists tightly together and twisted her head away so nobody could see her face.

Charles stood. He threw down his bow. It wasn't ever a good one, anyway, but he must have cherished that bow and thought a lot of it—and it showed how crushed he was for him to throw it away. He made an effort to smile. He went to his sister, giving her a clumsy sort of half punch and half pat. She rubbed her eyes with her knuckles, with a queer embarrassed look at me. Charles shrugged his shoulders. "Eh bien," he said. I didn't know what that meant; I didn't have to. He'd lost a good supper.

He nodded at me. "Viens," he said wearily.

Even as he spoke, that blasted rabbit again poked its head from the bushes. It wriggled its ears. It ducked back in. All three of us considered each other. I think, for a minute, I was just as sorry and disappointed as Charles and Suzanne were. That rabbit acted like it was taunting us. We saw another group of bushes move, off by the tree, as the rabbit passed under them.

I don't know what came into me. I don't want anyone to tease me and say I was showing off in front of Suzanne, because I wasn't—at least, not this time.

I was sorry for both of them. On an impulse I pulled out that big German pistol from under my jacket. Charles' eyes opened. "Oh!" he gasped.

Suzanne stepped back. "Un gangster!" she exclaimed. Maybe I ought to tell you that because of our American movies Frenchmen have the idea America is filled with gangsters and Indians and cowboys and movie stars and nobody else and the word for "gangster" in French is precisely what we have. Any other time I might have laughed.

I went after that rabbit with the big pistol. I could see the movement of the bushes. It was like shooting a coyote in chaparral. I lifted the pistol and cocked it, this time. I waited. I aimed low down on the bushes. The next time the bushes rustled—I pulled the trigger.

There was an almighty bang from the pistol. It had a tremendous kick. It nearly knocked itself out of my hand. Suzanne yelped. After her yelp, that rabbit in the bushes made the oddest sound ever to come from a rabbit. It let go with a grunt. After a grunt it squealed. It continued to squeal and it was still squealing, only not as loud, when it staggered out from the bushes and laid down in the clearing and stopped moving. Charles took one look at it. He put his hands to his head, rocking his head back and forth as if he'd become afflicted by a sudden splitting headache. "Ai! Ai!" he groaned.

Suzanne ran into the clearing. She looked down at what I had shot. She had eyes big as saucers. "Ah! Ah!" she ex-

It staggered out from the bushes and laid down in the clearing

claimed, absolutely horrified. "C'est le cochon de Monsieur Capedulocque!"

And so it was.

Instead of shooting a rabbit for Charles' and Suzanne's supper I'd gone and let fly at that conceited, trained, truffe-hunting pig belonging to the mayor of St. Chamant.

I wanted to sink right down through the earth and never viens up again.

Suzanne gasped, "Oh, j'ai peur. J'ai peur."

Charles had one more look at the pig and muttered, "Moi, aussi. J'ai peur. J'ai peur."

I didn't know what that "J'ai peur" meant, but from the way they said it anyone could see they were nearly scared to death. A mayor of a French village is an important object in France, much more important than in our own towns. I wasn't happy, myself. I was scared, too; and if "J'ai peur" meant "I'm scared," that was what I was, aussi. A lot. Afterwards I learned it almost meant that. Only the French say, "I *have* fear" instead of "I am afraid." "Je" was "I" and "ai" was "have" and "peur" was "fear"; and when Charles was saying, "J'ai peur," he was saying, "I've fear." But right then I didn't take time to do any cyphering of what he was saying.

Charles pulled my arm. "Viens!" he said, and ran across the clearing, Suzanne following. "Viens!" they called. "Viens vite! *Vite!*" You didn't have to hear that "Vite!" more than once to know it meant "quick!" And, je viens vite, too. But not vite enough. Before I reached them Monsieur Capedulocque stepped through the bushes and saw his dead cochon and began to roar at us and groan and tear at his whiskers with his hands.

8

LE TROUBLE VIENT

I can understand a man losing his temper because his prize cochon had been shot but I never witnessed a man go on about a cochon as much as that mayor of St. Chamant did. He collared Charles and Suzanne. He shook them. He yelled at them as if they were murderers. I stepped across to explain it was my fault. That didn't help any—because Monsieur Capedulocque didn't understand what I was saying.

I realize now that neither Charles nor Suzanne tried to unload the blame on me, either. Just as easy as anything, they could have told the mayor everything happened because of me, when I didn't know what they were saying. But never once did they point at me as you might think foreign kids would've done.

The mayor was panting and shouting. Charles was active, limber enough to slip away. But the mayor hung on to Suzanne. He shook her some more. I could see her biting her lips to keep from crying out loud. I shoved closer, forgetting my leg. Loudly as I could, I said, "I did it." That didn't even dent the mayor. He'd shake Suzanne—he'd look at that cochon in the grass—he'd yell—he'd groan and pull at his beard and rage. It was an awful thing to see him carry on as he did.

I figured a dead cochon wasn't nearly as important as the fact a live Nazi was probably hanging around somewhere right now, listening to all the commotion that angry little fat mayor was making. To distract him away from Suzanne, finally, I waved the German pistol at him. I wanted him to see the pistol and to realize what it was. But do you think he understood what I was driving at? Not at all. I'm hung if he didn't gawk at that pistol, as if he hadn't noticed before I was holding it.

His little eyes widened. His white beard sort of flared out. He let go of Suzanne. He stumbled back, waving his hands at me, shouting at me. Once more, I tried to persuade him to take the pistol and see for himself what it was. He let out another yell. He grabbed a knife in his belt and brandished it at me.

Automatic pistols are different from revolvers. Once an automatic pistol shoots, it cocks itself—and it's ready to fire again. So, when I happened to grab more tightly on to the pistol, I must have accidentally pulled the trigger.

The pistol went off a second time with a tremendous bang. It knocked itself out of my hand. The bullet slammed through the mayor's hat, lifting his hat right off his pink bald head.

For nearly a whole minute afterwards, there wasn't a sound in the clearing except the echo of that shot. The pistol fell at my feet. I was so pulverized by what had happened I didn't budge. The mayor opened his mouth; his face turned scarlet. He didn't say a word. He felt himself all over. He touched his head. He found his hat was gone. He looked around. He picked up his hat and he eyed the hole in his hat made by the bullet. He pointed his finger at me. "Assassin!" he shouted. "Tu es un assassin!"

The mayor rushed at me. He slammed me to the ground. Charles promptly tackled him. Suzanne tried to bite him. He grabbed all of us. He sputtered. He pointed down the montagne. "Descendez!" he ordered, drawing himself up like a judge speaking to three criminals. "Charles, Suzanne et Jean! Descendez la montagne! Vite!"

We must have taken about half an hour. We descended right down through the forest and across the vineyards on the lower slope until we came into la rue entering le village de St. Chamant.

By now, all three of us, Charles, Suzanne et moi, were pretty much scared. My leg hurt. I can't tell you how much it hurt. I don't believe it had hurt that much since Monsieur Simonis had dug his fingers into it. I'd never have made it to le village de St. Chamant if Charles hadn't helped on one side and Suzanne on the other.

We came into le village, the mayor walking behind us, puffing and roaring, letting everyone know what had happened, waving his hat, pointing to the hole in it. Before we reached the workshop mon oncle heard the noise. He ran to us. I'd fallen down a lot. I was scratched. Probably I was pretty much of a sight to behold. He took one look at me. He gave a jump. Although I was nearly as big as he was he picked me up. The mayor rushed at mon oncle, again shouting I was an assassin.

Mon oncle swung around. He took one hand from me. He gave the mayor such a shove that the mayor fell backwards and rolled into the ditch. He got to his knees, all covered with mud. If that man had been angry on top of the montagne, it didn't compare with what he was now. He was so out of temper he didn't even have time to take himself from the mud. He shook his fist at mon oncle. He started swearing and cursing and shouting and shoving at the people who tried to help him.

Mon oncle carried me to the hotel where Madame Graffoulier met him. They loaded me on the bed upstairs. I
began explaining. Charles and Suzanne came right in, too.

Charles kept saying, "S'il vous plaît," apologizing for
interrupting. Mon oncle said, "S'il vous plaît" meant, "If
you please—" and Charles was asking please let him give
his version.

Mon oncle listened to Charles. I gathered Charles was
taking on the blame. According to mon oncle Charles
claimed it was his fault because *he* asked me to shoot the
rabbit.

I said that wasn't anywhere near the exact truth. I said,
"S'il vous plaît," to Charles and explained *I'd* wanted to
shoot the rabbit.

Mon oncle's face sort of lightened. "You didn't try to
scare the mayor by shooting at his hat?"

"Oh, no!" I said.

Mon oncle couldn't help it. He broke into laughter. He
said he wished he'd been there. He told me, "Bien fait!
Bien fait!" and laughed some more and said "Bien fait!"
was French for, "Well done!" and by and by became more
serious and admitted he shouldn't have laughed. He
wrinkled his forehead.

"Ah, oui. I zink perhaps this is more serious than you
understand, Jean." He paused. From downstairs we could
hear the sound of men's voices. Every now and then we
heard a louder roaring noise. That was the mayor.

Evidently, he had at last hauled himself out of the mud
and followed us to the hotel. A couple of times Madame
Graffoulier stuck her angular head in through the door and
spoke to mon oncle and pulled her head back into the hall,
again, shutting the door.

Mon oncle continued, "You must tell me the truth, Jean."

I said, "I am. Monsieur Simonis is hiding up in the ruins."

He became patient and calm. He said, "Jean, I zink that experience you had in Paris has upset you. Monsieur Simonis is not in these hills. You are imagining things. You must not imagine things, s'il vous plaît. This is serious."

I said, "I wasn't imagining anything. Maybe it isn't Monsieur Simonis, but it *is* a German."

"You did see a knapsack? A German knapsack?" said mon oncle.

"Oui," I answered. "It was right behind the door. Why doesn't somebody look for him? Why doesn't somebody go up there? They'll see the knapsack."

"And that pistol *was* a German pistol? Not some old French pistol you happened to find in the mountains?"

"It was a German pistol," I said. "It's up in the clearing now, where I dropped it."

Mon oncle asked Charles some questions.

Charles ceased looking quite as glum. He nodded. He said, "Dans la montagne, oui, Monsieur Langres. Oui." He was backing me up about where I'd dropped the pistol.

"Very well," said mon oncle at last. "I'll arrange to have the men from the village search the mountain. But once more," he said, now as solemn as a preacher, "I must tell you that you have to tell me the truth. This cannot be a prank of yours, Jean, to hide the fact you may have picked up a French pistol accidentally dropped by French soldiers last winter when they were searching the mountains for Nazis. The mayor of St. Chamant is not only angry at you for killing his pig, but he is very angry at Charles and Su-

zanne for what happened. He blames all three of you, right
or wrong."

I said, "It wasn't any prank. I *am* telling the truth. Cross
my heart and hope to die!"

"I hope you are," said he, still solemn. "Because Charles'
and Suzanne's mother owes money to the mayor. If he
wished, he could take their vineyard away from them this
fall if they cannot sell enough grapes to pay him as well as
keep themselves from starving through next year. I will
arrange with the mayor to send armed men to the mountain. If you have not told the truth, it will be even more
difficult for all of us. The mayor has never liked the Langres or the Meilhac families. We were much more important families before the war than he was. Now I am afraid
he has become rich and would like to see us come crawling
to him."

"You find that knapsack," I said, "and you'll see a German has been there. The bread is fresh. *That* ought to be
proof."

"It *will* be proof," said mon oncle.

Charles and Suzanne gathered around and spoke to me,
friendly and cheerful. Mon oncle took a minute longer
to explain they were telling me they wanted to see me
again and were sorry they had to go now and that they
were glad the cochon was dead because it was a bad cochon
and proud and conceited and rooted all around the vineyards, destroying many of the vines. The villagers had
been afraid to do anything because it was owned by the
mayor. I told them I'd get up now and go with them and
mon oncle. I started to get off the bed.

"Non," said mon oncle, beginning to smile. "Have you
forgotten you have a lame leg, mon neveu?"

"By jiminy!" I said, "I got down this far, didn't I? I'll go back up with you if you'll help me. I'll show you where I left the pistol and where I found the knapsack. And you tell Charles and Suzanne I can pay for the cochon. We can't let that mayor take their vineyard, can we?"

Mon oncle had a way of inspiring everyone with his own cheerfulness. He spoke rapidly to Suzanne and Charles. He stuck his big nose over me, and said, "You are not angry, then, because I left you on the mountain?"

I'd forgotten all about the trick he'd played on me. . . .

And here I was. I had descended la montagne on my own legs, even if you count the lift I received from Charles and Suzanne, and the shoves the mayor had given me with his kicks.

I didn't have to reply to mon oncle's last question. He saw the answer in my face. The only person I was angry at was the mayor.

Mon oncle winked. He snapped his fingers. "Pouf!" said he. "Have no worries, if you tell the truth. We Langres stick together, hein? We shall search the mountains. For any Nazis found, there is a reward of ten thousand francs. Charles knows the mountains better than any man in the village. I shall pay off that cochon de maire! We Langres stay by our friends, oui?"

"Oui!" said I, and saw them all go, wishing mightily I could go with them, too. After they'd gone, though, I realized I'd have only been in the way. My leg started hurting more. I tried to go downstairs for dinner and fell.

Madame Graffoulier had to help me back into my room. She gave me a hand, and we got to the window and looked out. I saw a crowd of about fifteen men in the market

place, more coming, all with muskets and guns or pitchforks. Madame Graffoulier said, "Tout le monde quitte le
village. Tout le monde court de la ville. Tout le monde va
à la montagne."

I didn't know what that "tout le monde" was, but she
gestured and signified it was everybody. The whole village. And that was true.

Everyone was running from (de) the village or la ville
—town, as it was sometimes called as well as village. Everyone—that is, all the men—were going to (à) la montagne.
Tout le monde except the mayor.

He was off to one side, looking sour and angry. He
wasn't court-ing de la ville; he wasn't va-ing à la montagne.
No, he was arguing. He kept saying, "Non, non." He was
attempting to persuade the people—everybody—tout le
monde—that no Nazi was up there, out of sheer meanness
I guess, to prove anybody having anything to do with mon
oncle, avec mon oncle, was wrong.

Probably he'd been responsible for spreading the story
I'd simply happened upon a French pistol and first had
emptied it into the cochon and next at him, encouraged by
the two Meilhac youngsters. But the men marched off,
anyway, leaving him in la rue, scowling. Mon oncle already had gone up the montagne, accompanied by le forgeron and Charles and Suzanne. I imagined they'd take
Suzanne across the montagne to her mother's, and after
leaving her, go on up into the montagnes, searching for the
Nazi who was hiding.

Madame Graffoulier brought my dinner into the bedroom. Her nephew and niece tagged in after her, standing
around. They'd heard the news, and were half scared by
it. They tried to ask me questions. Little Philippe stood

next to the bed. He asked, "Jean voit un Nazi? Jean voit un Nazi?"

I shook my head. I hadn't *seen* a Nazi. I had seen the knapsack and the pistol. I said, "Moi—" remembering that meant "me." I said, "Moi voit a pistol et a knapsack."

That stumped the kids and Madame Graffoulier.

I tried again, recalling the word Suzanne had used for "I" when she said, "Je viens." I said, "*Je* voit a pistol—"

Philippe clapped his hands. He corrected me. "Je *vois* un pistolet," he said.

By this time it was nuit. Wind moaned. Darkness hid everything in la rue. I thought of those men sur the montagnes, searching. I wondered if Charles and mon oncle had found the tracks of the Nazi yet. I could imagine them up there and I could imagine the Nazi hiding from them, or waiting for them, maybe with another gun. Part of me was glad I hadn't gone; that was the scared part. Another part of me longed to be up there with them. It would have been a noble adventure, finding a Nazi, something I could write about to Bob Collins, back home. I thought of that reward mon oncle had mentioned. If the French government was offering ten thousand francs for finding any Nazi still holding out, certainly Charles Meilhac as well as mon oncle had a chance of getting it. I hoped they'd get the reward.

Well, the hours passed. The old clock downstairs knocked off ten o'clock. Next, eleven o'clock. Still none of the men returned. The kids were sent to bed. Along about midnight little Philippe snuck into my bedroom. We lit a candle and waited. It began to rain. By and by we heard some men in the street. They were talking in loud angry voices.

A little later mon oncle entered my room. Philippe jumped up, knowing he oughtn't to be in there. He ran out like a scared rabbit. Mon oncle shut the door and sat down —slumped down, I ought to say. He was tired. He was about done for. His pants and shoes were muddy. He was carrying a rifle. He laid that against the plaster wall. He rubbed his hands together as if they were practically frozen. I didn't ask any questions. From his attitude I could see he hadn't found the Nazi. I waited for him to do the talking.

It was worse than I had anticipated.

Not only had he failed to find the Nazi—he hadn't found either the knapsack or the pistol! Both were gone. There wasn't any proof that a German had been using la maison de ma mère as a hiding place. The men in the village considered that Charles and Suzanne Meilhac and me had made up a thumping lie to cover the fact I had, somehow, found a French pistol and had shot the mayor's cochon and the mayor's hat.

Of course, I realized what had happened. That Nazi *had* been there all the time. He'd taken the knapsack. More than that—*he must have followed me*. It hadn't been my imagination at all when I thought someone was tracking after me. He'd followed me. First, the cochon and the mayor, afterwards the two Meilhac twins, had prevented him from coming after me. That much I'd played in luck. But he had picked up his pistol. Now, he was armed again. He was there, hiding, waiting. And no one believed he was there.

Mon oncle had me go over everything again that had happened. I want to say this for him: When I was through, *he believed me*.

Maybe it was because I was part Langres and he'd been brought up to think that people in the same family have to stick by each other no matter what comes. He said, "Jean, I do believe you. But I am afraid—j'ai peur—no one else in le village will believe you unless we manage to find that Nazi. We must take care now, too. I zink he will know you suspect he is hiding. It is not good at all."

He got up and walked around the bedroom, the candle flickering, throwing his shadow upon the wall. After a long time he said if I wished he would write my parents in London and suggest perhaps I should leave St. Chamant and go to England. He said it was beyond reason to believe Monsieur Simonis ever had come here to grab me, but it was possible I'd happened upon the hiding place of a Nazi up there in the montagnes. He could understand such a thing was frightening for me and he wouldn't blame me if I wanted to leave.

Well, oddly—I didn't exactly want to leave. I was beginning to find that St. Chamant wasn't as dull as I'd first imagined. Besides, mon oncle's avion was almost completed. I looked forward to seeing it voler—fly, that is. And now I'd met Charles Meilhac—Suzanne, too—I'd have someone my age to go around with.

I'd gotten over imagining someone at nights hung around below my window. I knew by now those noises were caused by the wind and that the shadows I'd seen were merely shadows of trees in the moonlight. So, I said I figured I'd like to stay if mon oncle could stand the trouble I'd caused him.

At that, he laughed.

"Pouf!" he said, snapping his fingers. "There is no trouble you can make for me, mon neveu! And shall we

admit we Langres have been beaten by a fat stupid mayor?
Ah, non. And the promise I have to ta mère that you will
walk and write a letter in French and win the bicycle? I
will do this," he decided. "I shall write them at once and
explain what has happened before they depart for their
trip to Scotland. I shall say neither you nor I zink there is
danger, but if they wish, they are to write to tell me to
send you to England. How is that?"

I said, "Bien fait. Je suis content—" as I recalled he
would sometimes say to le forgeron when they were working on a piece of the avion. That is: "Well done, I am content." And I was contented with what mon oncle had decided.

"Bien," said he, his eyes twinkling. "Aussi—also," he
continued, "I will do this without informing tout le monde
à St. Chamant—without telling everybody in St. Chamant.
I will write to my friends in the Paris police and let them
know we zink a Nazi is hiding in our montagnes and it is
best they send quickly somebody here very secretly. How
is that?"

"Excellent," I said. "Super. Swell."

"Bien," said he.

"They'll send a real detective?"

He winked. "Tu vas voir—you are going to see."

And just as he promised, he wrote that nuit. Next jour
he mailed a letter to mon père—my father—and one to
Paris. Neither mon père nor ma mère replied. We thought
they'd concluded to allow me to remain, but we didn't
know they'd gone on to Scotland and our mail wasn't
reaching them. . . .

9

CHARLES VEUT VOIR L'AVION DE MON ONCLE PAUL

The following jour it was sunny and warm again after last nuit's rain. Soon as I had breakfast, I headed for the workshop. I took my crutches, mostly by habit. Half-way there I decided I wasn't going to depend on crutches any longer. If I could descend a montagne without crutches, I didn't require them on a level rue—street. Mon père had promised me the bicycle avec the high gear and the low gear on condition I was able to walk two miles as well as any other boy could.

By now the time I had to meet that condition was almost a third gone. I figured it was more than two miles from the ruins to le village. I'd gone that far—yes. But I hadn't met the condition mon père had set. I'd fallen. I'd been helped by Charles and Suzanne—as well as by the kicks from Monsieur Capedulocque. Afterwards, I'd been tuckered out, and stiff as a board. Even so, just getting down the montagne proved to me I still had a chance. My leg *was* getting stronger. The best thing to help it grow stronger was to stop using crutches. So, I made the rest of the way on my own feet.

Right away, inside the workshop I noticed the workmen were gone. Only mon oncle and le forgeron remained. Sunlight streamed through the windows upon the outstretched wings. By now, the framework to the two wings was nearly completed. If you can imagine a big "V" laid flat on the hard brick floor, the point of the "V" toward the door, you'll begin to understand how mon oncle's avion appeared—in French they'd say, l'avion *de* mon oncle, or—the airplane of my uncle. You can't beat those French to figure the most awkward way in the world to say something. Same with everything else; the house *of* my mother, instead of my mother's house; the pig *of* the mayor, instead of the mayor's pig.

Each side of the "V" was a wing. Each wing was about seventeen feet long and six feet wide. The result was like the framework to the most enormous butterfly you ever saw. According to mon oncle an avion built in this fashion, without a tail, practically flew itself. At nuit I'd heard him say, sometimes, he could plant a baby in his avion and shove the avion off, and that baby would be as safe and comfortable as in its own bed. Mon oncle was dead serious, too, when he claimed that. Naturally, every jour I was in a fever of impatience, hardly able to wait to see the avion done and tried out.

This morning mon oncle and le forgeron were occupied attaching spruce ribs to the longerons of the right wing. Four ribs were placed within every foot, all cross-braced with spruce battens and piano wire drawn tight by big turnbuckles. In that shaft of sunlight the partially completed wing stretched out from wall to wall of the workshop. Already it looked like a wing, even without the linen cloth covering which went on last.

"Bon jour, Jean!" called le forgeron in his big booming voice. Mon oncle was holding one of the ribs in his hand while he adjusted a wooden clamp. He gave me a quick smile. I waited until he was finished. He ruffled his black hair. I asked where the other workmen were.

"Oh, the ouvriers have quit," he said carelessly. "It is of no importance."

Le forgeron shoved his beard up over the left wing and rumbled, "Jean, tu vois? Pas d'ouvriers. Ce sacré Monsieur Capedulocque!"

The blacksmith had said there weren't any workers—something I'd already remarked—and blamed the mayor. I asked mon oncle, "You don't mean the mayor prevented them from coming?"

Mon oncle shrugged. "It is no matter. The mayor has offered them higher wages to work in the vineyards. I shall save my money by having them go. We shall not permit that mayor to see that he annoys us, because it would only please him the more." He picked up another rib, glancing at me over his shoulder. "He shall not beat us, never! That mayor wishes to be clever. He wishes to wait until he zinks we forget about his dead pig, too. Then he will attempt to surprise us with more trouble. You watch. But we will be ready for him."

I asked why the mayor had it in for us all the time. Was it simply because he hadn't been able to buy the Langres property and because I'd accidentally shot his cochon? I didn't understand. Mon oncle showed his white teeth. He said perhaps it was because the mayor was easily disturbed and enjoyed showing his authority, and I wasn't to worry —but I did worry.

Mon oncle showed me how I could help, screwing the wooden clamps. He said I could take the place of one of the workmen; and I did, too. But even though I didn't speak about it again to mon oncle, I worried and wished I could think of some way to stop the mayor from trying to plague us. It seemed to me if I hadn't ever seen that confounded Nazi knapsack and pistol and excited the village and stirred up trouble that perhaps the mayor wouldn't be so angry with mon oncle.

For the next few jours nothing much happened. The mayor didn't say anything more about the cochon I'd shot and I hoped he'd forgotten it. Mon oncle received a letter from his friends in Paris, thanking him for the information that a Nazi might be hiding round about St. Chamant. They said it wasn't anything to be disturbed about. After the war, quite a few Nazis had hidden away in the montagnes of central France, afraid of being captured. The letter assured mon oncle all efforts were being made by the authorities to handle the situation—and that was all that could be done.

Mon oncle gave a grimace when he finished translating it. "There you are, mon neveu. There is nothing to do but wait."

A little shiver passed down through me as if a cold wind had blown up and vanished. I said, "I'd think le village would be worried."

"It would be worried," he replied, "if that mayor was not such a pighead and was more interested in protecting his town than in proving you and I are fools."

There you are. As long as that Nazi remained hidden and didn't cause any trouble, le village would go on thinking I was a muddlehead, and mon oncle was a worse muddlehead for believing me. Of course, I didn't exactly want that Nazi to sneak down on le village at nuit and cause trouble, but—

Anyway, for a time nothing happened. It rained a lot,

too. That kept us inside the hotel or the workshop. I didn't have much of an opportunity to practice walking for a week. I helped mon oncle. While I helped I studied over in my head all that had happened to me, from Paris to St. Chamant, and it seemed to me there ought to be a means to prove to le village that up on la montagne somebody who was dangerous, armed with a pistol, was hiding. . . .

During that time, we rigged up the controls. We covered the wings with linen and varnished the linen until the cloth was tight as a drumhead over the ribs. I hoped mon oncle might find an opportunity to take me across the montagne where he said the Meilhacs lived. But without workmen he was too busy. He was concerned, too, I guess, more than he let on to me, because it was taking longer to build the avion than he'd expected. His money was running short. Often at nuit I'd hear him playing his flute behind the closed door of his room.

A couple of postcards arrived, signed by my father and mother. They were walking through Scotland. If I needed to reach them in an emergency, I was to have mon oncle cable the American Embassy in London; the Embassy knew how to locate them within a day or so. But there wasn't any emergency. I decided the mayor wasn't going to cause the trouble mon oncle had anticipated, either, about the cochon I'd accidentally shot.

Nothing happened. Nobody hummed under my window. The nuits were empty and peaceful. When I wasn't helping mon oncle I learned French from little Philippe Graffoulier in order to write that letter to my mother. From him I learned to say, for example, "it is not." The French are certainly peculiar. They have two words for our "not," sticking "ne" or "n'" in front of the verb, and "pas" behind. Very queer. If I was to say, "the air-plane is broken" I'd say: "L'avion *est* cassé." But to say, "the airplane is *not* broken," I'd have to say: "l'avion *n'*est *pas* cassé." And, "the airplane is *not* going to fall" would be: "L'avion *ne* va *pas* tomber." French can be perplexing.

On Wednesday, Suzanne Meilhac bicycled into le vil-lage to market for her mother. We had lunch together. We tried to talk to each other and laughed and I had more fun, that noon, than I imagined anybody could have with a girl. By gestures and by words she managed to make me understand that Charles was working from dawn until nuit in the vineyard in an effort to obtain a large enough crop to prevent the mayor from taking their place.

When she mentioned the mayor, she scowled. She drew down her mouth. Almost, for a second, she looked like he did. We both laughed. Madame Graffoulier had fixed a special lunch for Suzanne. Suzanne ate everything before her, as if she was tremendously hungry. When she finished, Madame Graffoulier put more vegetables in Suzanne's basket as a gift; and Suzanne thanked her and her eyes glistened a little as if she was so pleased she was nearly ready to cry.

I tried to tell Suzanne I'd come to see them soon as I could. When she bicycled off I wished my leg was strong enough to have gone with her. After she left le village seemed suddenly lonesome and deserted.

Then, all at once, on a Friday morning, the mayor and his lawyer came into the workshop. They had a long argu-ment with mon oncle. When they finished talking, I saw mon oncle was doing the best he could to contain his temper.

He turned to me to translate. He explained the mayor

wanted 2000 francs for his dead cochon. That was nearly a hundred dollars. Mon oncle said even for a trained truffe-finding pig it was an outrageous price. Before I could say a word he swung his nose around at the mayor. In a voice like a nail sliding over glass, not at all loud, but with something in it that made you shiver, he answered in French. I didn't understand but I saw that little fat mayor's face slowly become purple.

When mon oncle had finished speaking the mayor bellowed. The mayor roared. He pointed at me. He roared some more. He said "assassin" several times, so I knew he was referring to me. Mon oncle folded his arms. He listened. He cocked his head. Almost—looking at him—you'd take him to be polite and deferential. All he said was, "Bah! Je n'ai pas peur!" which meant: "Bah! I have not fear!"

That knocked the wind out of the mayor who was trying to threaten him. The lawyer tried speaking. The mayor—le maire, as the French call it—got so angry he couldn't wait for the lawyer to finish. He stuck out his hand and grabbed mon oncle's nose—and then *twisted* it, hard!

Mon oncle became perfectly white with rage. He jumped back. Next he jumped at le maire—the mayor—and picked up le maire by the coat and seat of the pants and threw le maire out of the door. Le maire landed in that same mud ditch in which he'd landed before, with a splash which must have been heard as far away as Paris. The lawyer danced around mon oncle, saying, "Monsieur Langres! Monsieur Langres!" Mon oncle simply looked at him. The lawyer ran to the door and into la rue and helped le maire up and the two marched away, le maire shouting back the most awful sounding French threats ever to be heard. I was glad I didn't understand them.

Mon oncle felt at his nose. He caught me eyeing him. He winked at me and tapped his big nose and calmly said, "Have no peur, Jean. My nose remains. It will take more than a Monsieur Capedulocque to detach the nose of a Langres!"

Afterwards, le forgeron tugged at his black beard and spoke to mon oncle with a grave, anxious expression on his face. Mon oncle merely laughed. I asked mon oncle what Monsieur Niort had said.

"He zinks the mayor is so angry my festival will be stopped."

"Festival?" I asked. "Do you mean you are going to have a festival?"

They'd promised him a festival—une fête, in French—on the jour his avion flew. Le village planned to invite hundreds of people from all the towns and cities nearby and mon oncle counted on it, because he expected several rich manufacturers might be attracted, too, to see him voler. He told me, "Le village has made a promise. The mayor cannot back down on the promise."

He began whistling, as if he'd enjoyed throwing the mayor out of the workshop. By and by le forgeron started chuckling, as if he was remembering the way the mayor had landed in the mud. Pretty soon both were laughing like two kids. In the afternoon the sun came out, bright and hot. Mon oncle told me I'd spent too much time indoors. He packed me off for the afternoon.

As an experiment I decided to see if I could walk to the lower cow field, below le village, and back. The cow field was about a mile away. I started fine. But three-quarters of the distance, my leg gave out on me. It began hurting. I reached the meadow, but I was limping. Here it was, well into the middle of the summer, and I couldn't even go half the distance I had to go to meet the condition set by my father. I flung myself down into the grass and wondered if ever I'd be able to walk like other boys.

Le jour was beau. It was beautiful. It was fun loafing under one of the trees, the birds chirping. My leg had stopped hurting. Everything was peaceful. I could hear the faraway buzzing murmur of old Monsieur Argeau's sawmill, east of St. Chamant. I remembered how scared I'd been the first week or so after arriving, imagining I'd seen Monsieur Simonis, imagining he'd tried to climb into my window, and thinking I'd heard Albert humming. All that was gone. It was like a bad dream. After that jaunt of mine up the montagne side with mon oncle, where I'd found the German pistol and shot the cochon—after that, except for le maire causing trouble, everything else had become peaceful and easy. I almost wished everything wasn't quite so peaceful. If that Nazi whom I *knew* was up there would only scurry down here a nuit or so, things would start popping. Le village wouldn't take so much stock in what le maire—the mayor—said every time. They'd have more belief in mon oncle. . . .

Upon returning, I learned from Madame Graffoulier that Suzanne Meilhac had been in town, marketing. She'd asked for me. When I saw mon oncle I asked if we might go to the Meilhac place one of these days. He said it was something he'd been planning to do. He hadn't realized so many jours had passed since I'd last seen Charles. He promised to take time out before next week.

At evening, as the men folks trooped back into le vil-

lage, I noticed they didn't shout as good-naturedly to mon
oncle as they used to. They walked by, avoiding him in
the shop, scowling to themselves, whispering. Little Philippe spent about half an hour to make me comprehend
what the trouble was. According to what he'd heard from
his aunt, le maire had passed word around that mon oncle
and I were attempting to cheat him out of the money due
him for the dead cochon. You know how stories spread.
He was doing his best to blacken the Langres name, never
mentioning of course the huge price he'd demanded for his
dead cochon.

Just before dinner, when I was upstairs in my room, le
maire and his lawyer again waylaid mon oncle, asking him
for the money. Afterwards, mon oncle informed me an-
grily they planned to lay a complaint against him and me
and try to stick us in jail, because he'd refused to pay the
price.

By now, I didn't care how much le maire asked. All I
wanted was to pay him. I dug out my purse in a hurry.
I hadn't used any of the money mon père had given me. I
gave it all to mon oncle and his lean face flushed. He said
le maire was robbing us. But, he supposed, there wasn't
anything to do except pay. He walked out of the hotel
and a little later returned, glum, his pride hurt. He'd paid
a hundred dollars. I had two hundred left. I hadn't used
any of it yet to pay Madame Graffoulier my bill and I
wondered when she was going to hand me my account.

Perhaps Madame Graffoulier realized how mon oncle
felt. Anyway, she had prepared an especially good dinner
for us: potato potage, potato pancakes, fresh lentils in
cheese, black bread, real cow butter, and the first meat
we'd had for five or six jours.

I don't believe I've ever tasted meat as good as the meat Madame Graffoulier served to us that night. Maybe I ought to explain: In France, and particularly in the part of France where I was staying, which was about the poorest and most backward section of all France, meat was something rare. Even before the war, I've learned, they didn't have meat very often. Chicken and ducks, yes; but fowl wasn't held to be meat. What we had was regular steer meat, served in long thin slices, covered with garlic sauce. That meat melted in your mouth. I noticed there were tiny black granules in it, a little larger than grains of pepper. At first, I took them to be dirt. I didn't say anything, mainly because the meat was so good I didn't care if Madame Graffoulier had dropped a peck of dirt in it by accident.

But the granules weren't dirt. I happened to taste one. It was like biting into a very solid bit of mushroom. No— not a mushroom. I don't know that I can explain. If you can imagine a tiny chunk of gelatin, about ten times firmer than gelatin should be made, not having any particular taste at first but leaving in your mouth after you've swallowed it a very rich taste of meat—why then, that's what I had. I must have paused, after swallowing that black granule. I'll admit I was surprised. The taste remained. It stayed. It filled my mouth. It became the most extraordinary and wonderful taste, fragrant and appetizing. It was as though that small particle had magically enlarged, becoming a whole mouthful of the finest steak ever cooked. I blinked.

For the first time in hours mon oncle's face relaxed. He ceased looking as grim as he'd been looking. He asked, "Don't you know what *that* is?"

I shook my head.

"Truffe!" he said. "Madame Graffoulier has cooked *truffes* in this meat. It is very good, I zink. Non? You see now why the mayor is so angry when you have killed his trained cochon."

Good? That nuit when I wrote to ma mère I told her it was one of the best meals I'd had since leaving Wyoming. In my letter to mon père I wrote him I was improving and now could walk about a mile without limping too much and hoped in a year or so if he and my mother—ma mère— ever again went on another walking trip, that I might be strong enough to join them. I said I hoped they were enjoying their trip. I was writing to them steadily, nearly every nuit, even if I knew there'd be a delay in forwarding my letters to them from London.

The next jour someone had tacked up signs all through le village de St. Chamant. With an air of suppressed excitement, mon oncle translated one of them for me. The government was offering a reward of 10,000 francs to be given to anyone responsible for capturing Nazi soldiers or sympathizers supposed to be hiding in the montagnes of the Cantal. He wagged his head. "Now," said he, "perhaps that will stir them up here in the village, if the mayor isn't too much of a pighead."

As we varnished the spars of the avion that morning, I kept thinking about the reward and how wonderful it would be if mon oncle or Charles Meilhac might be able to collect that reward. I asked mon oncle why he didn't go back up to la montagne and sort of scout around? He gave me a quick grin, replying that he had more important things to do than find a Nazi. But that must have started him thinking about it.

After lunch, instead of returning to the workshop mon

oncle sniffed the fresh montagne air. He stretched. He looked at me. With a kind of sheepish expression he asked if I'd like to take a ride up the montagne with him? Did I! That was like asking if I wanted to hunt ducks. Well, he ran up to his room. When he returned his coat bulged as if he'd stuck a gun in a shoulder holster hidden under his coat. I didn't say anything. However, the thought of mon oncle meeting with a Nazi didn't, somehow, appear too cheering. I remembered a jour or so ago I'd wished for something to happen. Now I started wishing as hard as possible that nothing would happen today.

He borrowed a bicycle for the afternoon from le forgeron, riding me on the handle-bars. He pedaled by the stone church, whistling, past the cemetery, and out by the big whitewashed tower and house belonging to le maire Capedulocque. Behind the tower and the house, surrounded by a whitewashed wall, were wooden sheds containing ducks and chickens. They clacked and gobbled at us as we went by. A donkey shoved its head over the wall and brayed. Another donkey inside Monsieur Capedulocque's house stuck its head through a window and looked at us. A cow must have been inside, too, because a cow shoved its head out through another window.

I looked back. There in a third window was le maire himself, scowling, watching us pedal up the lane. Mon oncle glanced back. Mon oncle laughed. "Voici!" he said —meaning, "Here it is," or "There you are." He wagged his nose. "The donkey, the cow, and the mayor. All fit company. I zink I do not like le maire Capedulocque one little bit, non!" We followed the path we'd taken a couple of weeks ago in the oxcart. As he pedaled higher, the air became more clear. The trees were green as paint. Mon oncle stopped to rest. We picked black figs; they were sweet and juicy.

I thought we were going to la maison de ma mère. The truth is, I became a shade scared. Even though I was with mon oncle, somehow I didn't much relish the thought of going to that high and lonesome meadow where the Nazi might be waiting. After going part way on the bicycle, we started walking. Because of my leg, mon oncle went slowly. Once, we halted in a clearing while mon oncle lit his pipe. He told me something of his plans for his avion as we rested. He said if all went well, even without workmen, he and le forgeron would have the avion ready by the middle of the month, a week or so from now. He planned soon to take it up to the meadow on ma mère's and his land, and set up a big wooden slide for it to glide away from, over le village to the cow field on the other side. I asked if there would be as many as a hundred people at the festival. I looked forward to seeing that festival—or fête, I should say.

"A hundred?" he said. "There would be a thousand, perhaps. Two thousand." He turned away, his face going a shade darker. "But it has been decided not to have la fête."

"Not have it?" I cried. He didn't answer right at once. I said, "That mayor won't let le village have it?"

"Bah!" said mon oncle. "It is nothing. Two thousand people would be very confusing. Monsieur Capedulocque has told everyone—tout le monde—in le village that my airplane will not fly and that it would be foolish and a waste of time to march up la montagne to see it. Voilà! We do not have la fête."

Even though he tried to hide his disappointment and

joked about it, I could see it was a stunner for him. He'd counted on people coming to see him voler. It meant a lot to him. It might be a chance to sell the avion. I said, "It all goes back to me finding that German gun and shooting the cochon, doesn't it?"

"Bah!" said mon oncle, again. "It is because the mayor is a pighead."

I insisted, "If we could only *prove* someone was hiding up there, wouldn't that help things? Wouldn't le village realize its maire was an awful pighead?"

"Ah, perhaps today I will find the Nazi," said mon oncle, attempting to be cheerful. "Who knows? Viens, Jean. We lose time."

He fooled me. He didn't take me with him to see la maison de ma mère. He swung off the path and we trudged over a hill. I thought all the time we were scouting for that Nazi. I began to be scared. My leg started aching. We crossed the other side of la montagne. We didn't see a sign of the Nazi. But down below on the slopes, I saw a vineyard and a big stone house beyond the vineyard with noble shade trees and flowers in the sunshine. In the vineyard were two figures working. Both of them had red hair.

I let out a whoop. Right away, Charles and Suzanne dropped their hoes. They answered with French whoops. They scampered up the slope. Charles flung arms around me, kissing both cheeks, French style, jabbering away like a washing-machine motor. After him, Suzanne flung *her* arms around me, as if it was the most natural thing in the world for her to do. It was the first time in my life I'd been hugged by a girl. I ducked back. She only kissed one of my cheeks. As it was, probably I went red as a beet.

Mon oncle waited, smiling to himself. It was the finest

surprise anybody could ask for. After greeting me, the Meilhac twins piled questions on to mon oncle. I knew they were questioning him about his avion because I heard that word repeated. Mon oncle kept on smiling, enjoying himself, and answering them. Finally, I heard Charles say, "Je veux voir l'avion, s'il vous plaît."

I asked what he'd said.

Mon oncle replied, "You know what 'je' is, by now?"

I did: "Je" was "I" in French.

He explained, " 'Je veux' is 'I wish.' And 'voir' is 'to see.' And you know what 's'il vous plaît' is. That is 'please,' or 'if you please.' "

It was like fitting a puzzle together. All at once it was simple. "Je veux voir l'avion, s'il vous plaît," fitted together perfectly: "I wish to see the airplane, please."

Next, mon oncle glanced at his watch. He told me he was leaving me with the Meilhac twins for a couple of hours. He'd pick me up around six o'clock. He waved, said "Au revoir," and trotted off, covering the ground between the vineyard and the forest about ten times faster alone than when he'd come down with me.

I didn't have time to worry over mon oncle because Charles and Suzanne kept me busy. They showed me the grapevines. In a few more weeks the grapes would be ripe. I said, "Monsieur Capedulocque—" and pointed at the vines.

Suzanne understood. She knew what I was thinking about. She clenched her fist. She frowned. She said, "Monsieur Capedulocque est un cochon!" and explained to Charles. Both of them were worried for fear the mayor would grab their vineyard this fall if the grapes didn't sell for enough.

By and by I tried out my French. I said, "Je veux voir ta maison, s'il vous plaît." It worked like a charm. They understood at once I'd said "I wish to see your house, please." Their maison was down toward the bottom of the mountain, set at one end of a long meadow, with trees planted on each side of what must have been years and years ago a broad coach road. Their maison was perfectly enormous. It had two stone towers and a high peaked slate roof. Most of the windows and doors were now locked or boarded. Around the big house still showed traces of long ago gardens, rose bushes grown wild, pear trees untrimmed and shaggy.

Madame Meilhac was short and jolly, with wonderful red hair, very neat and clean. The way she acted you wouldn't suspect she cared about being alone in a vast empty house with two children and no money any more for servants. She appeared to think it was a game, like camping out. Most of the rooms were closed off. I had glimpses of furniture covered with cloth, protected from the dust. In one long hall were rows and rows of pictures of Meilhacs, the last one smaller than the others, of a man in a modern army officer's uniform. Charles simply said, "Mon père." It was of his father, killed in the war.

All their misfortunes had happened after the death of their father. The Germans had robbed the bank containing the Meilhac money. The Meilhacs had been forced to sell most of their property. Now all they had was this house and the vineyard, with Madame Meilhac trying to keep that. You might have thought they'd be sorrowful. If they were, they never let on. They all were gay and cheerful. You wouldn't ever have guessed they knew they were poor.

They treated me as if I was a visiting noble or duke. They brought out four slices of thick black bread and spread goat butter on it. Madame Meilhac opened a stone crock. She scratched in it with a wooden spoon. She managed to locate a few grains of brown sugar. She gave me most of the sugar, smiling all the while as though she had a hundred barrels more of sugar hidden away.

I felt so sorry for them I nearly choked, eating that black bread and butter with brown sugar sprinkled on it. But it was a treat for Charles and Suzanne. They licked the crumbs off their fingers. I let on it was a noble treat for me, too. I'd have rather died than have them believe I didn't appreciate what they were doing to welcome me and to feed me in their maison.

After eating, Madame Meilhac and Suzanne cleared the table. They shoved Charles and me outside. He fetched me another bow and arrow he'd made, saying "peau-rouge" a couple of times. It was going on toward late afternoon. He signified he was through working in the vines today. He meant to entertain me; I was his guest. He thought I'd enjoy playing Indian. Well, it struck me funny to play Indian thousands of miles away from home. We crawled up to the vineyard. Charles and I shot his arrow at the vines and whooped and did our best to pretend we were wild Indians—but somehow it didn't go over.

By and by, without saying anything, we simply stopped playing. Both of us were melancholy. I could imagine Charles thinking about his vines, worrying, hoping le maire Capedulocque wouldn't take them away this fall. It seemed to me le maire must be the greediest man alive, or the meanest. He was after my mother's and my uncle's property up higher in the montagnes, even though there weren't any vineyards there—and he was after the Meilhacs', down here. You'd think it was more than just grabbing land. It was as though he was determined to rid le village for good of both the Meilhac family and anyone belonging to the Langres family. I couldn't understand such hatred. In some respects he was worse than Monsieur Simonis had been—meaner, too.

Once more I got to thinking about le maire, wondering if there wasn't any way to make le village appreciate what a pighead he was. You know how it is when you moon along, idly, thinking about something, almost dreaming what could happen in your head?

Well, all at once, it appeared to me I'd stumbled upon a solution. I knew exactly how to wake up the entire village to the danger that Nazi was to them. I had discovered a way to excite them and worry them and send them tramping through those montagnes until there wasn't an inch left for a man to try to hide himself in!

10

L'AVION EST CASSE

It seemed to me much of our grief resulted from that German—or whoever owned the German knapsack and the pistol. I wouldn't have shot le maire's cochon or knocked off his hat if I hadn't found the pistol. If I hadn't found the pistol and knapsack I wouldn't have told tout le monde a German was up there. Mon oncle wouldn't have sent le village chasing into la montagne; le maire wouldn't have lost his temper at me and mon oncle. Of course le maire was set against mon oncle before that—but by what I'd done I'd given le maire more convincing reasons to say mon oncle and I were muddleheads.

I figured if the people in the village got worried enough to spend a week or so searching the montagnes they were bound to locate whoever was hiding nearby. My idea was to manufacture the worry for le village. It was a good idea; it was simple. You see, I remembered those ducks and chickens belonging to le maire. Charles and I would wait until it was nuit. We'd hide in the cemetery which was across from la maison de Monsieur Capedulocque. When it was good and dark, we'd sneak across. This was where I'd require Charles. My leg wasn't yet strong enough to wriggle over le maire's wall and carry me to the chicken and duck roosts and get back before being seen. I reckoned on staying outside the wall, acting as guard.

Now, you might wonder how on earth doing all that would arouse le village. I'll tell you. That was where my plan was bound to succeed because it was so almighty simple. The thing was, we had to convince Monsieur Capedulocque a German had sneaked down from the montagne to rob his chickens and ducks for food. And I'd figured how to convince le maire that the robber was the German —and not local people or tramps. I'd use a few of the German coins from my collection.

We wouldn't actually be thieving from le maire because I planned to drop ten or twenty pieces of French money on the ground, too, as well as the German coins. And, I'd have Charles scribble a note in bad French, just as if an ignorant German had spelled it out, warning le maire not to tell anyone the chickens and ducks had been taken, on pain of death—a regular pirate's warning, in fact.

The note could say the German was leaving pay for what he'd taken. That would explain why the money'd been left, as if the German hoped by paying for what he'd taken to keep Monsieur Capedulocque from talking. Of course, I expected le maire to disregard the warning; I expected him to shout he'd been robbed by a Nazi, being scared by the fact he now had proof a Nazi *was* sur la montagne. You can see for yourself how simple that plan was. I think you'd agree a plan as simple as that one ought to have been sure-fire. Certainly it wasn't my fault if things got more complicated than I expected.

As if he thought something was wrong with me, as if I had a sunstroke, perhaps, all during this time Charles was eyeing me. Once I was finished working out the plan I was in a fever to get started. I needed Charles. I had to contrive of a means to explain his part in it and manage to get him to stay overnight with me at the hotel.

Right then, mon oncle appeared near the forest and shouted down at me, "Viens, Jean! Viens!" He waited for me to come. Suzanne came running out and all three of us joined him and, speaking part of the time in French and part of the time in English, he made known to us that he'd searched the ruins from top to bottom, this time. He hadn't found a thing to indicate anyone might still be living there.

But he had done something a person not as smart as he was mightn't have thought of. He scraped away the loose dirt on the floor of the cellar. When the Germans set fire to la maison they'd exploded it, too, with hand-grenades and bombs, and the explosion had half filled the cellar with dirt. Well, he scraped along the walls and had discovered where somebody had made a fire at one time, and cooked food there. To mon oncle, that was additional proof someone had been living in the cellar when I'd happened on that knapsack. He didn't believe, though, anyone in le village would consider it as very important proof.

It was growing late. There wasn't anything now to do but go home. I had mon oncle assure Charles and Suzanne I'd try to get back up here in a few days; and with his help I thanked them and asked them to thank their mother for giving me the treat with the bread and sugar. They walked as far as the top of the montagne. There they waved and called, "Au revoir, reviens vite!" which means, "Good-by, re-come quickly." We'd say "return" but the French say "reviens," probably because nobody ever taught them any differently.

Mon oncle waited until I'd climbed to the handle-bars of his bicycle. We coasted down the path, a long glorious swoop of ride. Now mon oncle had searched la maison I

was more than ever convinced the German had simply re-
tired to the forest and was hiding out there. What was
required was to have the entire village go through that
forest and get him before he could do any harm. I was determined to figure out some way to go back to the Meil-

*We coasted down the path, a long glorious swoop
of ride*

hacs' tomorrow and draw Charles off to one side and get
him to go partners with me in a hurry on my scheme. The
scheme itself was simple as onions, but I was plagued by
the way trifles kept coming in and complicating it before I was even ready to start.

At the hotel I asked mon oncle if I couldn't return to
see Charles tomorrow. I said I believed I could walk it this

time, if I went slowly. The practice would do me good, too.

"I should like you to help me tomorrow," he said slowly. I couldn't very well refuse.

He must have noticed, however, I was mighty eager to see Charles again. He explained, "I have not told you, but in a day or so I will move the airplane to the meadow. I shall finish it there. You will see Charles often."

Then he again hesitated. Finally he said he'd decided to leave the hotel and remain sur la montagne avec his avion. Le forgeron would help him erect a shelter for both the avion and himself. He got embarrassed. You know how proud he was. The fact was, as I finally got through my head, he was running out of money. To save expenses, he proposed to camp sur la montagne the rest of the time until he'd tried his avion. He asked, "You will not be afraid to stay here in the hotel alone, Jean?"

I wasn't afraid, but the idea of camping sur la montagne seemed gaudy and wonderful. I asked why couldn't I be with him.

He hesitated once more. He made excuses: He said I required a good bed and a roof over me when it rained. When I still protested, the real reason came out. In le village it was safe at nuit. While he wasn't worried about himself, he didn't care to expose me up there in case a German was somewhere around. He became firm. He said he was sorry; it was best for me to remain here at nuit. Le forgeron would take me up each day and bring me back at nuit. . . .

At dinner I saw Madame Graffoulier had two more people in her hotel. She'd set two tables. A traveling salesman from Tulle was staying several days. A fat, good-

natured, black-haired fellow had taken a room, saying he
was on a vacation from Toulouse and had come here to
fish. She introduced me to both of them, calling me "le
garçon Americain—" which meant "the American boy—"
although the French do it backwards, "the boy American," like that. Those French people never do work out
an easy way to say things.

I didn't get much sleep that night. I was still figuring
about my plan, checking it up and down to make sure it
would work. The more I thought about it, the more I
liked it. It began raining during the nuit. When I awakened, it was pouring. I couldn't go to the Meilhacs' in the
rain, even if mon oncle hadn't needed me. While we had
breakfast, mail arrived, with letters from mon père, ma
mère, and one from Bob Collins, back home. Mon oncle
also received a letter from ma mère, as well as a whole flock
more which resembled bills to me. He said we might as
well stay in the hotel and read our mail before going to
work. That suited me.

One letter was from mon père, and two from ma mère.
Mon père had written from some little out-of-the-way
spot in Northern Scotland where ma mère and he had
stayed on a Sunday during their walking trip. He told me
he'd stopped in Edinburgh, a big Scottish city, to look
at a new stock of bicycles in a shop there. He'd found a
new bicycle, one of the first to be made after the war,
which not only had a high gear and a low gear—but a
middle gear as well. This special middle gear was for riding in town. He said he'd arranged with the dealer to hold
it for him.

As soon as he saw me, and witnessed whether or not I
was able to walk the two miles without tiring or limping,

he'd cable to Scotland and have the dealer put the bicycle on a boat to be shipped to Wyoming. It would be waiting for me when we arrived.

In ma mère's first letter she wrote more about the scenery, as most mothers probably would do. She added a couple of things, though, that were exciting. First, mon père's work had been about completed in England. There'd be a chance he could leave the army and return with us to Wyoming. Secondly, she'd put in her order for the electric lighting dynamo and was ready to have it shipped along with the bicycle as soon as I could write her that letter in French!

Her second one was written pretty hastily, evidently just after she'd mailed the first one. She wrote:

Your uncle Paul's letter just arrived telling us a German may be hiding in the mountains. I am very much concerned. Your father says he doubts if any German soldier will bother you, but if there is the slightest trouble, please have Paul cable the American Embassy in London at once so they can reach us. We expect to return to London next week—we're taking a week longer than planned because your father received an extra week's leave. Then, as soon as your father turns over his job to Colonel Burton, we plan to cross to France and come to St. Chamant for you. Please take care of yourself. . . .

I'd almost forgotten the letter mon oncle had written to ma mère. I considered by now she must have received the letters I'd written to her and would know everything here was swimming along peacefully—too peacefully for me, but I hadn't told her that. I noticed mon oncle had finished his letters. He got out of the chair and said to come along as soon as I was ready.

I opened Bob Collins' letter. It contained all the news from back home. He was working on the range, right along with the other hands. Old Jake had been made foreman of the combined ranches. Dr. Medley had asked Bob to be sure and inquire of me if my leg were improving. Everybody sent their best. Bob had received the letter I'd written from Paris and the one from St. Chamant. He thanked me for sending him those French coins. And he admitted he was envious of the chance I was going to have to fly a real airplane.

For a minute, I stopped reading that part of his letter, feeling my cheeks grow hot. I remembered I'd written him when I first arrived, boasting about the fine time I was having here and I'd indicated, too, not exactly lying, though, that I expected to pilot mon oncle's avion. Well, he'd believed me. More than that, in his letter he told me he'd passed the news on to everyone in town. The editor of our newspaper, Mr. Sulgave, had printed a piece about me, and wanted me to send him a photograph of me in the machine. Whew! I didn't know what to do about that.

There wasn't much more to Bob's letter except to say he'd gone to his first dance, taking Jane Sulgave with him. I never expected the time would come when Bob Collins would go to a dance with a girl! Me and Bob had decided never to go with girls. No sir, we'd sworn a pact to keep clear of girls and grow up and buy ourselves a ranch—and, there it was. Right down in his own handwriting. He'd taken Jane to a dance. He'd danced with her. I could recognize he was changing on me while I was away. It wasn't right. For the first time in weeks, I started feeling homesick.

I folded the letters, the rain beating outside. As I looked

up I noticed that the fat jolly black-haired man had taken a chair by the window. He was watching me. Soon as I looked at him, he swung around, back to me, untangling an old fishing line, as if he hadn't been aware I was even in the room. Probably if he'd said something, I wouldn't have marked anything at all. But because he acted as if I'd caught him looking at me when he hadn't wanted to be noticed, I paid more attention to him than before.

It almost seemed to me, now I considered him, that I might have seen him some place. Of course, that couldn't have been, though, because I'd never been in Toulouse. If I hadn't spent so much time reading my letters I might have asked him if he'd ever been in the United States. However, I was in a hurry. I slammed out, going through the rain, entering the workshop. Here, mon oncle and le forgeron were making preparations to move the avion as soon as the rain stopped. I put my plan about the Nazi in the back of my head until I could see Charles, and worked right along with the two men on the avion.

As we worked mon oncle said ma mère had written him, saying she was worried. He promised to write her tonight to tell her there wasn't any need for her to be concerned. If a German was hiding, he seemed to want to hide and do nothing to be found. Mon oncle wagged his head at me and said, "Besides, if your mother takes you away from here now, you will never win that bicycle, hein? It would be a great misfortune."

I agreed with him there. By now, I was nearly certain I'd be able to walk those two miles. What concerned me more was winning that electric lighting dynamo by writing a letter in French. My French didn't seem to improve a third as much as my leg was doing.

The following morning, Tuesday, I think it was, le forgeron and I made the first trip to the meadow in the oxcart. Monsieur Niort did most of the unloading of the tools and the lumber and canvas for the slide and shelter. To launch the avion, mon oncle counted upon building a kind of runway, about ten feet from the top of the ground at one end. The avion would coast down this runway and gather speed before it took off to sail over le village.

Partly by speaking French, partly by making signs with his hands when I didn't understand, Monsieur Niort let me know he meant to remain up here and erect the shelter while I drove the oxcart back down to le village. He led the ox around. He switched the ox. He waved at me, thundering away in his big voice, "Au revoir, Jean! Reviens vite!"

I'd hoped I might encounter Charles or Suzanne as I descended vers le village—toward le village. But I didn't see a sign of either one. Probably they were working over on the other side of la montagne. I was a shade uneasy, first because it was a new thing to drive that big lumbering ox—secondly, because I was still not too sure la montagne was as safe as I'd made out in my letters to ma mère. Just the fact that someone *was* somewhere up there, hiding, wasn't calming to the mind.

It required about an hour for that huge ox to haul the cart down the montagne into le village. It was a fine experience for me. I'd never driven an ox before. Fact is, I let the ox take its own head. It knew the way. It was slow as molasses, never going faster than a walk, but nothing could stop it. The cart had two big squeaking wooden wheels, high as my head. A mile off, you could hear us coming.

Mon oncle was ready for me at the shop. You might expect it to be difficult for one man and a boy my age, with a lame leg, to lift that avion onto the cart. It wasn't difficult at all. Even though the frame of the avion was put together, and the wings stuck out on each side all of thirty feet wide and more, all of it didn't weigh more than a hundred or a hundred and ten pounds. It was marvelously constructed to be both light and strong as possible.

An avion with a motor is a different affair altogether. The motor whips around a propeller. The propeller sets up a breeze. It drags the avion across the ground faster and faster until the avion leaps into the air. An avion with a motor has wheels. Mon oncle's avion didn't have any wheels. All it had were two short skids under the wings to land on. In the center of the wings was slung a canvas belt, which was the seat. Mon oncle planned to sit astraddle of this seat, the steering wheel in front of him, and take off from the runway. The avion was supposed to voler through the air and voler over le village and the crick and descend into the meadow. To do all that without a motor, it had to be light as possible.

Consequently, I didn't have to do any lifting to speak of when we put the thing on the oxcart. Mon oncle merely crawled under the wings until he was in the middle. He straightened up. He carried his avion to the cart. Next he hauled it upwards, the long wings vibrating and trembling like the wings of a bird.

The ox snorted a little, not knowing what was happening. My job was to steady one end of the wing.

While the oxcart squeaked up la montagne we ate goat's cheese and black bread and had our first wild cherries of the season. You'd be surprised how good such simple food can be. By the time we arrived in the mountain meadow, le forgeron had begun to erect the canvas shelter. He marched over towards us to give mon oncle a hand with the avion.

I climbed down one of the big wheels to steady a wing. As they lifted the framework, the left wing circled toward the ox. Nothing probably would have happened even then, because ordinarily an ox is as steady as stone, if at that second my leg hadn't decided to take a rest of its own accord. It flopped. I fell against the ox. Startled, the ox lunged forward. The wing cracked.

The ox didn't move more than a couple of feet. But the damage was done. Instead of rushing to save his avion, mon oncle had jumped to me, picking me up, being concerned about me. He carried me under a tree and sat me down and rolled up my pant's leg. I wasn't hurt. I'd had falls like that before. I was ashamed and grieved about what I'd done to the avion.

Mon oncle inspected the damage. He came back to me. He said, "Oui, l'avion est cassé."

I knew what "cassé" was—"broken."

"But—" And he smiled. "But not very much. The tip of the wing. Pouf!" He snapped his fingers. "By demain—by tomorrow I will fix it. By demain, l'avion est réparé. You will see. I do not joke."

He said "réparé" almost like we would say repaired. I understood that word. By tomorrow, or, demain, he was telling me, the avion is repaired. I wasn't sure if the break was as unimportant as he made out. I thought he might be trying to spare me grief. But he gave me a light whack on the back. "Voyons!" he exclaimed—look here—see here. He told me to come and see for myself. He showed me where the linen cloth was ripped at the tip of the wing. Demain—tomorrow—he'd glue on a new patch. That was all there was to it. I felt better. Even my leg felt better. "Very soon," he said, cheerfully, "the airplane will be ready to fly—prêt à voler. You will see."

"Prêt? That means ready?"

"Oui," said he. "The airplane will be prêt. And you —toi? Will you be prêt to win your bicycle?"

That was one thing I didn't know. Sometimes I figured I was sure to win. Other days, I'd still have cramps in my leg. I'd lose hope. . . .

I didn't have a chance to see Charles about my scheme for a couple of days. Mon oncle and le forgeron were as busy as could be, erecting that slide. They built it about fifty feet below the ruins of the maison. On a beau jour I could stand next to the great stone walls of the maison and look down across the meadow and over the valley and voir—see—the river and le village and the cow field and meadows and voir men no bigger than ants working in the vineyards. Some of the leaves were beginning to change to yellow and red. It was hard to believe I'd been here for so many weeks.

The way I was when I first arrived, I'd never have stayed in a hotel without mon oncle or somebody kin to me even if I'd received a hundred dollars for doing it. I guess, without my realizing it, I had improved some.

I'd go down to St. Chamant with le forgeron. Here, I'd eat dinner with the Graffoulier kids, spending the evening with them, sweating on my French, experimenting even by trying to write a letter in French. I knew quite a heap of French words, now, too. The trouble was, I didn't know the right words to join together for a letter. Sure, I could ask for things. I could make people understand me. I could get around in the language. But to sit down in cold blood and attempt to compose a letter to ma mère all in French—why, it was harder than learning how to walk.

After mon oncle left the hotel, I learned something he'd done. I gathered enough spunk to ask Madame Graffoulier for my bill, how much I owed her. Well, do you know what? Mon oncle had gone and paid for me out of his own pocket! She told me he had. I didn't know what to do. There he was, poor as a church mouse, slaving on his avion, probably no one coming to see it voler when he was ready, not much chance of anyone knowing if it would be any good because of what le maire had done—and yet, he paid my bill. He figured I was his guest. According to his lights, he was supposed to pay. I never knew a man as proud and touchy about what was right and wrong in matters of honor as was mon oncle.

Of course, I asked mon oncle when I saw him, telling him mon père had given me money to pay my own bills. But he wouldn't hear any talk about it. He said it was understood I was his guest. His black eyebrows clamped down over his big nose. He asked, "Am I so poor I cannot have my own neveu for a guest, hein? Ah, non!" Then, he changed back. He smiled. He said when he came to visit me, I would have to pay for him. He clapped me on the arm and walked away, whistling, as if everything was agreed to between us. It wasn't. But I couldn't argue with him. I guess nobody could argue with mon oncle when he was set upon something. I didn't know how to explain to ma mère, though, after she'd cautioned me to keep an eye out for him. . . .

Business was picking up at the hotel as summer moved toward early fall. The fisherman still remained, leaving often before daylight, coming back late at nuit. The sales-

man from Tulle moved on. A blind pots-and-pans mender
stayed there for a time. He set up shop in the courtyard.
The women of le village brought their pans to him and he
heated his solder and fixed the pans, all by touch. Day or
night didn't make any difference to him. Sometimes at
night I'd hear his sad sweet voice, singing old songs out in
the courtyard, while he worked.

Finally, the framework for the wooden runway was
nearly finished. I spent the noon exploring the cellar in the
ruins. Mon oncle went with me. The Germans had bombed
the place. The cellar was dark and gloomy and with his
flashlight mon oncle showed me how the earth had piled
in after the explosion. Under a pile of dirt in one corner
we found a couple of rusty tin cans with German words on
them, German rations. And we found rabbit bones, too,
where whoever had stayed there had eaten. That was on a
Thursday, I think. On the way to St. Chamant, I asked le
forgeron to let me off before we reached town. I tested
myself. I walked in. The distance was nearly a mile and a
quarter.

I was late for dinner but my leg had plugged along,
giving me no trouble at all. I decided to increase the distance—maybe Friday, try to walk over to the Meilhacs'
to see Charles. It bothered me how the jours were racing
by, with me having no chance still to do anything. That
Thursday evening I was tired and sleepy. I didn't spend
much time with little Philippe on French. I went to bed
early. A queer thing happened. Along about midnight I
awakened, with the impression someone near me was humming that same silly tune Albert used to hum back in Paris.
Probably it was because I was so tired. Pretty soon the
humming ended. I fell asleep. For the first time in weeks

again I dreamed of the long white face of Monsieur Simonis. Friday morning I awoke, feeling depressed.

When le forgeron and I reached mon oncle, we found
he was stirred up over something, too. During the night
someone had stolen some wood—not much, half a dozen
sticks. He kept shaking his head and said he didn't understand it. The people around St. Chamant weren't dishon-
est. If someone had wanted wood for a fire, he was certain
he'd have been asked. I almost told him about the dream I
had last night and how I'd awakened, thinking Albert was
passing outside in the hall humming that silly tune. But in
broad daylight, the fresh montagne wind blowing down
upon us, everything seemed different. I could see how
foolish I'd sound, worrying mon oncle that I was beginning to imagine things again just as he thought I'd recovered from all those fears. I had enough sense to keep
my mouth shut—leastwise, that Friday morning, I *thought*
I was being sensible.

Evidently, mon oncle noticed I'd been listening to him
talking to le forgeron. He realized I was slowly learning to
understand French conversations. Right away, he broke
off speaking to le forgeron, saying it wasn't important losing a little wood; and he shooed me off to the shelter to
fetch more nails. The sun broke through the clouds along
about ten o'clock. By eleven, the big wooden runway had
been completed. We hoisted the avion on top of the runway, mon oncle attaching it in place with a rope, so it
wouldn't slide down.

I walked around it and looked at it up there, shimmering
in the sunlight. I could hardly see where the wing had been
fixed. He nodded his head at it. "Oui," said he, pleased. "Je
suis content. L'avion n'est pas cassé. L'avion est réparé.

L'avion est prêt à voler. L'avion va voler très *loin*. Do you understand enough French for all of that, Jean?"

I said I'd understood most of it. "The airplane is not broken. The airplane is repaired. The airplane is ready to fly. The airplane is going to fly—" And then I said I was stuck on that word "loin."

"Far," he said. " 'Très loin' is 'very far.' The airplane is going to fly very far. L'avion va voler très *loin*."

"Ne volez pas *trop* loin, mon oncle," I said, which meant "fly not *too* far, my uncle." We'd probably say in English, "Don't fly—" but in French they use that "ne volez pas" with the double "not's."

He smiled. "As-tu peur? Have you fear?"

I looked across the meadow to where the cliff dropped away, and le village was small, so far below; and I said maybe he ought to try out his avion not very loin at first, just a little jump. He laughed. "La peur n'est pas bonne, Jean. You will see. L'avion va voler dans le ciel—in the sky —for beaucoup de minutes. For many minutes!"

While we were talking in the shadow of the ruins, Suzanne and Charles marched across the crest of la montagne and saw us and hallooed and whooped and came court-ing or I should say "courant" in French, actually, for "running," because "court" just means "runs." It was a wonderful surprise. Here I'd been planning on asking mon oncle to go to their maison this afternoon and was afraid he might refuse—and now they were here. I saw this was my chance to get Charles to one side and make him understand he'd have to sneak down the montagne tonight and meet me outside the hotel for my scheme.

Before I could say anything, they did the same thing they did the other time. Charles gave me a quick hug, and kissed me on the cheeks. Suzanne gave me a hug and I might as well admit it, I'd been here so long and seen it was the natural greeting, that I gave her a quick hug back and probably didn't do any more than turn all the colors of the rainbow.

Meanwhile, Charles was rapidly explaining to mon oncle.

Mon oncle repeated it to me. Because the Meilhac twins hadn't seen me for so long, this morning they had gotten up before daylight to do their work. After finishing, they'd started over la montagne to visit me at the workshop in St. Chamant and luckily saw the avion up on the wooden runway and came here instead.

For the next half-hour, I didn't have an opportunity to signal Charles I had to talk privately to him. Mon oncle showed Charles and Suzanne the avion, telling them about it, how it was supposed to coast down the wooden runway and gather enough speed to leap off into the air and voler. Le forgeron was splitting stakes with an ax. He laid the ax on the slide and came over to boom away on his own hook, probably boasting how loin the avion would voler once it was in the sky—le ciel.

Resting on top of the runway, the avion somehow appeared larger than when it was in the workshop or simply on the ground. Perched so high above us, more than ever before it resembled a gigantic butterfly, the wings quivering a little from the wind, the bracing wires thrumming a low soft steady note.

To demonstrate to the twins how it would fly, mon oncle climbed into the cockpit located in between the wings. The cockpit was open to the air. Mon oncle straddled the canvas sling serving as a seat, his feet touching the

*Mon oncle climbed into the cockpit, in between
the wings*

wooden runners of the runway. On either side of him were the skids to the avion. Le forgeron climbed up to the top and took a piece of soap from his pocket. He demonstrated how he would rub soap on the runners for the skids to coast down.

Charles' eyes goggled. "L'avion ne va pas tomber?" he asked.

Mon oncle said, no, it wouldn't tomber—fall. It would voler dans le ciel—the sky. He was absolutely confident. I wished I could feel as confident as he did, now the time was almost prêt for him to try it out.

The thing that made me angry, however, was that because of le maire there wouldn't be a crowd invited or any famous people. Mon oncle might go and risk his neck and voler all over the place. No one would ever know about it or buy mon oncle's invention of a stable avion. I simply *had* to manage some means of grabbing Charles off to one side this afternoon and informing him everything depended upon him helping me tonight.

Suzanne asked, "L'avion est prêt à voler?"

Mon oncle explained it was prêt, but he planned to wait until early next week before trying it out. He wanted to wait until the wind blew up a storm. The more wind he had, the better he could prove to himself that his design of an avion was absolutely stable. That didn't make sense to me. If I was an inventor I'd want to pick a day still as doom for my first attempt, before risking my neck in a storm. But mon oncle wasn't built along cautious lines, I guess.

As mon oncle hoisted Suzanne up to the avion, to have a better look at it, Charles passed around toward me.

I grabbed at him, pulling him under the wooden runway. Hastily, I whispered, "Tu viens *voir* moi. Nuit," hoping he'd understand I wanted him to come to *see* me tonight. I added, "Nuit. Nuit. Hôtel. Tu viens? St. Chamant."

"Moi?" he said, pointing at himself, his mouth gaping in astonishment at the idea he was supposed to come to the hotel in St. Chamant tonight. "Tu *veux* je viens à St. Chamant?" That "tu *veux*," you remember, means, "you *wish*."

"Oui!" I said. "Tu viens. Hôtel. Nuit. Le maire. Secret. Très secret!"

It's altogether astonishing how few words you require to explain something when it's an emergency and you have to hurry and you've got somebody like Charles Meilhac who was trying as hard to understand as I was to make him understand.

II

MONSIEUR SIMONIS VOIT CHARLES ET MOI

"Hola!" called mon oncle. "Where are you two?"

Charles et moi—Charles and me—ducked out from under the runway. I said, "Ici. We're ici—here."

Suzanne bent down, suspiciously gazing at us as if she knew we were talking secrets together. Charles tried to appear unconcerned. He said, "Il fait beau aujourd'hui," and peered up at le ciel. He stuck his hands behind his back. There wasn't anybody, I guess, as good-hearted as Charles, but whenever he tried to hide anything from Suzanne, just the opposite happened—he always gave himself away by overdoing it.

Fortunately, mon oncle was like a child with a new toy. He was too busy showing us his avion to notice Charles et moi might have conspired privately. He asked us to climb to the top of the runway. "Pousse Jean," he told Charles— and Charles obeyed; he pousse-d me up—pushed me up. Suzanne didn't say anything. She was too smart to ask us questions. But I could sense her thinking. I could feel my scheme again growing complicated.

As Charles scrambled beside us he nearly tripped on the ax. Le forgeron waved his hands, warning us to be careful. Mon oncle said the ax was sharp, not to touch it. When the time came le forgeron was to use the ax to cut the rope attaching the avion to the top of the runway.

168

Mon oncle was sitting in the cockpit. In front of him was a wooden post with a small wooden wheel, something like the kind you put on one end of a broomstick to steer a coaster wagon. He explained, to va to the right or to the left, you simply turned the wheel. To descend, you pushed forward. To voler up, you pulled back. That was all there was to it, he said. It was as simple as driving an automobile. You didn't have to concern yourself about the avion falling off to one side or the other as most avions did. His avion balanced itself because of how the wings were constructed.

He had built two rudders, one at each end of the wing. Ordinary avions have ailerons—flaps in the wings which keep the thing from tilting to one side or the other. Mon oncle's avion—l'avion de mon oncle, I suppose I should say—also had flaps. But they were attached to the rudders. They automatically moved when you worked the rudders. The whole purpose of his design was to construct an avion anyone could voler in.

He told us, proud and pleased with it, that you couldn't have an accident in it. For example, you couldn't make it dive so steeply it would smash into la terre—the ground. If you poussed too far farward on the post, why, the avion would merely dive a little and speed up and come level of its own accord.

Another thing, he explained. If his calculations were right, all the trouble and danger of landing that ordinary avions had were ended with his. His avion was designed to descend gently *vers* la terre—*toward* the ground. It practically floated down, no faster than a parachute, was his claim.

It must have been nearly four o'clock in the afternoon

before he finished keeping his promise to show Charles and Suzanne his avion. He allowed each one of us, too, to climb into the cockpit for a minute.

I straddled that piece of canvas. The wings stretched out on either side of me. For a second or so it was almost as if I were voler-ing. I could look ahead and sight down the wooden runway and see where the meadow dropped off, to the cliff. Beyond was nothing but le ciel—sky—and air and wind. Far, far away was le village, small, the houses no bigger than toy blocks. I had a moment of peur. The wind caught at the wings. I thought someone might accidentally have cut the rope holding the avion and it was starting to slide down the runway. Of course, it was only the wind. But it made me uneasy. I climbed out in a hurry.

Mon oncle jumped down, light and easy, and came to me. He said, "Why do you not ask Charles to stay avec you tonight at the hotel? I zink your father would not mind at all if you use your money to pay for your guest."

"Oh," I cried. "That would be wonderful! *Can* he? *Will* he?"

I couldn't have asked for anything better. Immediately, mon oncle explained to Charles. Charles' face lit up. You almost could see his freckles dancing around for pure joy. Probably, he thought this was my secret and what I'd been trying to tell him under the runway when I was saying for him to come to see me tonight at the hotel. I didn't mind if he was a trifle muddled on it. Once I had him at the hotel there was plenty of time before midnight to outline the entire scheme to him—and make him understand, too, French or no-French-not, as you might put it.

Charles said, "Oui, je veux rester avec Jean la nuit!"— nodding his head.

The only one who wasn't content was Suzanne. Of course, being a girl she couldn't come with us. She knew that. But, also, she suspected we were up to something. Probably, most girls right then and there would have blabbed out their suspicions. It's only fair to say, as vexed as Suzanne must have been, she didn't say a word to mon oncle about what she might have figured Charles et moi were up to. No, she just set her lips together. She scowled. She dug the point of her wooden shoe into the ground. She walked away, pretending she was more interested in picking flowers than listening to us.

Mon oncle proposed that Charles let Suzanne go with le forgeron et moi as loin—as far—as the ridge in the oxcart. When we reached the ridge, Monsieur Niort would wait while Charles court-ed to la maison to ask his mother permission to rester la nuit avec moi.

All of us piled into the oxcart, le ciel changing slowly from a clear blue to pink and salmon colors. The clouds floating in le ciel were white, like big lazy sheep drifting through the air. We waved to mon oncle. He called, "Au revoir!" We watched him walk back to the avion and stare up at it, his hands clasped behind his back, no doubt thinking and planning ahead to that jour when a big wind would blow and he was prêt to make the flight.

At the ridge, Monsieur Niort clucked at the ox to stop. The twins jumped out. Charles let me know he believed his mother would grant him permission to come avec moi, particularly since mon oncle had asked him also—aussi, I should say, I guess. With dignity, Suzanne hoisted herself out of the oxcart. She didn't say anything to us at all; she just walked away, all by herself.

I called, "Au revoir, Suzanne."

She didn't even turn her head.

I can't tell you how sorry I suddenly felt for her, leaving her out. If she'd been a boy, I'd have invited her at once. She acted as if I'd run out on her and played her a mean trick, which was absolutely unreasonable of her to believe. Once more I called, "Suzanne! Au revoir, Suzanne."

But Charles didn't give a hang about leaving his sister at home. He swung over the oxcart, blue eyes sparkling, his hair red as paint. He told me excitedly, "Je reviens. Je reviens, vite!" That was: "I re-come, quick!" as the French have to say it. He raced by her, not paying any attention to her at all.

What she did was to stick out her foot, tripping him. He fell headlong. Before he could get up and catch her she'd darted ahead on the path, her red hair streaming, running as fast as a deer. I don't know how I happened to think of it at that moment, but I wished Bob Collins had been here. If he could have seen Suzanne then, I'll bet he'd have thought she was prettier even than Jane Sulgave. It never occurred to me before, somehow, that Suzanne Meilhac was awfully good-looking even if she was a girl and had red hair and was so thin.

While we waited, Monsieur Niort filled his pipe and smoked and talked French at me. Sometimes, I longed to be in a place where tout le monde—everyone—spoke nothing but words I understood.

You can't conceive how tiresome it became now and then to be where someone would say, "Eh bien, ça marche, aujourd'hui, hein, mon garçon? L'avion va voler, je crois. Ça m'amuse bien de voir l'avion voler loin, parce que je veux voler moi aussi. Est-ce qu'un forgeron comme moi ne

peut pas voler, hein?" and stuff like that, not spoken slowly
either, but rattled off, faster than a man hammering
tacks.

I wondered if ma mère expected me to speak like that
when she saw me. I hoped not. Just when I was getting
confidence that I might be able to speak the language—
along would come a volley of words such as le forgeron
shot at me, innocent and all, not realizing he was pulveriz-
ing me with every syllable he let go.

In about fifteen minutes, Charles revient. His mère had
given him permission to rester la nuit à l'hotel avec moi. I
noticed he was wearing a new coat. The coat appeared stiff
and bulky. He had difficulty climbing into the oxcart,
holding his stomach as if he had an ache. I tried to ask what
the matter was. He gave me a quick nudge, whispering,
"Sh-h!" which is one word, at least, meaning the same
thing in English it does in French.

I discovered what was wrong with his coat when we got
out of the oxcart, halfway down la montagne, for me to
walk the rest of the distance to St. Chamant on my own
legs. He waited until Monsieur Niort and the cart and ox
had vanished around a clump of oak trees. Mysteriously,
he pulled me next to an old stone wall, and lifted up his
coat—and extracted his bow and arrow. He had on a grin a
mile long. "Peau-rouge!" he said, absolutely tickled pink.
He considered we were going to play Indian tonight! He
thought *that* was our secret.

Well, as we walked to le village, I had to make him realize my secret was deeper than merely playing "peau-
rouge." With all the French I could muster I began out-
lining the scheme.

You can realize it wasn't such an easy thing to do when

Charles didn't know a lick of English and probably I didn't
know more than three or four hundred words of French.
Ordinarily, I'd have been stumped before starting. But this
time, I simply couldn't let myself be stumped. And Charles
saw I was up to something important. He did all in his
power to help me and to grasp whatever I was saying. We
made progress, but we reached le village way too soon. I
was so intent on what I was doing, I never realized I'd
walked all that distance without even a cramp or a pain in
my leg until I found myself smack in front of the hotel,
little Philippe Graffoulier sitting on the door-step, drawing pictures with chalk on his slate.

I was able to explain without too much trouble to Madame Graffoulier that Charles was going to be my guest
tonight—Charles va rester avec moi à l'hôtel, la nuit, something like that.

She understood. She was wonderful to him, too. She
treated him as if he were the most important person she
had staying in the hotel. She gave him the other corner
bedroom, the biggest one in the hotel. Between us was the
room that the fisherman occupied. The blind peddler had
taken mon oncle's little room in back.

Little Philippe tagged after us, hardly giving us a moment of peace before dinner. I noticed his slate. I signed to
him I'd like to borrow it. I decided I might be able to use
the slate to draw pictures for Charles when I couldn't explain any other way. Philippe was perfectly agreeable.

We washed. Charles hid his bow and arrow in his room.
We came down to dinner. He laid into the potage and
vegetables and thick bread and slices of broiled goat's meat
as if he hadn't eaten for a week. Come to think of it, the
Meilhacs were so poor, probably he hadn't had so much to

eat at one time since his father had died and he and Suzanne and Madame Meilhac had returned to St. Chamant.

After he'd stuffed himself, we went out into the courtyard for a little time to enjoy the sunset. The blind man was there, squatting on a stool, heating his soldering iron over a charcoal fire in a brass pan.

"Bon jour, monsieur," said Charles, pleasantly. The blind man showed us how he mended the pans, feeling for the holes, placing just the right amount of solder in each hole. Philippe sat down beside us and piped up in his squeaky voice, saying when he grew up he was going to mend pans, too. The big black-headed fisherman stuck his head through the door while we were talking. I could see him out of the corner of my eye.

It was growing darker, all the time. Shadows filled the courtyard, too. The fact is, except for that one morning, I'd never had a very good look at the fisherman. He was either going somewhere in a hurry with his rod and tackle, or returning, climbing up the stairs, shutting himself in his room. But as I noticed him now, he had the same bulk and shape of—I couldn't think. Not old Jake, back home. Old Jake was leaner. I didn't know.

Now, a curious thing happened. I think it's worth mentioning. Probably the fisherman assumed all of us in the courtyard were too occupied to pay attention to him. Charles and Philippe were arguing about one of the pans. The blind man had the soldering iron in his hand, the hot iron sizzling.

But just as the blind man was picking up another pan, I saw him turn his head a little. His ears seemed to prick up, too. Of course, it might have been because of the shadows and the dull light, but for a second I could have sworn that the blind man—had *looked* out through his dark glasses straight at that fisherman. The fisherman had closed the door quickly by the time I turned.

Up until now, the blind man had been perfectly good-natured, explaining to us how he fixed the pans. Now, all at once, his voice got harsh. He said we were disturbing him; for us to go away.

It was time for Philippe to go to bed, anyway, and it gave me an excuse to beckon to Charles and pull him upstairs into my bedroom. I locked the door. Because I could hear the fisherman moving around in the room next to mine, I spoke to Charles in a low voice. After lighting a candle I took Philippe's slate and chalk and while Charles sat on the bed, I went at him again about my scheme.

I drew a picture of a chicken house. I pointed and said, "Monsieur Capedulocque," and it was clear to whom the house belonged.

I drew more pictures. Gradually, Charles began to understand. Finally, I drew a picture of what I imagined a Nazi would be. It was a pretty ferocious picture. The man had spiked moustaches. "Nazi," I said. I drew montagnes. "Nazi dans montagnes," I said. I made the Nazi come from the montagnes and go into the chicken house. "Nazi," I said again. "Le maire. Nazi. Ici."

"Quoi?" exclaimed Charles suddenly, jumping off the bed.

"Oui," said I, believing he was understanding.

"Le Maire Capedulocque—Nazi?" insisted Charles, once more, as if he couldn't believe what I'd said.

Of course I replied, "Oui," just as anyone would, after having gone to all the trouble of explaining such a simple scheme.

Well, from that instant on you never saw such a change come over a person. Charles acted as if the world had fallen upon him. He concentrated on every last word I said. His jaw stuck out. In the candlelight, his eyes had turned a cold blue.

I was pleased, myself, to see he'd finally gotten through his head most of what I wanted but, I'll admit, I was a trifle puzzled to know just what it was that I'd said finally to bring him around in such a hurry, all at once.

The only part of my scheme remaining was for me to explain to him about the note. But do you think Charles would listen? No. He marched up and down the room, whispering fiercely, "Ah, ce Monsieur Capedulocque! Le cochon! Le cochon!" I began to wish I hadn't stirred him up quite so much. Finally, I attempted to construct the note, myself. That didn't go. I simply didn't know enough French. I gave it up.

I'd scatter the German coins as I'd planned and trust le maire would see them and think a Nazi had left them there. It was all I could do. I tiptoed to my bureau drawer, Charles watching every step I took. I got about ten German coins and half a dozen French francs. Charles brought the candle to the bureau and saw the coins in my hand.

"Qu'est-ce que c'est que ça?" he whispered.

It was enough to discourage the most patient man in the world. Charles was supposed to know already why I had to take German coins. I showed them to him. I said, "Nazi—Nazi—" and he bent his head down and picked up one and looked at it and in the candlelight his round face became perfectly furious.

"Ah!" he said. "Le maire?"

"Oui," I replied.

"Ah," he said. "Le cochon!" and threw the coin to the floor.

That was a preposterous thing for him to do. I didn't understand. I was wondering if he was off on one track and I was off on another. I picked up the coin and stuck it in my pocket. He appeared puzzled. I didn't have any more time for explaining. If he hadn't absorbed all the points, it wouldn't be my fault for not trying; he'd have to come along and do the best he could. I blew out the light and whispered, "Tu viens?"

That roused him right away. Noble and fierce as if this was something he was staking his whole life on, he whispered back, "Oui, je viens. Je suis patriote!"

It was a fine thing for him to be so enthusiastic, but I didn't see why he had to tell me he was a patriot. I concluded he was acting so fierce because it was natural for the French to excite themselves easily.

We went softly into the hall. We listened in the darkness. Madame Graffoulier and the two kids slept on the other side of the courtyard. They wouldn't hear us depart. The room next to mine was dead silent—not a sound came from it. I figured the fisherman was asleep. I headed for the stairs. In the darkness, Charles reached out and touched me—and I gave a little jump. I hadn't appreciated I was so nervous. He whispered, "Un moment, Jean. Je reviens, vite."

I waited more than a moment in that dark creaky hall for him to re-come, quickly. In about three minutes he glided noiselessly to me, carrying something in his hands. We got down the stairs without arousing anyone. There we halted, peering toward the courtyard. But the blind peddler had packed up his kit and gone to bed long ago.

We passed out into la rue, walking over the cobblestones, keeping close to the maisons. We heard a dog bark.
As we crossed to the right, toward the church, moonlight
slid down through the trees, shining on Charles. I stopped
dead.

I saw he was carrying his bow and arrow. *That* was
what he'd gone back into his room to get. For my scheme,
he didn't require a bow and arrow. They'd be a nuisance.
I searched for some words to tell him to get rid of them.
He stepped closer to me, an unholy grin on his freckled
face, all white and round in the moonlight. He lifted up
his bow, wagged his red head, whispering fiercely, "Voici!
Bien, hein?"

It wasn't bien at all. I might have stopped longer to
argue with him, if we hadn't heard the sound of footsteps
on the cobblestones. We ducked in behind the church in
a hurry.

It didn't seem possible anyone would be up at this early
hour in the morning. We didn't wait to see who it was.
We streaked along the side of the churchyard and hoisted
ourselves over the cemetery wall, landing in soft terre—
earth—and staying there, not making a noise, scarcely
breathing. I wondered if it could be the fisherman arising
this early.

I guess Charles didn't like being here any more than I
did. We drew close together, picking our way along one
of the old brick walks. Le maire's place was opposite the
graveyard, on the other side. We stole along through those
gravestones, hearing the wind come sighing to us. I'd never
realized how spooky a graveyard could be at night. We
approached the middle of the cemetery, the old part,
where the trees grew more thickly. Their leaves were like

a blanket overhead, shutting out most of the pale moonlight. We had to grope our way on the brick walk, feeling for the rusty spiked fence.

For a couple of minutes we must have got lost, wandering around in that cold darkness. Instead of coming out

We stole along through those gravestones, hearing the wind come sighing to us

directly opposite le maire's place, we emerged from the graveyard three or four hundred yards north, near the corner of the stone wall. Here it was a little brighter. The leaves weren't so thick. The moon shone down with a flat paleness on three or four old mausoleums, erected next to the wall.

I drew Charles' attention to le maire's place across from

the cemetery on the other side of the road. I signified to him, best as I could, that we were to make a rush across the road and crouch under the opposite wall as our next move. He got that part of the plan, too. He nodded. "Oui," he said in a whisper, his voice more steady than mine was.

Just as we were about to jump for it, we heard those footsteps again. They came down the main rue and turned, right, and clop-clopped past the church, coming closer and closer to this side of the wall surrounding the grave-yard. We risked peeking above the wall, to see who it was. The trees shaded us so much that it was perfectly safe as long as we didn't make any noise.

But the minute I raised my head and saw who it was, coming toward us, I nearly fell over backwards. I can't ever express how uncanny a thing it was to see that blind man approach, the moonlight upon him. He clopped-clopped in his wooden shoes along the deserted road, his head up, the black glasses covering his eyes.

He walked on by and went on toward la montagne. It seemed as though the entire nuit stood still, the leaves mo-tionless in the trees, the wind empty. That peddler was blind, but he walked that road with his head up in the moonlight! When he reached the turn beyond Dr. Guere-ton's vineyard, why, *he* turned, too, although how he knew it was there was a miracle to me.

We waited a long time after the peddler was gone. I guess just seeing him, uncanny and lonely in the solitary road, had dampened our spirits. An owl hooted somewhere behind us. Both of us jerked. Finally, his voice shaky, Charles whispered, "T-tu viens?"

I whispered, "Oui." We slid over the wall and rushed

across the road, diving for the tall grass growing beside the wall enclosing le maire's property.

From somewhere near us, a rooster started crowing. That noise split out through the darkness so loudly I thought the entire village would hear it and wake up and know we were laying low near le maire's place. By and by, the rooster gave up. But another took on, crowing even more loudly. A donkey brayed. After that a dog barked faraway. A dog in le village next barked. A wind blew down from the montagnes with a cold freshness of early morning. I could feel Charles shivering against me, waiting for the next move—and, probably, I was shivering just as hard, or harder, against him.

I reached into my pocket for the German coins. I shoved them at him. Well, he didn't conceive of why he should take a handful of German coins! That was the most bitter shock of all to me. Here I'd thought he understood my scheme perfectly and at the very crucial moment, when he was supposed to take the coins to carry out the scheme, I had to discover he was still ignorant of their purpose.

The wind got colder. Morning was coming closer. Already the stars in the sky weren't quite as bright. I knew if we waited much longer it would be too late and we'd never have this chance again. I could either give up because Charles was obstinate and refused to understand at the last minute what he was supposed to do—or I could change my scheme. Instead of me standing guard, I'd have to take over and sneak across the wall and grab a couple of hens and ducks, scatter money around, and shove for it.

I took a big breath. I whispered, "Tu restes ici, s'il vous plaît," telling him to rest here, please, expecting him at least to stand guard for me.

I scooted across the wall, landing fortunately on my feet. Right away, there was a soft scratching noise against the wall. I whirled. It was Charles. *He* clambered over it, too, not leaving me for a second. My plan was scattering all to nowhere. *That* wasn't what he was supposed to do at all!

You might have expected me to order him back. Well, I didn't. It's fine to plan things. Once you're in the middle of doing a thing such as I was tonight, I found it a lot more comfortable to have Charles sticking along with me even if my original scheme called for one of us to be guard.

The back yard of the maire's place was covered with gravel. In the space between the maison and stables and chicken and duck sheds, were a cart and a dilapidated buggy and a pile of junk. We snuck as far as the cart when a dog tied near the stables started barking as if it were going crazy.

I'd never counted on a dog giving us away. Soon as it began barking, of course, the donkeys let loose; they brayed. I hope I may never again hear so many animals all going at the same time.

With all that noise, I knew in a minute that le maire was bound to be awakened. My interest evaporated in the scheme I'd constructed. I lost all interest in it fast. All I wanted to do was to get back to the hotel, into bed. I stood, preparing to make a run for it to the wall. But Charles still crouched beside the big cart. I hauled at his arm, trying to let him know my scheme wasn't as perfect as I'd figured.

Do you know, he didn't budge. He stayed where he was. I bent down to whisper at him. He made a sudden move, caught me, shoved me clear down. "Hsst!" he whispered, pointing.

Then I saw what I hadn't noticed before. A light was

showing through the cracks of the rear door. Now, I could see a light might be burning in the rear room. The windows were shut tight with shutters. You had to look sharp before realizing the maison wasn't dark. And as I stared, the crack opened wider and wider—the door swung out.

There, framed in the candlelight from the room, stood le maire himself. Late as it was, he was dressed. He wasn't wearing a nightgown. He stepped forward, peering in the darkness toward the sheds. He asked, "Qu'est-ce que c'est que ça?" It came very plainly to where we were hiding, as if he were addressing a question to someone behind him, asking what was the matter.

And as I watched, I felt my heart practically turn to stone and stop beating.

A tall thin man came out from the room and stood behind le maire. He was head and shoulders above le maire, with arms like bean poles. I couldn't believe my eyes. My throat tightened.

I only knew of one person who could be that tall and thin, who moved with a kind of series of jerks as if made out of wood. Le maire asked the same question again, nervous and startled. The tall man behind answered in a voice I recognized—a voice I'd never forgotten. In that rusty whine of tone, the man said, "Va voir!"—go see. *It was Monsieur Simonis!* It was Monsieur Simonis in le maire's maison, talking to le maire, telling him to go see what was causing all the commotion from the animals and chickens in the sheds.

I laid flat to the ground, under the cart, Charles next to me. I felt as if I were about to perish. I knew if Monsieur Simonis ever put hands on me I was finished.

Le maire stepped down from the door, hesitating. He

turned back. A second man came from the room. This was the worst of all, because, quite calmly Monsieur Simonis ordered this second man, "Albert, va avec le maire!" And when Albert came into the light I saw at first the black-haired fisherman who was staying in the hotel, and as I heard the chuckle, as I remembered Albert's chuckle, it was as though the shape of the fisherman was changing even as I stared. It was Albert—wearing a black wig or dyed hair, his thick eyebrows trimmed and dyed black, and his moustache shaven. No wonder I'd thought I'd seen the fisherman before.

Le maire and Albert started along the path toward the sheds. Le maire saved us. I think he must have been nervous, not liking to be seen even at nuit in company with Albert. About a hundred feet away from the cart under which we were hiding, he suddenly halted. He told Albert, "Non, ne viens pas avec moi. Va à la maison."

They argued. The donkeys were braying even more loudly. The dog chained next to the duck shed was leaping against his chain, smelling us, wanting to get us.

If we were ever to clear from here, this was our single moment. I nudged Charles and whispered, "Viens!" and took a quick breath and made a leap from under the cart toward the wall. I got about halfway before I heard the men suddenly shouting. I looked behind—saw Charles behind me, running—and, my leg tripped. I went over on my head and shoulders and rolled. Monsieur Simonis' great creaking voice was hollering to le maire, "Ai! Ai! Là! Tu vois! Albert!"

They'd seen us for certain.

Instead of slamming by me, Charles whirled. He stopped and hauled me to my feet and in the moonlight his face had a wild terrible grin on it. The minute I got to my feet, he faced Albert and le maire. He shouted at them, "Traître! Conspirateur! Collaborationiste!" which meant precisely what the words sound like—Traitor! Conspirator! Collaborationist!

After that he did the bravest thing any boy of his age could do. In a flash, he strung up his arrow to the bow. He pulled back. He let fly. That arrow wobbled across the yard. Either this time Charles' aim was lucky, or Albert was so huge nobody possibly could have missed him. Anyway, that arrow hit Albert right in the mouth between the teeth!

Albert fell back, choking, yelling for help, pulling at the arrow that had gone on in his mouth and cut the inside of his cheek. He collided against le maire, and both of them plumped down into the gravel.

Charles ran for the wall. He gave me a hoist and a pousse. Over we went, into the grass. We streaked across the road, as Albert and le maire climbed over the wall. We headed for the cemetery, because that was the darkest place there was to hide in.

12

"L'AVION EST PRET A PARTIR!"

We must have had, maybe, a minute's head start. We ran straight for the middle of the graveyard and before we reached the middle, we became confused by the darkness and all the branching paths, and found we were lost. Somewhere behind us we could hear the noises the men made following us.

My idea, and I suppose it was Charles' too, was to try to work across the graveyard to le village and arouse the inhabitants there, before we were nabbed. To understand where we were, you'll have to understand that old graveyard was an entire city in itself. St. Chamant wasn't very big, probably not over a thousand people living there, but one way or another it had been in existence since way back during the time of the Romans and the Limovices.

The graveyard was roughly in the shape of a vast square, the southwest corner next to the church. The road to the montagnes ran along the west side, and le maire's place was situated about a quarter of a mile north of the church, on the west side of the graveyard. Consequently, we'd ducked in a good distance north of the church and le village, and something less than a quarter of a mile from the upper or north side of this old cemetery. The brick paths had been laid out in a series of two passing from west to east, and two from south to north, forming checkerboard squares. Branching off from the brick, fenced-in paths, were little lanes, wandering through each of the squares. After so many years, dirt and grass covered the bricks in places and there were great gaps in the iron fences.

Charles and I ran along the upper brick path, crossing the cemetery from west to east, planning to hit one of the north to south paths and go down it to the church and to le village. Now that I'm telling about it, it seems easy. You'd think we couldn't have made a mistake. But we were scared practically to death. Albert was blundering through the brush behind us, having already lost the path. It was black as pitch under the trees. The stone grave-markers stood up all around us in the darkness, nearly invisible until we crashed against them.

I don't know where we got off the brick path. The voices behind us had dropped away. We didn't hear any more noise for several minutes. Charles took my arm and said, "Hsst!" and we stopped, listening, trying to figure where we were. When we peered up through the leaves we could make out a faint whiteness in the sky where the moon was shining. Charles must have decided he knew where we were, because after a moment he said softly, "Viens, Jean," and I heard him move. Well, I made to follow. I stepped onto something rounded and lifting up a little from the ground, harder than the earth. My foot went on through the soft dirt and I couldn't help from yelling. If my life had depended on me not yelling—and perhaps right then it did, too—I couldn't have stopped myself.

I can't explain how I felt, when I realized I'd wallowed down into an old grave. The crumbly dirt poured in on me. I struggled up in the blackness, finding I'd fallen four or five feet downwards into a hole filled with old leaves and rotted pieces of wood from a coffin, and other articles which weren't old leaves or wood or dirt—more like pieces of cow bones such as I'd picked up in Wyoming. Only these bones didn't feel as bulky as cow bones. It took me about a second to realize what kind of bones they were— and then I nearly went crazy wanting to get out.

"Hsst, Jean!" whispered Charles anxiously from somewhere above me. His hands groped down into the hole and touched mine. I gave a kind of gasping lunge, with Charles pulling on me. Next we heard Albert's shout somewhere off in the darkness among the trees. My yell had given us away. In order not to lose each other, Charles and I grasped hands and we started to run.

Le maire's voice was calling, "Albert? Albert, où es-tu?"

We didn't stop to wait to find out where Albert was. We ducked around a couple of more tombstones and came out on one of the brick paths. We didn't know which one it was. We simply streaked along that path, and it was like running in a dark tunnel. Pretty soon, the trees spread out a little. Moonlight filtered down on us. Charles halted, bringing me up with a jerk. He stood silent, listening. I strained my ears. There were voices and noises, but much fainter now. They came from a distance, somewhere still in the center of the graveyard.

We continued along the path until we came out from under the trees and were bitterly disappointed to find we'd completely mixed up our directions. Instead of being at the south side, the side closest the village, we'd come out way up at the northeast corner, the forest and vineyards and montagnes ahead of us.

We reached the group of stone mausoleums. Here we got our breath. "Ça va?" whispered Charles, asking how everything was going with me. I was still able to move. My bum leg hadn't given up on me. The weeks of exercise and walking had strengthened it more than I realized, now we'd run into a real emergency. "Ça va," I whispered back.

We crawled behind the mausoleums, heading toward the road. We could see the dim outline of the trees, shaking their whiskered leafy heads in the wind. A cloud rolled across the moon, blotting out most of the light except that which came down from the sprinkle of stars. I shivered. We reached the northeast corner. Now all we had to do was work down, south, toward the church and le village, following the descent of the road. We got over the wall, in the low ditch, between the wall and the road.

We moseyed south, easy and soft, taking our time, keeping our ears pricked for all sounds. We couldn't believe we'd escaped Albert. It didn't seem possible. We were afraid he was stealing behind us, taking *his* time about it, too, planning to surprise us with a quick jump at us the second he got close enough.

Ahead we could distinguish the faint blurred shape of le maire's tower. We heard a cackling of chickens. We knew we were coming closer to le village. We never did get any closer that nuit. It was lucky for us that dog of le maire's wasn't a regular hunting dog and didn't know enough to keep quiet when it smelled our scent. It set up a barking. We risked standing up in the ditch, to make sure it was le maire's dog and not simply a stray dog of le village. Down ahead of us, in the moonlight, we saw the long angular figure of Monsieur Simonis, his shadow falling aslant on the wall, with the dog held by a leash in his hand. The dog lunged toward us. Monsieur Simonis shouted, "Albert! Albert, viens vite! Capedulocque, vite!" and started to run toward where we were hiding.

He took awkward stiff steps, as if something was the

matter with his joints or bones. Charles wheeled. "Viens!" he told me, and we cut back, from where we'd come, going around the northeast corner of the graveyard wall and on up through a vineyard. My breath was coming in tearing gasps by the time we'd reached the upper end of the vineyard. We sighted back. We saw Monsieur Simonis and Albert and le maire in the road below us, gathered together, evidently holding a quick meeting about what they should do.

Charles touched me. We crawled over another fence, climbing upwards on the lower ridges of the montagne. He said, "Ton oncle, Jean. Va à ton oncle!" He realized we'd never be able to reach le village tonight, and proposed for us to climb la montagne and awaken mon oncle. It was all we could do. We descended a gully and climbed up again, going toward the forest. As we entered the forest, once more we looked back. We could see the figures of two men coming across the vineyard half a mile below us. One was dumpy and squat and the other figure was big —le maire and Albert. They had the dog with them now and we could hear its bark clearly.

The road wound around a bend, vanishing behind a lower hill, and we couldn't see Monsieur Simonis. We didn't know whether he'd taken the road, to block us, or if he had returned to le maire's house to wait for Albert and le maire to bring us to him after they'd nabbed us.

We plunged into the forest. Here we had a big advantage. Even at nuit, Charles knew this forest, knew his way. All I had to do was keep up with him and follow him. That was enough. The land under the forest was at a slope. We had to climb and the way became steeper every minute. Now and then, Charles would stop for a few seconds to let me catch my breath. My leg was beginning to hurt. More and more, I lagged behind.

Charles came back to me and made me put one arm around his shoulder, and we continued in that fashion. Pretty soon, we came out from the forest and here Charles halted. I hadn't realized where we were. Charles had headed toward the northeast, going at a diagonal away from the graveyard and le village. Now, instead of finding ourselves midway up the montagne, we were directly under the enormous rise of cliff, bare and craggy in the moonlight. High above us, a thousand feet, perhaps two thousand, was the long meadow land of the Langres family and the ruins of the Langres maison. I could imagine mon oncle up there, sleeping peacefully, perhaps dreaming of le jour when he would go volering in his avion.

But how Charles ever expected us to mount that practically perpendicular face of cliff was beyond me. It lifted in front of us like an enormous wall, blocking further progress. I thought he'd become lost. And somewhere behind us, the dog tracking us, were Albert and le maire and maybe Monsieur Simonis, coming along steadily and surely, up and up, until they'd have us. I felt myself waver. I nearly slumped down to the terre—the earth—believing we were beaten.

In the moonlight, Charles had a queer smile. "Ah, non, Jean," he said, reaching down a hand toward me. "Ton oncle est là—" and with his other hand, he pointed upwards. "Viens." I shook my head.

I knew I couldn't climb that cliff. He didn't realize how whipped I was. I signified for him to va—to go on. I said, "Laisse moi. Laisse moi!" Leave me. Leave me.

"Non," he said.

He put his hands under my arms and lifted me. "Viens," he ordered, his chin shoving out, stubborn and square.

And we didn't go directly up the face of the cliff.

Charles crossed through a creek and I followed, the water wetting us to the skin. We climbed up along a ridge, covered with second growth oak. We turned right, along the side of the cliff, with Charles pausing every now and then, considering the lay of the land, looking for something. It was getting on toward morning. The stars were growing paler and the moon was going down.

Somewhere from below us, in that forest which covered the land like a black cloud, I heard the sudden yelping of a dog. It was le maire's dog. They'd climbed closer to us.

But Charles took his time. Pretty soon he found a kind of path, leading between two rocks each as high as our maison back in Wyoming. "Viens," he said again, now confident. We took this path, if you can call it a path.

I guess it had originally been made by goats, centuries ago. Probably people from the montagnes had come upon the path and used it for hundreds of years to descend to le village or to return to their homes in the montagnes, taking this short cut instead of the long way around.

The path wandered back and forth up the side of the cliff. Once you were on the cliff, you saw it wasn't simply a sheer rock, dropping away hundreds of feet to the forest below. No, it was weathered rock, crumbling, with pockets, with little cleared spaces about as big as a city lot where goats might have grazed. I heard the sound of water tumbling down. Birds flew up and lighted near us in the darkness and chirped brightly, as if they knew morning was about due.

I suppose it must have taken us almost an hour to climb

We crossed the creek, the water wetting us to the skin

along that path to the top of the cliff, what with all our rests and halts. All the time, we had the terror of knowing those men were somewhere below. Perhaps le maire knew of the goat path. Perhaps even instead of wandering in the forest, looking for us, they'd found the path. The dog might have led them to it. Charles didn't dare rest for very long at any stop. We'd come to a cleared space and I'd sort of tumble into the grass or against a pile of rock and take long breaths, feeling my lungs ache, my foot tremble and quiver from the effort of climbing. Next Charles would say quietly, "Viens—" and off we'd go for another five or six minutes.

By and by the sky—le ciel—seemed to lose its darkness. A paleness spread over le ciel. The morning air turned colder, fresher. As we neared the end of the climb, we passed several trees, stunted and twisted. The sun lifted above the horizon, le ciel turning pink. We came to more trees, not much taller than we were. Dirt and rocks had tumbled from the ragged edge of the cliff above us. Charles hauled himself onto a rock—pulled me up after him. "Tu vois?" he shouted at me, above the wind, pointing downwards. In the morning light, I saw far below, coming along the faint line of path from the base of the cliff, Albert and le maire and the dog. They had found the path. It would take them a good fifteen more minutes, hurrying upward as fast as they could go, to reach us.

The sight of them made me forget about my leg. We scrambled up to the top of the cliff. Here the ground was all broken, crumbling. Charles motioned me to go on toward the meadow where it was safer. I watched him pick up a piece of rock and lug it beyond the line of stunted trees, almost to the edge of the cliff. He let the rock drop.

He threw a couple of others after it—peered over, hanging on to a tree. I heard him laugh. He ran to me, still laughing and said something in French which must have meant he'd either hit or frightened those men below by the rocks.

When we gained the thick grass of the meadow, we simply tumbled forward in it, feeling it soft and sweet around us. For a couple of seconds we couldn't have moved if Monsieur Simonis had jumped in front of us and commanded us to with his pistol pointing at us.

"Aiy! Aiy!" said Charles, shaking the red tangle of hair from his eyes, getting up. A third of a mile or so ahead of us lifted the wooden platform of the runway, the avion on it, its wings shimmering like gold in the morning light. Behind the runway and the avion were the massive gray stone ruins of the maison Langres, trees green in the background. The meadow never looked more peaceful and inviting than it did that morning. Next to the wooden runway was the canvas shelter. We could see the canvas swelling and flapping in the wind.

All that was like a magnet. I forgot how tired I was; I forgot my leg. At the same time, both Charles and I started running for it. Probably Charles didn't let himself out full-speed, keeping me in mind.

I wobbled along with him, determined not to give out on the last stretch. As we got closer we saw mon oncle was already awake and up and working. He was half sitting in the cockpit, one leg hanging outside, a wrench in one hand—and a white cup in the other. We shouted.

He looked up, surprised. As we shouted we saw somebody with red hair pop up from the other side of the avion. It was Suzanne. She was standing on the platform with mon oncle, holding one of those earthenware pots. Evidently she'd awakened early this morning and fixed hot chocolate and a breakfast for him and tramped up here to give it to him. She waved at us, as did mon oncle, neither of them appreciating we were shouting warnings in dead earnest.

All that shouting of ours, along with the running, left us exhausted when we reached the wooden runway, practically collapsing for want of breath. Never suspecting all the terror steadily marching up that cliff toward us, Suzanne bent over to good-naturedly jeer at her brother. She said he was a sleepyhead. Charles made gasping noises at her, pointing violently toward the cliff.

At last, mon oncle recognized something was wrong. Probably I must have been a sight to be seen, wet from the creek, scratched by branches, muddy, my face red, my eyes no doubt sticking practically out of my head.

"Hola!" he said. "What's this? Don't shout all at once. What are you trying to tell me about the mayor?" He set down his cup. He stooped, reaching a hand for me. "Porte Jean sur tes épaules," he told Charles—put John on your shoulders. Charles grunted. He poussed—and mon oncle pulled, lifting me up to the top of the platform.

"Voici," said he. "Now, what is it— Ah! Take care, Jean!"

I was so weak, coming to him on the platform I'd nearly tripped on the sharp ax. Suzanne picked up the ax. Puzzled, she first gazed at me and next down at Charles. By now Charles had recovered enough breath to shout up at us, "C'est le maire, Monsieur Langres. Le maire est un traître!"

"What's this?" asked mon oncle. "The mayor is a traitor? Here, sit here, and explain why you are here." He placed me on the side of the cockpit of the avion, where I perched, clutching a wooden strut.

"They're coming after us!" I cried, the terror of last nuit again filling into me.

"Gently," said mon oncle. "Perhaps I should tell you the detective was here earlier this morning—"

"Detective?" I was so astonished I forgot my fear.

Mon oncle nodded. "I did not wish to alarm you, so I did not tell you there has been an agent of the French government in St. Chamant for several days. It is more serious than I zink, Jean. If anyone has frightened you and Charles, we must immediately inform Monsieur Joubert, the detective, who—"

Suzanne gave a scream.

Mon oncle whirled. Monsieur Simonis appeared from around the ruins, and walked toward us, a pistol pointing at us. Monsieur Simonis had come up the montagne by the road, to head Charles and me off. "Bon jour, Monsieur Paul Langres," he said, polite as you please, his green eyes glittering.

Mon oncle produced an astounded sound from his throat—not even a word, simply a queerish little noise. Quick as a cat he jumped from the wooden runway, landing on his feet, and ran toward Monsieur Simonis with outstretched hands, to grab him, ignoring the pistol.

"I will shoot," said Monsieur Simonis calmly. But instead of pointing it at mon oncle, he pointed it up at Suzanne, smiling steadily as if this was the greatest joke in the world. "I will shoot the girl first, Monsieur Langres."

Mon oncle halted, slowly lifting his hands.

Monsieur Simonis laughed. "Bien," he said. He pointed the pistol at mon oncle.

As someone from over near the cliff yelled, he lifted his head. We saw Albert running clumsily across the meadow toward us, the dog leaping after him. Behind, more slowly, followed le maire. Monsieur Simonis waited until the two men reached him. Le maire was puffing hard, sweat running down his fat face. Albert sighted up to the platform and saw me and shook his fist at me. Next he noticed Charles and stepped toward him. Albert's mouth was bloody from the arrow. He looked perfectly horrible, scratched by the bushes, covered with muck and dirt where he'd fallen across the graves, hot and sweaty, with the black dye on his hair and moustache streaking his face. He made a grab at Charles—but Monsieur Simonis delivered an order, low and soft. Albert halted, grinning, just opening and shutting his big hands, as if waiting for the occasion to use them.

Without moving the muzzle of his pistol away from mon oncle, in that falsely polite voice Monsieur Simonis told me, "There you are again, foolish American boy! You have caused me much trouble, you know."

Because he was speaking to me in English, mon oncle asked him in English, "What is it you want?"

"What do *I* want?" said Monsieur Simonis, all the politeness fading from his voice, leaving nothing but a kind of dead coldness. His green eyes left mon oncle and searched the grounds and again jerked up to Suzanne and me and back to mon oncle. "Why, if you wish to know, my dear sir, I will inform you. I should like to use that spade of yours for an hour or so, which you have so conveniently brought up here. And I believe also I can use that ax, which the young girl is now holding. If you are sensible, my dear Langres, and don't force me to shoot you immediately, I will request your services, too. And the boys appear quite strong. You and the two boys can proceed to the cellar and dig in a spot I shall indicate for a large sum of French gold which Monsieur Capedulocque and I managed to hide while I was *gauleiter* in this part of France during the war. Albert and I have waited much too long to obtain the money as it is. If only you had been reasonable enough to sell me this land—" And here his eyes got even greener. He laughed. I don't want to hear that laugh again, ever. He didn't finish his last sentence.

Now mon oncle observed le maire. Mon oncle said the same thing Charles had shouted back in le village. With contempt he said, "Traître!"

The traitorous mayor puffed out his flabby face. He tried to laugh. His laugh was weak. Charles was edging around the runway, and now he made a lunge toward Monsieur Simonis. Albert caught him, knocked him flat with one blow. Monsieur Simonis didn't even appear to notice the interruption. Once more he looked up at us. He ordered, "Descendez! Get down. Vite! Hurry. Both of you."

"Oui, monsieur," said Suzanne, with sudden docility.

She acted as if she was scared of being so high. She balanced back and forth, holding the ax in one hand. I was trying to lift myself off the avion when I heard her whisper, her lips barely moving, "L'avion est prêt à partir!" which meant, "The airplane is ready to depart—" and the next instant, before anyone could guess her intention, she whirled around, swung down hard with the ax and—*she chopped the rope in two which held the avion to the platform of the runway!*

There was one awful instant after that when I heard her

scream, "Va, Jean! Va! Vole à St. Chamant!" The avion
gave a jerk, throwing me back into the canvas seat of the
cockpit.

Have you ever ridden down a roller coaster? Well, the
start was like that, mixed up with tearing shouts, with loud
explosions from somewhere, with a yell from mon oncle,
another from Charles. "Vole à St. Chamant!" Suzanne had
screamed—fly to St. Chamant, as if she expected a miracle
to happen; and all I had to do was clutch the sides of the
cockpit and pretty soon find myself in le village. That's
the trouble with girls. They take too much for granted.

I wasn't hardly inside the cockpit, with my legs hanging
down each side of that canvas sling serving as a seat, the air
rushing against my face, before the avion had rushed clear
down to the bottom of the slide. Next, it followed up the
incline, still just as if I was in some kind of a crazy roller
coaster. The thing was rocking back and forth, the wings
fluttering, the wires humming, with the blast of wind increasing to a perfect gale. That little steering wheel was
vibrating back and forth, hitting me in the face. With a
jerk, I bounced harder down into the canvas sling. Next
second, there was a tremendous rush of air *under* me. All
the rocking and bouncing ceased. Suddenly, everything
was very still. The avion had shot free of the runway.

I looked down—and practically died, right there. *We
were off the ground*. We were—that avion et moi—about
twenty feet off the ground, sliding through the air from
the momentum gained after the coast down the runway!

The terre streaked by below me, like a length of green
carpet. I saw the shadow of the avion scooting along, up
and down the gullys. The dog was there, chasing after
the shadow as fast as he could go, his jaws slavering.

I humped into the canvas sling, hanging for my life to the side of the cockpit. All at once a gust of air struck us from the side. The avion lifted a little, like a sailboat hitting a swell. It dropped and sidled off, and turned into the wind again, the big wings curving gracefully. I risked looking down once more—and wished I hadn't.

The green carpet of grass had changed to yellow rocks. The dog was way behind our shadow, losing speed. Presently, trees flashed below us, lots smaller than trees ought to look; and after that, it was as if the whole world was dropping away. The avion leaves the mountain—l'avion laisse la montagne! Now, the avion flies in the sky—l'avion vole dans le ciel!

A rush of air flowed upwards from the base of the cliff. It tossed the avion higher. This time, the avion rocked more violently, as if caught in greater swells. I felt my head spin. I thought for certain this was the end. This was the finish. It was fine for mon oncle to talk of building an automatic avion, one even a child could fly—but it was a different kettle of fish to be the first to voler in it. I'd trade places any day with the first child to climb up here and ask me to let him have it.

Now the air was steady and direct in my face, as if I were in front of a strong fan. I opened my eyes. We were still in the air. We were going along, too, easy and smooth, those outstretched yellow wings like great comfortable sails. Why, I think those wings were almost alive. You could see tiny shadows ripple and dance on the surface where the air passed over the cloth. The wires had dropped to a strong even humming sound, as if they were settling down to their job.

A bird winged past me. It turned around. It flew close

to me, perhaps to see if it recognized the new bird or if there was any message to be received. We hit another puff of air. The avion tilted down, calm and gentle about it as if it knew its business now, correcting its position, the little wheel in front of me moving back and forth again, quite urgently. You'd almost imagine that wheel was trying to attract my attention.

I gripped so tightly on to the wooden spars that I must have pressed fingerprints into them. I managed to shift a little—nothing happened. We remained on even keel, still soaring along steadily. I shifted more. I looked back. I saw the face of the cliff far behind me, like the prow of the most enormous ship ever launched, rising up and up, a thousand feet from the forest which was like a green sea.

There—standing on the topmost edge of the cliff—was one man. He was about a fifth of a mile away, already receding, going further and further away each second. But in that brilliantly clear morning sunlight I could see enough of that black figure, like a black toothpick, to know it was Monsieur Simonis. Evidently he'd run after the avion as far as he could, leaving Albert and le maire to guard mon oncle and the Meilhac twins.

Even as I twisted my neck, gazing back, floating along so high above the forest, a faint crack of noise came to my ears—like a tiny stick being snapped. A second later something whined and buzzed. There was a sudden plop—and about three feet to my left, a hole opened in the taut linen covering of the wing.

Monsieur Simonis was shooting at me!

13

LE JOUR DE LA FETE

Maybe he shot again, I don't know. The avion was going too fast, leaving la montagne too far behind for me to hear. By now, I was getting somewhat accustomed to riding along through le ciel in an avion. I recognized at least for a little while I was tolerably safe. That little wheel in front of me moved again as the avion tilted into the wind and gently rocked back on even keel.

I saw the wheel move every time the avion did. I remembered a little of what mon oncle had told me. I took hold of the wheel, and in a way, it was like riding a bicycle. I mean, I sat astraddle the canvas sling, my legs dangling below the avion, holding on to the little wooden steering wheel as if it was a pair of bicycle handle-bars. I pushed the wheel forward to see what would happen. I considered I'd given it a gentle push—but whoosh! I thought the whole bottom of my stomach was going to cave in as the avion suddenly stuck its nose down and dived.

I let go that wheel as if it was a hot iron. I clung to the frame. Well, mon oncle had been right. The avion tilted upwards again, even and smooth, the way a horse does when you've accidentally raked it with spurs, jumping suddenly, then quieting down again after teaching you not to be too impetuous. I suppose by now we'd been voler-ing five or six minutes. Maybe less—it's hard to judge when seconds seemed to last half an hour.

We were coming down in a long flat slant. A mile or so ahead of me, I could see le village unfolding, like a tiny flower growing and opening up in the middle of a crumpled green sheet. The rush of wind was so strong in my face, my eyes watered. I had to keep blinking them. I tried the wheel again. This time I was careful not to shove it forward more than half an inch.

The avion now was docile as an old mare. It dropped its head a trifle; it merely picked up more speed. Next, I hauled back on the wheel. The avion lifted upwards, its speed slacking off. If it hadn't been for the fact that those men had mon oncle and the Meilhac twins back on the meadow, perhaps right now shooting them, or making them dig for the stored treasure, I might have enjoyed that ride as I gradually lost my fear. I turned the wheel to the left—the avion swung toward the left, with no trouble at all. When I twisted the wheel to the right, the avion did the same thing, although the wind came more from this direction, and we rocked a little, the great wings rippling, the wires stretching tighter, the humming noise coming more sharply.

Of course, without a motor we didn't voler nearly as fast as an avion hauled along by an engine and a propeller, but it seemed to me we were traveling a lot faster than I'd realized. When I looked down the next time, I saw that le village had opened up. It was closer to me. The church steeple looked about a foot high. I could see people swarming out in la rue. Off in the distance, men working in the vineyards and fields had dropped their rakes and hoes and were looking up, shading their eyes. In that clear air, I heard their shouts—every noise distinct, but far away. I had the impression of being a giant, walking hundreds

of feet above le village and checkerboard fields and meadows and streams, with a crowd of tiny human beings way
down below me, everything in reduced size, the voices reduced in volume, a cow about an inch long making a low-
ing sound that came up to my ears almost as a squeak.

I heard a faint put-putting, very much as if a little model
airplane motor was traveling along somewhere a couple
of feet below me. I peered across the other side; I saw a
little automobile colored green, the size of those pressed
iron toy automobiles which kids half my age buy in toy
stores. As I watched, I saw the smallest arm imaginable lift
up from that little figure in the toy green automobile. It
was Dr. Guereton's green automobile. Probably he'd had
an early call and, returning to St. Chamant, saw the avion,
thought mon oncle was in it, and believed he was waving
to him. I tried to shout down at him, "Hey! Stop. Reste
là!" wanting him to wait there until I could get this thing
to terre—to earth. An automobile could get back up la
montagne in a hurry—almost to the top.

But it wasn't any use to shout. I was too high. By now,
I must have been voler-ing nearly eight minutes or more.
I began to be worried. The avion had been too well designed. It wasn't coming vers la terre—toward the earth
fast enough to suit me. I didn't dare think of what might be
happening all this time back there on the meadow behind
me. When I peered over on the other side, I saw the avion
was now passing directly above le village. I could hear the
tiny cries of people below me but they couldn't hear my
shouts at all. It's a funny thing, that noise will travel
upwards a lot better than down. I saw the oxcart and the
ox, plain as could be, right in the middle of la rue where le
forgeron was starting toward la montagne. Le forgeron

was standing up in the oxcart, jumping up and down, waving both hands. He probably thought mon oncle was in this avion, too, just as Dr. Guereton did—just as everybody else no doubt did. At least, one thing was proved: le village could see mon oncle hadn't been a muddlehead when he boasted about his avion.

But the thing wouldn't stop. It kept on, sailing away as if it enjoyed the experience. Le village slipped behind me. The avion crossed the stream, about four hundred feet high, the cows now larger in the field, their frightened moos coming more loudly. I became desperate. I could see myself going around all morning in this avion, giving all the time in the world to Monsieur Simonis and his gang on that montagne. I shoved the wheel forward; I shoved it forward as far as it would go. The avion gave a sickening lurch. I shut my eyes. The wind roared in my ears. I clenched my teeth, determined to keep the wheel shoved forward until we were a few feet above the ground.

But just as mon oncle had told me, his avion wouldn't continue diving. It lurched downwards ten or twenty feet, speed increasing—brought up its head with a kind of thump, the wings trembling, the wires screaming with the strain—and flattened out, shaking itself, the wheel jerking in my hands as if it was attempting to inform me I was to let it go. Now we sailed over the bridge, the long stone fence unreeling under me. I shoved harder on the wheel. Once more the avion lurched down—came up—lurched down again—wallowed—the wood groaning, the linen covering drumming loudly from the pressure of air.

We passed over the cow field and I twisted the wheel. The avion wheeled around and came back toward the cow field, low and lower, in a series of jerky dives and leaps, fighting to keep clear of the ground as if it was alive. That avion may have been built only of wood and wire and cloth, but mon oncle's brain had gone into it; and right now, in the air, that contraption had twice the sense I had. It knew it wasn't supposed to fling itself headfirst on the ground. It did all it could to coast down gently, despite my fever of impatience to reach earth—la terre—and find help in a hurry.

A tree appeared. It got bigger. Cows enlarged. They ran. The tree increased in size and shot up from the ground. The avion faltered. A gust of wind hit it. The avion tilted and seemed to give out a sigh and headed straight for that tree. I twisted the wheel to the right. As though it was making its final effort, the avion awkwardly wheeled a little to the right—hesitated about fifteen feet off the terre —dropped—slammed into the tree with one wing and after that there was an almighty crash and thunder. Somewhere a cow was mooing very loudly and for the next few seconds or minutes I didn't know what was happening at all.

When I opened my eyes, at first I thought I was out of my mind. You remember that blind peddler—well, *I thought I saw him bending over me*, asking me questions in French, and he wasn't wearing his glasses! I must have given a kind of yell. I shut my eyes. Next, when I opened them, Dr. Guereton was kneeling before me. The peddler wasn't anywhere around. I'd been dreaming. I saw a blur of more people and found I was sitting propped against the trunk of the oak tree. Near me was one wing, tipped upwards, like the sail of a boat. Half of the other wing was wrapped around the oak tree and lower branches, the torn cloth snapping in the wind. When I attempted to move,

pain sheared me from my left shoulder to my elbow. Now
I noticed my left arm was crooked, bent out of shape. Dr.
Guereton touched it. I yelped. He said gently, "C'est
cassé. Cassé." He was telling me it was broken. Broken.
My arm was broken.

*That blind peddler—I thought I saw him bending
over me—and he wasn't wearing his glasses!*

People were crowding around me. Men were running
from the fields, climbing the stone wall. They were lifting up parts of the avion, exclaiming to themselves. Dr.
Guereton was asking me a whole string of French words
I didn't understand. Right then, le forgeron came leaping
across the field, his black beard fanning out in the breeze.
His big arms cleared a way through that crowd. He got

to me. I was never so glad to see anybody in my life as I
was to see Monsieur Niort.

I wriggled away from Dr. Guereton. I didn't care if my
arm was cassé. I didn't care about anything but to make it
clear to Monsieur Niort that mon oncle and the Meilhac
twins were in mortal danger. He shoved closer to me. He
was the first one in all that crowd who had enough wits in
his head to realize mon oncle never would have allowed
me to make this first flying attempt with the avion. He
roared, "Où est ton oncle?"

I cried, "Mon oncle est sur la montagne avec le Nazi!"

"*Quoi?*" bellowed Monsieur Niort.

"*Oui!*" I said. "*Le Nazi est sur la montagne! Aussi!*"

He started back, making a noise like thunder. There
wasn't an instant when he didn't believe me. He realized
I'd never have taken off in that avion if something grave
wasn't taking place right now up there sur la montagne.
He jumped up. He spread out his arms, calling tout le
monde to attention. He shouted. He bellowed. He got the
facts across to them, too, this time.

"Mon automobile!" yelled Dr. Guereton, starting to
run, forgetting all about me.

"Hey!" I said, as the men streamed away from the tree,
toward the road and the automobile. It wasn't my idea to
be left behind. I managed to get to my feet, feeling dizzy
and weak. Women of le village took hold of me. I shook
free of them. I started running, the excitement pounding
through my blood. I saw men piling into Dr. Guereton's
green automobile. "Hey!" I yelled with all my breath.
"Hey!"

It was like hearing thunder again when my name,
"JEAN!" was shouted. Le forgeron jumped from the

automobile. He grabbed me and he said, "Je ne laisse pas Jean!"—I will not leave Jean! His arms were big around as small barrels. He cleared that wall, carrying me with him, in one leap. I know it's hard to believe. All I can say, I *know* he did, because I was there. He laid me gently on a man's lap and stepped on the running board, and off we drove toward la montagne.

We rocketed through la rue de St. Chamant, careening at the crossroads, past the church, past the cemetery, past la maison de Monsieur Capedulocque, the donkeys braying at us, the chickens and ducks clacking and screeching. In the rear, all the men de St. Chamant trailed after us, on foot, on horse, in carriages, in carts, with muskets they'd picked up from their homes, or with pitchforks and rakes and clubs.

"Vite! Vite!" thundered le forgeron, leaning over, holding me against the man sitting in the seat, as the automobile pounded up the narrow road.

Dr. Guereton turned it into the montagne path. After that, the automobile labored. It groaned. Finally, it stopped. I hadn't paid any attention to who was riding along with us, but as the men jumped out—for a second, I was startled. Plain as life, I saw that blind peddler get out, too, and go hurrying up the montagne ahead of all the rest, as if his life depended on it. And he wasn't wearing the dark glasses. I began yelling! That blind peddler wasn't blind. He was a fraud.

Le forgeron thought I was telling him not to leave me behind. I was afraid that blind peddler was one of Monsieur Simonis' gang and I kept trying to tell le forgeron, but it wasn't any use. I didn't have the French to do it. Le forgeron hoisted me to his shoulders—épaules. I wrapped my legs around and under his arms, with the one hand clinging to the black bushy beard. I was in a sweat to reach mon oncle. I was dead certain the peddler had streaked up there to help Monsieur Simonis. You can't imagine what terror I had as le forgeron carried me up that path on his épaules.

Halfway there, we heard somebody above us shouting in mortal fear. Next moment, out from around a turn leaped Albert, running as if a pack of tigers were after him. He saw us—dug his feet into the terre in an attempt to stop—and mon oncle appeared, right behind him. Mon oncle gave one leap. He landed on Albert's épaules. He slung him to the ground, slammed him on the head a couple of times, jumped off, picked him up, hit him, and let him loose. Albert slumped to terre, eyes streaming tears, all the dye leaking from his moustache. It was the most awful, cowardly spectacle you ever saw.

Mon oncle noticed us. "Hola!" he said.

Le forgeron advanced, with me riding high on his épaules. "Qu'est-ce que c'est que ça?" asked le forgeron, the doctor and the other men from the car following. Two of the men picked up Albert and held him.

"Where's Monsieur Simonis?" I asked. "Did that peddler try to hurt you? Where's Suzanne? Where's Charles? The Meilhac twins aren't dead—are they?"

"No. The Meilhac twins—they—" he said, with peculiar emphasis, "*they* are very much alive. They are all right. Where is mon avion?"

"Ton avion," said le forgeron, "est cassé."

"Cassé?" said mon oncle, not a muscle moving on his dark face. He glanced up at me. He told me, "Never mind. I shall make another one. Are you hurt?"

By now, more people from le village were arriving.

Mon oncle was explaining to them in French. I saw the men holding Albert grip on to him more tightly. Albert was shouting, "Kamerad! Ich bin ein guter Mann!" which wasn't French at all—I knew that much—but German. Mon oncle wanted to take me, but at that le forgeron laughed. You see, of all those people, mon oncle was the smallest. I still don't see how he had the courage to leap on Albert who was nearly twice his size, or why Albert didn't stand and face him instead of running away. I guess that is the difference between someone who's brave, as mon oncle is, and someone like Albert who gives up and quits the minute he knows *his* game is ended.

The blacksmith—le forgeron, I mean, he told mon oncle, "Jean reste ici, sur mes épaules!" and he held me on his shoulders. Mon oncle half smiled. "Viens!" he told tout le monde, proud and fierce, as if he'd elected himself the general of them all. In about ten more minutes we reached the meadow.

Charles was sitting on le maire's head. Every time le maire moved, Charles thumped him and told him, "Silence, traître!" Standing in front of le maire was Suzanne, holding the ax.

And over to one side, leaning on the wooden framework of the runway was—the peddler. He was smoking a cigarette, hands in pockets, and seemed to be enjoying the spectacle. Monsieur Simonis wasn't anywhere in sight. I was perfectly dumbfounded. I was overcome.

"Voici, Jean," said Suzanne cheerfully when we arrived.

I yelled at mon oncle, warning him that the peddler was a fraud and dangerous and to take him quick. Mon oncle didn't appear to hear me. He stood in the center of the

crowd and made a little speech in French. Then he called
to that peddler who came forward, easy and careless. He
said, "Monsieur Joubert—" and more words in French, as
if he was introducing the fellow.

Mon oncle caught sight of me. He called, "Oh, Jean.
Meet Monsieur Joubert. He is the detective. He stayed at
the hotel, perhaps you saw him?"

Perhaps I saw him?

Monsieur Joubert waved at me. "Ah, Jean," said the detective. "Bon jour! Ça va?" He laughed.

Things were coming too fast for me. I simply stayed
where I was and gawked and tried to listen.

The detective pulled Albert free from the men holding
him. Albert staggered forth and saw le maire, who had
been lifted off the ground. The detective prodded Albert,
evidently ordering him to talk and to talk quickly, if he
knew what was good for him.

Albert began accusing le maire. I gathered he was claim-
ing le maire had worked in cahoots with him and Monsieur
Simonis, the German who had been the local governor of
this part of France during the war. I wanted to ask mon
oncle why they wasted time here, questioning the two
men, instead of hunting for Monsieur Simonis—but mon
oncle was too busy to hear me.

Le maire didn't have any more heart left in him than a
chicken might have. To save his neck, he was willing to
confess everything. Of course, I didn't understand more
than every tenth word, but I knew enough of what had
gone on to obtain the general drift.

With fifty or sixty of the men from le village around
him, more coming sur la montagne every minute, le Maire
Capedulocque confessed all he'd done. Perhaps he

wouldn't have been quite so eager, but every time he hesitated Charles sort of stepped toward him, grinning—and, I noticed now, somehow, Charles had in his hand the ax that Suzanne had been holding. At the sight of that sharp ax le maire would shudder. He'd choke. He'd step back, lifting his hands. He'd blurt out more of what he and Monsieur Simonis had schemed to do.

During the time the Germans took over this part of France, le maire stayed here in le village, pretending to be a patriot. In secret, he had worked with Simonis. The German had raided the banks of St. Chamant and the nearby town, Argenta, getting all the gold and silver the people had stored there, all the money that had belonged to the Meilhacs, to Dr. Guereton, and to anyone else who had attempted to do any saving. However, that Simonis had been disloyal to his own people, just as le maire was to France. Between them, they'd kept the money, Simonis making some sort of excuse to his German superiors in France that the local banks hadn't had any gold.

Then, Simonis and Capedulocque had packed up the gold one night, getting Albert to do the real work. Albert had been an orderly—that is, a German soldier assigned to act as Simonis' servant. With Albert helping, they'd taken the gold and silver in a cart up to the Langres maison, dug a place to hide it in the cellar, and to conceal what they'd done, deliberately blown up the cellar, setting fire to the maison. They planned to lie low until the war was ended and everything was peaceful. Afterwards, Albert and Monsieur Simonis were to return, disguised as Frenchmen, just as they'd done.

From le maire, they'd understood mon oncle, Paul Langres, had been killed during the war. Of course, le maire hadn't heard correctly—mon oncle had only been severely wounded, but they didn't know that. Also, from the same source, they were informed the other owner of the Langres place was ma mère. She was supposed to be thousands and thousands of miles away, in the United States, so loin—so far—she wouldn't ever come here, and would be willing to sell. They'd counted on buying the land cheaply, setting up there in the maison, melting the gold and silver, and escaping safely, all three of them, with their stolen fortune. It was a good plan, I guess, and simple in the details; but, like mine, it got complicated toward the end.

First, they discovered mon oncle hadn't died. He was recovering from his wounds. Monsieur Simonis didn't want to take the gold and silver coins from the maison, as they were, because other Germans in other parts of France also had stolen French money and now the government had the police and special agents on the lookout for all such money thefted from French banks. By melting the money into gold and silver bullion, it could be taken out of France and resold in Spain without much difficulty. But to melt all that money down into bullion meant that they had to have time and be undisturbed in the maison. Consequently le maire, acting under orders from Simonis, attempted to buy the land from mon oncle. Mon oncle refused to sell.

Secondly, as you know, my family arrived in Paris. That upset all three thieves. Monsieur Simonis planted Albert in Paris, at the hotel at which we were staying, to spy on us. Albert was lucky enough to get the chore of pushing me in the wheel chair, which played smack into the hands of Monsieur Simonis. As you know, Monsieur Simonis

learned mon oncle and I meant to come to St. Chamant. He
had to prevent this at all costs. He made the effort to buy
the land. That failing, he determined to scare me from
coming, to get rid of one of us, trusting he could handle
mon oncle later. He failed when mon oncle rescued me
in le parc.

Well, Monsieur Simonis took the same train we were
on—got off that one—followed us, right behind us, snuck
up to our maison and for a time lived there in the cellar
until I happened upon the hiding place. I guess, by then, he
was nearly crazy with worry, blaming mon oncle and me
for all his misfortune.

Later on, when they'd put Albert in jail, Albert admitted to a few things le maire had forgotten. Albert was
ordered to drive me out of le village. He'd hummed under
my window. He had thrown stones at my window, to
make me nervous. He swore he hadn't ever attempted to
climb in, though. Maybe he was telling the truth about
that. Possibly, at that time, I was already so nervous and
scared, my imagination ran away with me, and I merely
thought someone actually was climbing in to get me. . . .

Anyway, when le maire finished his part of the whole
miserable scheme, le village might have strung him up right
there, if le forgeron hadn't stepped in and taken charge.
He reminded them France had laws for collaborationists.
That was what the mayor was—a collaborationist. He
would be punished, perhaps beheaded, or at least stuck in
prison for fifty years or so, the rest of his life, as payment
for all the suffering he'd caused. The people didn't have as
much hate against Albert as they did for le maire. Almost,
I pitied that maire. He resembled a balloon with all the air

drawn out from it. Monsieur Joubert, the detective I'd thought was a peddler, clamped handcuffs on the two prisoners.

The people milled around the mayor and Albert, Monsieur Niort thundering, mon oncle watching, smiling, his eyes shining. I still felt shaky. I sat near the framework of the runway, in the sunshine, thinking that it was fine to have le maire and Albert caught, but wondering how Monsieur Simonis had managed to escape. That didn't cheer me, at all. With Monsieur Simonis free, he'd never rest until he'd repaid mon oncle and me for all we'd done. My broken arm started hurting, too. Nobody seemed to notice me any more—not that I blamed them. They were too busy with le maire and Albert, keeping the two talking, explaining. I thought of mon oncle's avion, cassé, wrapped around that oak tree. It seemed to me as if about everything had gone wrong.

I happened to look up. I saw Suzanne and Charles in front of me. Suzanne reached down, and gently touched my arm. "C'est cassé?" she asked. I nodded. She ran to mon oncle. She spoke to him. He jumped around. Both of them ran back to me. He knelt in front of me. "Jean!" he exclaimed. "Why did you not say you were hurt?" He called to Dr. Guereton.

I didn't care about my arm as much as I cared that Monsieur Simonis had escaped. Maybe, after all that had happened this morning, I was a little out of my head. I remember, between them, mon oncle and Dr. Guereton carried me, planning to take me back to the automobile. I was shouting not to waste time, to go after Monsieur Simonis. Charles and Suzanne ran along beside me. Suzanne had practical sense, always. She saw I wasn't going to be satisfied or quiet until I knew how mon oncle and the twins escaped, and where Monsieur Simonis was. Very quickly, mon oncle explained how Suzanne had helped. He said, "Albert and the mayor guarded us while Monsieur Simonis ran to the edge of the cliff to shoot at you. Albert had a revolver. I zink we would right now be dead, maybe, in the cellar if Suzanne had not been so quick. When Simonis was shooting at you, all of us except Suzanne watched. Suzanne ran for the ax. The mayor ran at her. Charles tripped the mayor. Albert forgot me and pointed the revolver at Charles and I—" He snapped his fingers. "I jumped upon Albert and—voilà! That is all. You see the rest."

I guess I gaped at him. "How did you ever dare to tackle him when he had a gun?"

You know how vain mon oncle is. I guess it's born in him; he can't help it. For an answer, he simply snapped his fingers again, said, "Pouf! Am I not a Langres, hein? It was simple."

And I asked, "But where is Monsieur Simonis?"

"Oh," said mon oncle, his face changing. "I zink this afternoon we will send men to the bottom of the cliff and we will find him there."

"He got away by walking down—"

"Walking?" Mon oncle lifted one eyebrow. He rubbed his big nose. "Not by walking. No. I zink he was more interested in shooting at you than seeing where he was going. For a man who does not take care, it can be very dangerous to stand on the edge of a cliff. The rock crumbles." He eyed me. "You understand?"

I said, "Oh!" and for an instant, it was like being up in that avion again, and having it drop suddenly. Almost, I could see Monsieur Simonis, standing solitary and evil on the edge of that high cliff, concentrating with all his might on me and the avion, stepping forward, one step, another step, aiming his long pistol—and just one more step—

I said, "Oh." That was all I could say.

Mon oncle changed the subject. He said Monsieur Joubert wanted to see me a minute before he took le maire and Albert to Tulle, where a jail was waiting for them. While the doctor did what he could to my arm, and we waited for the detective to free himself from the crowd, mon oncle told me about Monsieur Joubert. The government had sent him here secretly, convinced someone in le village was aiding the escaped Nazis—but not knowing who it was. The detective had revealed himself to mon oncle, asking for assistance, pledging mon oncle to remain silent about him.

And the detective had heard Charles and me steal out of the hotel last night, not knowing it was us. He tracked us as far as the graveyard before losing us. After that, he'd gone up the montagne to awaken mon oncle and warn him, telling him something was occurring in le village—he didn't know what—but to remain on guard. After awakening mon oncle, Monsieur Joubert had climbed higher in the montagne, circling to the east, hoping to find traces of someone hiding in the forest, returning to le village about the time I made my unexpected flight in l'avion.

Now Monsieur Joubert approached.

But before he had time to question me, Dr. Guereton rapidly said something. Mon oncle said, "We will take you to the hotel first, Jean. You can answer questions later on. . . ."

I don't know, but I think I must have passed out. My arm hurt a lot. Probably I ought to add here, they did find what was left of Monsieur Simonis; parts of him, I understand, were spread over quite a distance. . . .

By the following day, Dr. Guereton had set my arm in splints, and I was allowed to come down to the main floor of the hotel. Charles and Suzanne were there, dressed in their best clothes. Madame Meilhac was with them, smiling, her cheeks redder than ever. I'd never seen anyone so happy.

Mon oncle informed me the gold and silver had been located. The men from the banks were up at the meadow right now, loading it into trucks. The banks would be opened. From now on, the Meilhacs wouldn't be poor.

I don't suppose St. Chamant ever had as much excitement as it did during the next week. By that second day, the news of what had happened had spread all over the country. In the big cities the papers carried accounts of it. A thing happened that neither mon oncle nor I had counted on. The reporters learned from the village people that I had flown the avion—a boy. At least, that's the account that was printed. The newspapers seemed to believe it was an extraordinary thing, a perfect miracle, for a boy who'd never before in his life been in an avion, to fly all that way down and almost make a perfect landing. It evidently caused talk all over France, because by the third day, the town was filled with reporters and tourists coming in from as far away as Toulouse and Brive and Marseilles and Bordeaux. Madame Graffoulier's hotel was packed.

When people asked him how a boy could fly his avion, mon oncle would snap his fingers and say in French, "Pouf! It was simple. I built the avion to be flown by anyone. Am I not a Langres?"

Albert and le maire had been taken to Tulle and jail by

Monsieur Joubert, who wasn't simply a detective, but chief of police there. After putting them in jail, he took a train to Paris to explain everything that had taken place to the police in charge of French security. He sent his assistant, a sharp-eyed little fellow, back to St. Chamant to interview mon oncle, the Meilhac twins and me. He was supposed to obtain the whole story of what Charles and I had done, to make everything official. Well, I didn't understand enough to do any talking. Charles did all the explaining.

Come to think of it, I guess this was the first time mon oncle had heard Charles' complete account of our adventure, except for what Charles had briefly told him up on the montagne. Now mon oncle's face became more and more puzzled. "Quoi?" he said. "*Quoi?*" He looked at me, blinking.

By and by this assistant to Monsieur Joubert gravely got up. He walked to me. He shook hands with me and made a long speech. It was all beyond me. After he finished, the two policemen accompanying him did exactly the same thing. All the time, Charles looked on and grinned, and acted as if this was the proudest moment of his life. When the police had finished with me, they shook Charles' hand, and seemed to be complimenting him, too. I wondered what on earth he'd told them.

And when all *that* was done, Monsieur Niort came to me. He said, "Un brave garçon!" which means, "A brave boy!" and *he* shook my hand. So did the doctor. So did about ten other men listening to what Charles had told the police. Every time they shook my hand I could see Charles visibly inflate with pleasure, as if he were basking in some sort of glory I'd acquired, I didn't know what. At last mon oncle said hoarsely, perplexed, astounded, bewildered:

"But Jean. Tell me. *How* did you happen to suspect the mayor was a Nazi accomplice? How, Jean? You must tell us. We are all ears to know how you managed such a stupendous thing."

I said, "What?"

Mon oncle said, "Monsieur Joubert was told by Charles, up on the montagne, what you had done." He added crossly, as if slightly vexed, "I wish someone might inform *me* now and then what my nephew does. Now, Monsieur Joubert has given specific instructions to his assistant to learn how you first suspected the mayor. Monsieur Joubert was unable to ask you when we were all on the montagne. Well?" finished mon oncle, giving me a peculiar look.

I swallowed. "You mean Monsieur Joubert believes *I* suspected the mayor of being a Nazi?"

"Yes," said mon oncle, baffled. "Charles has just told us. He has explained everything, how you told him that night he stayed with you that you'd discovered Mayor Capedulocque was a Nazi and how you showed him German money you'd found in the mayor's house as proof the mayor was a traitor."

I just sat there, with my one arm hanging limp, and my other arm in the sling, and my legs stuck out straight in front of me. I noticed Charles was smiling at me. He believed I'd discovered the truth about Mayor Capedulocque long before anyone else, and was pleased because at last he'd given me what he thought was the credit I'd earned. And the fact was, it never had entered my head that Mayor Capedulocque—le Maire Capedulocque, I mean—was a Nazi. My scheme hadn't considered him as a collaborationist. All I'd wanted was to make le maire think a Nazi was in hiding! When all along le maire *knew* a Nazi was in la montagne and was doing his level best to keep that fact hidden.

That's what comes of trying to explain a scheme to someone like Charles in a language you can hardly speak. Charles never had gotten my scheme at all in his head. Now I understood why he'd jumped up that night when I was saying, "Le maire—Nazi." I'd expected he'd realize what I was driving at—that we counted on frightening le maire by *pretending* to be Nazis!

Mon oncle asked me again, perplexed, how on earth I'd discovered le maire's secret when no one else had suspicioned it. The police were looking at me as if they wanted to know, too. A couple of reporters from Tulle came in closer. *They* were waiting for the mystery to be cleared as well. I simply slumped down and fortunately, Dr. Guereton entered and said I'd been questioned enough for today. So I escaped.

That night, I learned from mon oncle, he'd sent off a cable to my parents to inform them I was well and safe in case they'd seen any of the newspaper accounts of our experience. He was tremendously excited. He said le village had voted Monsieur Niort to be the new mayor. After that, le village had voted for a festival for the avion next Sunday. Invitations had been sent to everyone of importance in the district. I asked, "But isn't the avion cassé?"

"Ah," he said, mighty cheerful. "Only one wing. Six of the best carpenters in Corrèze are working on it night and day to have it repaired—réparé—for Sunday. Besides, I do not design airplanes that break, airplanes that remain cassé permanently. I design good airplanes. Pouf!" He snapped his fingers. "It is simple to have it ready to fly by Sunday. Am I not a Langres?"

By Saturday morning there must have been nearly two thousand people camped around St. Chamant, or crowded into the maisons and hotel, for the festival—for la fête. The weather was warm, with sunshine. Charles, Suzanne and I went to the workshop and saw the avion, with mon oncle explaining how by tonight the repairs would be completed. He drew me to one side and whispered, "Ah, Jean—" and seemed a shade embarrassed. "Between us, hein? Just *how* did you suspect the mayor?"

I didn't have time to tell him I hadn't ever suspected le maire, because the postmaster ran in at that moment with a cable he said had come all the way from London. It was from my father. He'd read in the Scottish papers about what had happened and had received mon oncle's cable, assuring him I wasn't harmed except for a broken arm. He had cabled to tell us he and my mother were leaving London Sunday and would arrive Monday.

We cabled back to try to tell them to leave at once, to be in time for la fête, Sunday. But evidently the cable didn't reach them in time. They weren't there, Sunday morning. Dr. Guereton took me as far up the montagne as his car would go. I walked the rest of the way, with Monsieur Niort—now le maire—on one side, and Suzanne and Charles on the other. Behind us came Madame Meilhac, Madame Graffoulier and the Graffoulier kids, and all the rest of le village—tout le monde—everyone, camera men, the people from the surrounding towns and villages. It was like being on a great vast picnic. They had the band playing in the meadow. Monsieur Niort made a speech. He called Charles and Suzanne and me to the platform on the runway, the avion—now repaired—right behind us. Mon oncle was there, too. All of us had to be photographed. It was the most wonderful day I'd ever seen, le ciel blue and clear, the wind blowing gently.

Suzanne wore a new dress, bought in Tulle. Her hair was curly, done up, and she was pretty as a picture. I couldn't hardly believe she was the same Suzanne I'd seen way early in the summer playing at "peau-rouge," until she gave me a quick pinch when nobody was looking. "Bon jour," said she, smiling.

"Bon jour," I said, pleased to see that same friendly smile. Actually, she and Charles had deserved the credit, all of it. Monsieur Niort finished his speech and turned to distribute the reward of ten thousand francs—about four hundred dollars—between the four of us, mon oncle, the Meilhac twins, and myself. They helped me down; the band played again. Monsieur Niort thundered to everyone that the moment was now here when Monsieur Paul Langres would this time himself voler in his avion.

I looked up at mon oncle Paul. I looked at the avion. Ah, I thought, the avion is grand—is big. The avion is ready to fly. Oncle Paul bent down at me and grinned and said, "Bon jour, Jean," as if we were together on a joke or secret. I asked, "Are you ready?" and he said he was prêt; he wished to fly very far this time, to make a record. "Très loin," he said gaily.

Seeing him up there must have reminded Suzanne of that other time when the avion was ready to fly. She became a trifle nervous. She called up, "The airplane isn't broken?" —that is, l'avion n'est pas cassé?

Mon oncle said, "It's repaired, don't worry, Suzanne. It's ready to depart." He said all that in French, but I understood that much. Suzanne said, "Good, but please don't fly too far," and everybody around laughed. By now,

We saw mon oncle land. Three men from the black limousine ran to him

mon oncle entre—entered into l'avion. He called, "Au revoir!" and Monsieur Niort chopped the rope and poussed—pushed the avion and away it slid, down the runway and into the air. I heard people in the crowd shouting, "Bonne chance! Bonne chance!" which was their way of saying, "Good luck!"

Mon oncle didn't voler right down across le village as I'd done. No, he gave all that crowd a show. He soared in the wind. The avion lifted higher and higher until it was no bigger than a bird. It swooped down low over our heads and we thought for sure it was going to land on the meadow—but no! It caught the draft of air rising from the face of the cliff, soaring once more. Oh! I tell you, it was wonderful to watch mon oncle in his avion that jour de la fête! By and by he soared toward le village. Monsieur Niort, the doctor, the Meilhacs and I went down the montagne in the doctor's car. We roared to the cow field, the others coming along behind. A big black limousine passed us on the lower road, went ahead and was waiting at the cow field by the time we arrived.

We saw mon oncle land, very gently, the wings hardly fluttering. Three men from the black limousine ran to him. Then the crowd surged into the field. I waited in the car. I saw Dr. Guereton and Monsieur Niort lifting the avion on their shoulders—portant l'avion sur les épaules—and carrying it above the crowd, so it wouldn't be broken a second time. . . .

That day of the fête passed all too quickly. That night we had a big dinner in the hotel. You know, I'd forgotten all about my leg. I realized my leg was well. It came to me, all of a sudden, as I was sitting at the table on mon oncle's right, hearing everybody talk and laugh and joke, with Charles and Suzanne sitting opposite me.

At the other end of the table, Monsieur Niort was introducing one of the men who'd been in the black limousine. He explained this man was Monsieur Parousse, a manufacturer from Toulouse, who'd read in the newspapers about mon oncle's avion and proposed to establish a small factory here in St. Chamant, if mon oncle was agreeable, where Langres avions would be built. Monsieur Toulouse said something about using rocket motors and producing an inexpensive avion anyone could fly, but I was getting sleepy and didn't hear much of that speech.

I half awakened when mon oncle leaned to me and said anxiously, "Jean! Jean! They are asking me again to explain how my nephew discovered that the ex-Mayor Capedulocque was—"

He didn't finish.

He didn't finish, because right then my mother and father walked into the hotel.

14

LA LETTRE

I doubt if you can conceive of the surprise and joy with which mon oncle et moi welcomed mon père et ma mère.

Both of them were browned from their walking trip. They'd received mon oncle's cable, asking them to come for la fête. They'd taken an airplane from London early last night, planning to reach Paris by midnight, transfer to another airplane early this morning to reach Tulle by eight o'clock and drive to St. Chamant in time for la fête. A storm had blown up over the channel grounding all airplanes. They weren't able to leave England until late this morning. As a result they lost hours, didn't reach Tulle until this afternoon. They again lost more time trying to locate a taxi to drive them here.

Because the hotel was packed, they took my room. Madame Graffoulier fixed up a place for me in the attic with little Philippe. While mon père et ma mère washed and brushed off the dust from their trip, for a few minutes I had a chance to be alone with them in the room. Of course, right away they both wanted to know about my leg and my arm. I assured them I figured my leg was cured and my arm didn't hurt very much. I rattled off as much as I had time for, about all that had happened.

When I'd completed the story, I told mon père how Charles had misunderstood my French. As a result, I was in an embarrassing position now, everyone—tout le monde

—considering I was the one who'd been the first to discover Monsieur Capedulocque was a thief and collaborator. They were asking me to tell how I'd found out. I wanted to know what to do. Worse, I'd been given one fourth of the reward money, too. I showed it to them, in a bag on the dresser—two thousand five hundred francs, about one hundred American dollars.

Mon père simply sat on that bed. He laughed until he was weak. Ma mère said, "Richard! Richard Littlehorn!" a couple of times. But she broke down. She began laughing too. Finally, mon père told me he considered I'd done enough to earn my fourth of the reward money. Even if I'd done it by accident, more or less, the money was mine.

However, as for telling them how I'd worked out a scheme which had been completely misunderstood by Charles—well, I had to handle that myself, he said. He couldn't help me there. He said it was too complex for him. On the one hand, if I admitted the plain truth, it might spoil all Charles' pleasure, after blowing about me, telling people nobody could compare with him and me as detectives. On the other hand, mon père said he didn't think I ought to lie about the facts, either. He couldn't see any way out. No, he said, once again laughing, it was too deep for him entirely.

Mon oncle was knocking, asking how soon my parents would be ready. Mon père said, "One minute, Paul."

I asked, "How long are we staying here? A week? A month?" I was just beginning to get into the swing of being here and hoped we didn't have to shove too soon.

"A week?" exclaimed ma mère.

Mon père delivered the bad news. We had to leave— *tomorrow noon*. His job in the army was finished. He had made reservations for all of us on a boat departing Tuesday from Cherbourg for home. He'd have to stay at Washington, D.C. a week or so to be mustered out of the army. We'd remain with him. After that, all of us would be bound for Wyoming. . . .

I don't know how my face looked, but ma mère noticed me; and my expression must have indicated something of my disappointment. "Why, Johnny," she said. "Aren't you happy we're going home?"

I said, "Sure. I guess so."

"You guess so?" said mon père, as if he was amused. "I thought you weren't going to like it here?"

I said, "I've changed my mind. I've got friends here."

"You've friends home, too," said ma mère.

"Tu viens, Yvonne?" called mon oncle from outside in the hallway.

They got up to go to the door. "We'll have a talk later on," said mon père. "Your mother wants to go up the mountain to see what's left of her home tomorrow morning, and I'd like to go with her. How far is it?"

"About two and a half miles."

"Could you walk it with me?" he asked, a curious expression on his face, half smiling. "Despite that broken arm of yours, do you think we might walk it together?"

I said, "Sure, I can walk it," without thinking. Of course I could. I wasn't worried any more about my leg.

We got downstairs once more, and there was more speech-making, my mother greeting old friends she hadn't seen for more than a quarter of a century. They cleared the floor. Mon oncle played his flute. Monsieur Niort sent for his accordion. I danced a couple of times with Suzanne, despite my broken arm. Doctor Guereton told ma mère

that it would help my arm, too, although for the life of me
I don't see how dancing can help a broken arm any.

Afterwards, along about eleven o'clock, way past
Charles' and Suzanne's and my bedtime, all of us, my parents, oncle Paul, Madame Meilhac, Monsieur Niort, everyone we knew, sat in front of the fire, still talking. By and
by mon oncle glanced at me and something seemed to
strike him.

"Ah," he exclaimed. "The bicycle!"

In French, immediately, he explained to the village people present how I was engaged to win a bicycle with a high
gear and a low gear and a middle gear and with a real
electric dynamo from my folks.

Mon père said calmly, "Johnny and I are to walk up to
the Langres house tomorrow. If he does that, I shall consider he has won my part of the bargain."

Mon oncle snapped his fingers. "Pouf! That will be
simple for him! Is he not Langres—" And he corrected
himself. "At least, half Langres? Assuredly, he will do
that. But the electric dynamo, Yvonne?" he said to ma
mère.

My mother—ma mère, I mean—gave me the merest
glance. I couldn't tell whether she was laughing or not.
She spoke seriously. She said she expected me to keep my
bargain with her if I was to receive the electric lighting
dynamo. And I hadn't written her a letter in French. She
was sorry.

Mon oncle protested. He said we hadn't expected them
to be here so soon. He translated back into French for the
benefit of the others present. Charles appealed to ma mère.
Suzanne said, "Oh, Madame Littlehorn, Jean vous écrira
bientôt!"

Ma mère shook her head. She said it was a bargain. She asked me if I didn't agree. Well, much as I hated losing that dynamo, I had to support her. I hadn't written the letter. Fact is, I was pretty certain I'd never be able to construct a whole letter in French. That was beyond me. Ma mère said when we reached Wyoming I could take up French at high school and perhaps in a year or so learn enough to write her the letter. Then she'd give me the dynamo which she already had ordered.

I jumped up, "You've *bought* it?"

She nodded, eyes sparkling.

I looked at mon père. "You've bought the bicycle—"

"With all three gears," he said, cheerfully. "Only you won't get it, young man, if you don't keep up with me tomorrow morning!"

Immediately, mon oncle translated our conversation to the others. Charles clapped his hands. "Bravo!" he said, pleased that I would have at least the bicycle, because he was just as confident as I was that I could walk those two miles. But Suzanne leaned forward a little, away from the fire. Her face became solemn. She spoke to mon oncle rapidly. He listened. He said, "Ah, oui." He nodded. He snapped his fingers. Ma mère understood French, as well as anyone there—and I caught her smiling.

Mon oncle suddenly told me, "Jean, in Paris I have made you a promise. I have said you will come here and not only walk but write a letter to your mother in French. Is that right?"

I said, "Yes," not comprehending why all the French people were beginning to smile, as if they had a secret.

"Eh, bien," said he, now very serious. "Very well. It is simple. Are you not half Langres? You will write the let-

ter tomorrow morning *after* walking to the montagne. Dr.
Guereton will wait at the halfway point in his automobile.
As soon as you have proved to your father you can walk,
you will rush back here to the hotel, *and you will write
that letter before noon!* Voici!"

I protested. I said ma mère was here. I couldn't write her
a letter when she was here. I guess ma mère was as eager to
see me win the electric lighting dynamo as anyone. In her
pleasant way, she suggested we make a trifle of a change
in the bargain. Instead of writing her a letter, she'd be satisfied if I wrote her six pages in French about any subject
I might choose.

"Six pages!" I exclaimed. That was impossible.

Mon oncle said, "Pouf! It is simple. You will write about
la fête and mon avion. That is easy. It is decided. I have
made a promise." And so it was decided.

That night in the attic, I couldn't do much sleeping.
I thought about the letter I'd have to write tomorrow
morning, between the time I returned from the montagne
and when my parents got back. And I thought about the
weeks I'd spent here and about Charles and Suzanne Meilhac; and about little Philippe who'd helped me most of all
with what French I did know; and about the doctor; and
Madame Graffoulier, who'd made such wonderful soup;
and about le forgeron—no—now—le Maire Niort, with
his black beard—and—oh—all the village—everyone. I'd
have to leave them. I might not ever see them again. It
might be at least years before I could return. I felt a great
sadness come upon me, that tomorrow I'd have to go. I
heard the roosters crowing early in the morning before I
finally fell asleep. . . .

It didn't seem more than a minute had passed before

Philippe awakened me. The morning light streamed through a little opening at the far end of the attic. I got dressed as best I could with my arm. When I went downstairs I found ma mère already had packed for me. Dr. Guereton was there for one more look at the arm. He peered over his spectacles at it and under his spectacles. He said, "Ça va, ça va," and I guess that meant my arm was improving.

I was surprised to find Charles et Suzanne waiting to have a last breakfast with me. They'd walked from their maison early in the morning. With the money in the bank, Madame Meilhac was able to employ men in the Meilhac vineyards. No longer did the twins have to labor there from morning until nuit and fear that Monsieur Capedulocque would turn them out this fall. None of us spoke very much. As the time drew nearer for us to say "good-by—au revoir" to each other, a silence fell upon us.

We finished breakfast by six-thirty. Mon père was waiting. Ma mère had gone on ahead with Madame Meilhac in the doctor's car. The twins, mon oncle, mon père et moi, all five of us set out, the air fresh and cool. My arm bothered me a little because it was in the sling, and couldn't move as my other arm did when I walked—but except for that one thing, I had no trouble. It was as if all the kinks had gone forever from my leg.

The fact is, I was more concerned by the letter than walking to la maison de ma mère. I tried to remember French words. They evaporated out of my head. Before I knew it we were in the meadow, with the women greeting us. Mon père looked at his watch. It was a few minutes before eight in the morning. We'd taken a little less than an hour and a half. He came to me and stuck out his big hand, looking down at me from his height, his face brown and lean and smiling, the scar showing red and twisted when he grinned.

"Okay, Johnny," he said. "You get the bicycle. Now your mother and I will remain up here until eleven. We'll ride down in Dr. Guereton's automobile, he has promised to come back for us after delivering you at the hotel. That will give you about three hours and a quarter to write your French. Good luck!"

Mon oncle was impatiently waiting. "Vite!" he said, "Vite, Jean!" knowing the sooner I reached the hotel, the more time I'd have to win.

Ma mère was watching. "Bonne chance!" she called at me. And then she said to mon oncle, "And no assistance, Paul, you understand. That wouldn't be fair."

Mon oncle shrugged. "No assistance, then," he said glumly.

If I walked up to the maison, I practically flew down to the place where Dr. Guereton was waiting for us in his automobile. Charles took one side, and mon oncle took the other side of me. Taking care not to hurt my arm, they rushed me down that slope so fast I still have to catch my breath whenever I think of it. We reached the hotel at twelve minutes after eight. Suzanne jumped out of the car and ran into the hotel and had pen and paper ready for me the second I entered.

I sat down at the table.

I thought.

I thought for ten minutes and I couldn't think of a single solitary word to put down.

"Ah! Ah!" exclaimed mon oncle.

Monsieur Niort appeared and sat down by the fire.

Little Philippe walked in and whispered to mon oncle, "Ça ne marche pas?"

Suzanne leaned her elbows on the table and told me fiercely, "Va! Va vite, Jean!"

More people drifted in. Fifteen minutes passed. I felt sweat roll down my back. Mon oncle sprang up and cleared everyone out of the room except Suzanne and Charles and Monsieur Niort. "Now you must write," he said. "Quickly."

"I can't think of how to start," I said.

In anguish, mon oncle pulled at his nose; Charles whispered over to him. Mon oncle listened. "Bon," said mon oncle. He told me, "Charles suggests you write very simply what happened yesterday when I fly. Can you not do that?"

I said, "I get mixed up when I think of myself. That's the trouble."

Mon oncle and Charles and Suzanne and Monsieur Niort put their heads together and had a discussion while the minutes raced along. Finally mon oncle said, "Ah, *now* we have it. You will not write about yourself! No. You will write about a boy named 'Jean.' Voici!"

I hadn't thought of doing it that way. I could pretend I was somebody else. I asked what time it was. Mon oncle looked at his big old watch. He sighed. "Nine o'clock."

I dipped my pen in ink.

I decided it would be all right to simplify some of the details about yesterday because I didn't know enough words to describe everything. At the top of the first page I wrote:

LA FETE

Charles looked at it. "Bon," he said.

"Sh-h!" said Suzanne fiercely.

"SH-H-H!" said Monsieur Niort.

I dipped my pen again into the ink. I thought a minute. I would start out by saying it's the day of the fête. I would say a boy comes from the house, remembering that little French "de" was tricky, meaning both "from" as well as "of." I'd say that boy was me—John. I began writing.

I was still writing when Dr. Guereton honked his automobile horn at the entrance into la rue—the street—to warn me he was bringing my parents back. I scribbled the last sentence as the door opened. I wrote "La Fin"—the end—just as ma mère entered.

I sat back. I watched her pick up all the six pages in my handwriting and read them and I saw her smile and she laid the sheets down and bent over and kissed me on the nose and said, "You win the dynamo, Johnny!" and Charles began to whoop like a peau-rouge, and that was like a signal. I guess half le village had gathered around to see us off. They cheered. Mon père said, "We've got exactly three-quarters of an hour to reach Tulle and get our train!"

They threw our bags into Dr. Guereton's green car. Charles flung his arms around my shoulders—épaules—and embraced me. So did Suzanne embrace me. Mon oncle said, "I must stay here because this afternoon I am expecting the men from Tulle to sign the contract for my airplane. But someday you will return, hein? You will come back. You are half Langres, you know, and always one with French blood in him returns!"

We got into the automobile and drove away, waving. I saw Charles and Suzanne and Philippe standing by the door of the hotel, waving. "Au revoir!" they called. I like the way the French say "good-by"—their "au revoir" doesn't actually mean "good-by" at all. "Revoir" means "re-see" and what they say is, "To the re-see . . ." that is, "until we see you again." So I called, "Au revoir."

All at once, I saw mon oncle give a start, as if he'd just remembered something urgently important. He loped after the automobile. He came up even with us. "Oh, Jean," he panted. "They are still asking me in le village. You have forgotten to tell me. How did you learn Monsieur Capedulocque was a traitor?"

I said, "How did I learn that?" I snapped my fingers just as mon oncle did. I said, "Pouf! It was simple. Am I not half Langres? Is not a Langres capable of learning anything? Even French?"

None of us said much until we were nearly to Tulle. I guess ma mère was as sad as I was about leaving St. Chamant. I kept telling myself I was going to grow up fast and return to St. Chamant as soon as possible, before Suzanne found some other— Before—

Anyway, before everything was changed. And I could write letters to them all. I asked ma mère, "You didn't lose all those French words I wrote out for you, did you? I'd like to keep the papers. I'd like to have them with me to help me remember."

She laid her hand over mine. "I have them here," she said. "You won't forget French. You'll learn more."

"Just the same," I said, "I'd be obliged if I could keep those French words, myself."

"Of course, Johnny," she said. "Do you have the papers, Richard?"

Mon père opened his leather case. Solemnly he handed them over to me and said, "Altogether it was a successful summer for us, wasn't it, Johnny?" I said it was a wonderful summer, the best ever. I looked at what I'd written down, all the French words, reading them again, seeming as clear as crystal to me, and I saw I'd never be baffled by them; I knew them; I'd lived them, just as I've been telling you all along. I saw I'd learn more French at school. In a few years, I'd be back here for a visit. Just looking at what I'd written for ma mère gave me confidence. Leaving wasn't quite as sad, having these papers in my hand.

And right now, back in Wyoming, as I finish this, I've got those six pages next to me. They're a memory and a reminder of France and St. Chamant and all my friends there, and of the little factory mon oncle is running; and when I read them, I can recall as if it was yesterday that day of the festival and how mon oncle took off in his avion, and it might be if you'll look at them, they'll do the same for you. So here they are, the pages about l'avion que mon oncle a fait voler—which means, translated exactly, "the avion that my uncle has made to fly," and is how a Frenchman would say the title of this book.

Here's what won me the electric lighting dynamo for the English bicycle with the high gear and the low gear and the middle gear I've been pedaling all over our county for the past few months:

La Fête

Par Jean Littlehorn

C'est le jour de la fête. Le garçon vient de la maison. Le garçon est Jean Littlehorn. Jean va dans la rue de St. Chamant. Voici Jean.

Jean voit un garçon. Charles est le garçon. "Bon jour, Charles," dit Jean Littlehorn.

Charles voit Jean. Charles dit, "Bon jour, Jean."

Jean dit, "Bon jour. Le jour de la fête de l'avion de mon oncle est joli!"

Charles dit, "Où est ton oncle Paul?"

Jean dit, "Mon oncle Paul est sur la montagne. Tout le monde va à la montagne."

Jean et Charles marchent vers la montagne. Jean voit la fille. La fille est Suzanne Meilhac. Jean dit à Suzanne Meilhac, "Bon jour, Suzanne."

La fille dit, "Bon jour, Jean. Bon jour, mon frère." Charles est le frère de Suzanne Meilhac.

Charles voit Suzanne. "Bon jour, Suzanne," dit Charles.

Jean demande, "Suzanne, tu veux voir l'avion de mon oncle Paul?"

"Oui," dit Suzanne. "Certainement, je veux voir l'avion de ton oncle Paul."

Charles remarque, "Suzanne, tu viens avec Jean et moi?"

Suzanne dit, "Oui, je veux! Je viens avec Jean et toi!"

"Bien!" dit Jean.

Aussi, Charles dit, "Bien!"

Suzanne et Jean et Charles montent sur la montagne.

Tout le monde est sur la montagne. Le forgeron, Monsieur Niort, est ici. Le forgeron est aussi le maire de St. Chamant. Monsieur Capedulocque n'est pas le maire. Monsieur Capedulocque est le traître de St. Chamant. Le docteur est ici. Le docteur est Monsieur Guereton. Philippe Graffoulier est ici; sa mère, Madame Graffoulier est ici. Et Madame Meilhac est ici. Tout le monde est ici et tout le monde est content.

Jean voit oncle Paul. Jean voit l'avion. Ah! L'avion est grand. L'avion est prêt à voler. Oncle Paul dit, "Bon jour, Jean. Bon jour, Suzanne. Bon jour, Charles."

Suzanne et Charles et Jean disent, "Bon jour."

"Es-tu prêt, oncle Paul?" demande Jean.

"Oui," répond oncle Paul. "Je suis prêt. Je veux voler loin."

"Très loin?" demande Jean.

"Oui. Très, très loin," répond oncle Paul.

Suzanne dit, "L'avion n'est pas cassé?"

Oncle Paul dit, "Oh, non. L'avion est réparé. L'avion est prêt à partir."

Charles dit, "Bon. S'il vous plaît, Monsieur Langres, ne volez pas loin."

Oncle Paul demande à Charles, "As-tu peur?"

Charles répond, "Non, je n'ai pas peur."

Mais, vite, Suzanne dit, "J'ai peur, Monsieur Langres."

Oncle Paul dit, gravement, "La peur n'est pas bonne, Suzanne. L'avion est complètement réparé."

Le maire, Monsieur Niort arrive. Monsieur Niort demande, "Prêt, Paul?"

"Oui," réplique oncle Paul.

Le Maire Niort crie à tout le monde, "L'AVION EST PRET! L'AVION VA VOLER TRES LOIN!"

Tout le monde regarde l'avion et l'oncle Paul. Tout le monde est content. L'avion va voler. L'avion va voler très loin. . . .

Oncle Paul entre dans l'avion. Oncle Paul crie, "Au revoir, au revoir!"

Monsieur Niort, le maire de St. Chamant, pousse l'avion.

Tout le monde crie, "Bonne chance, Monsieur Langres! Bonne chance!"

Ah! L'avion va. L'avion vole!

L'avion laisse la montagne. L'avion vole dans le ciel. L'avion vole beaucoup de minutes. L'avion vole très loin.

Suzanne a peur. Suzanne dit, "J'ai peur. L'avion ne va pas tomber?"

"Non," dit Jean. "L'avion ne va pas tomber."

L'avion descend. . . .

L'avion de Monsieur Langres descend vers la terre. . . .

Suzanne et Jean et Charles descendent la montagne. Tout le monde descend la montagne. Tout le monde court de St. Chamant. Tout le monde va à l'avion.

Voici l'avion!

Voici oncle Paul!

L'avion n'est pas cassé. Oncle Paul n'est pas cassé. Jean court à son oncle Paul. Jean embrasse oncle Paul.

Monsieur Niort dit, "Bien fait, Paul!"

Dr. Guereton dit, "Bien fait, Monsieur Langres! Je suis content!"

Tout le monde est content. Le Docteur Guereton et le Maire Niort portent l'avion sur les épaules. Tout le monde va à St. Chamant.

Oncle Paul dit à Jean, son neveu, "Je suis très content."

"Bien!" dit Jean. "Moi aussi. Je suis content!"

"Bien!" dit Charles.

"Très bien!" dit Suzanne.

Ah, tout est beau le jour de la fête de l'avion de l'oncle de Jean Littlehorn.

LA FIN